BROKEN ECHO

Happy reading!

KR Hanc...

K R Hancock

For Moose, EB, & Benji

BROKEN ECHO

CHAPTER ONE

NOW

"JAKE IS GOING TO DIE," SAM SAYS. HE STARES OUT THE kitchen window at the 1955 powder-blue Porsche Spyder showcased in the garage made of glass. "I know because I've seen it happen three times."

Sam and Mary Forester had asked to speak to me about their son but this was not the conversation I had in mind.

I wait for Sam to turn and wink but he doesn't and I wonder what got lost in translation between Sam Forester's American words and my Australian brain.

"I don't understand." I shake my head and some strands of my orange frizz fall into my eyes.

"We've tried to save Jake three times, and each time we've failed." Mary dabs at a fallen tear then continues to dry the dishes.

"Is he sick?" I ask and my fingers grip the kitchen chair in front of me, "Does he have cancer?" I speak my thoughts.

"No, it isn't like that," her head wags back and forth, "Jake dies in the Porsche." She nods toward the window and then it hits me.

"You had a dream about Jake in the Spyder," I say in a half-whisper. Mary spoke often of Dream Theory, a technique she encouraged with her patients during Art Therapy sessions.

"This is not about my dreams," she says and a crease of frustration lines her forehead.

"But you had some sort of premonition in a dream and now you've convinced Sam it will happen," I process aloud.

"Shay, we traveled back in time and…"

"You've traveled back in time?" I don't let her finish, "Really?" every muscle in my face tightens. "Why are you doing this?"

I notice my handwritten note resting on the edge of the marble countertop near Mary and my shoulders deflate. "I'm sorry I made that stupid list but I don't deserve this." I cringe at the paper laying bare every bizarre encounter I'd had with Mary and Sam since my christening as their prized Australian foreign exchange student, five months ago.

"Shay, we traveled back in time to save Jake and we failed. We've seen our son die three different times."

I stand and toss my backpack over my shoulders.

"This conversation is over." I walk toward the front door. "I'm leaving."

Sam cuts in front of me. "Wait," he says then extends his hand. A strange hum emits from a pair of black-framed glasses. "Put these on; they will explain everything."

I shuffle backward and away from him and walk swiftly toward the door.

"Please Shay, don't go."

I pause at the sound of Mary's desperation, then turn as the patio door opens. An Asian man dressed in black with a scar across his left temple walks into the room.

"Who is he?" I say, my voice wavering.

Mary doesn't answer but nods her head, sending the man back out onto the patio.

"What is going on? What is he doing?" A sense of unease fills the air. It replicates through the entire kitchen until I feel like I'm suffocating.

Behind me, I feel Sam open my gray backpack and place the humming glasses at the top of my bag then zip it closed.

"We didn't want to do this," he says, looking toward the patio door. I search for an escape but Sam steps closer, boxing me in.

The man returns with two people. A man and a woman have burlap sacks over their heads and duct tape around their wrists. They huddle close together, trembling.

"Who are they?" my voice cracks.

"Go ahead, Moses," Sam commands. The man in black pulls the burlap away from the victims' heads and I scream. Carbon copies of Mary and Sam struggle to free themselves of their restraints. The room starts to spin and I push past Sam then sprint to the front door.

CHAPTER TWO

THEN

"FLIGHT 782 FROM SYDNEY, AUSTRALIA, YOUR BAGGAGE has arrived at carousel three."

Somehow, I had fooled myself into believing that moving to the other side of the planet for six months—to live with a family I'd never met—wasn't completely bonkers. How the hell did I let Ingrid talk me into this?

My fingers find their favorite place and trace the tattoo on the inside of my left wrist. The four numbers inked in my skin hold a strange attraction for my nervous fingertips.

A woman approaches and I force a half-smile. I step forward but she walks past and I pretend to stretch my back but my body hunches over. It refuses to take any form other than that of the plane seat it was forced into the last fifteen hours. I lose my balance and shuffle backward over the gray carpet covered in cactus-shaped airplanes. Bile crawls up the back of my throat and mixes with the metallic taste coming from the chewed spot on my lower lip. I know if I'm not careful, I will spew over what now look like flying gherkins on the floor.

This was all Ingrid's fault. "Study abroad," she said, "there's a spot open in the foreign exchange program." She gave at least ten convincing reasons why I should apply, none of which that I can currently recall, so I hesitantly filled out the paperwork. I never dreamed I'd be taken seriously. Who would want a girl with such a sketchy past living with them for six whole months? A few weeks later, my application was not only approved but expedited with a candidate that matched my criteria; or a group of candidates, the Foresters.

I dodge a romantic reunion and find a vacant spot near the end of carousel three then take inventory of the wandering people around me. A mum with infant twins and a Dad with a toddler, nope. Mary and Sam Forrester have only one son, who, like me, is in Year 12—or Twelfth grade, as they say in the United States. A pink-haired woman with a nose ring and man with face tattoo, maybe? The truth is that I know next to nothing about the Foresters and the act of analyzing every passerby is brutal.

I refocus my energy and try to locate my navy duffle on the shiny bag mover. Maybe I'll get lucky and the Foresters will find me first.

Near Carousel four, an older bloke watches me through the glass doors leading to the street. We make eye contact and a wide line carves relief across his forehead like when you come up for air after being tossed around in a rip tide. The doors open and he turns the opposite way and exits the baggage claim.

5

A tap on my shoulder spins me around. A poster in the shape of Australia bobs up and down in front of me. I can't see who's holding the sign, only the words WELCOME SHAY! written in giant red letters.

"Shay?" A woman lowers the continent so that the Northern Territory rests below her chin.

"Mrs. Forester?" She looks like one of those celebrity housewives I'd seen on television.

"Please, call me Mary," she says then rests the sign at her feet and extends her arms. Long locks of her almond brown hair spill onto my shoulders, filling my nose with notes of sage and citrus. I rearrange my semi-limp arms around her waist, not anticipating the intimate embrace then give her a slight pat on the back cueing my release. She steps back and takes one of my hands in hers as if we are reunited mates and not complete strangers.

"We are so glad you are here," she says without looking away and I notice that her eyes are the color of the ocean after a storm.

I don't know what to say so I half-smile then turn toward the baggage claim.

"Sam, my husband, he's parking the car. And our son, Jake, he's at Lacrosse practice, but you'll meet him when we get home." Mary continues but I get lost in the word home.

Ingrid's small flat, near the beach, was the closest thing I'd had to a home in years. A sudden sadness grips me and my left hand grabs for the flask in the front pocket of my trousers; except there isn't a flask there and I instantly hate myself. My pocket has been empty for four years, three months, and ten days and I'm ashamed that I let my weakness get the better of me. As punishment, I drown myself in thought of self-loathing; you will always be an addict, you are the same hopeless screw-up you were fours years ago, the Foresters are going to see right through you.

My fingers fumble the recovery chip floating in place of where the flask used to be and it acts like a life preserver holding my head above water.

"Shay, this is my husband, Sam." Mary interrupts my pity party and I see a man resting his hand on her shoulder.

I try to hide my unease. It's the same bloke who'd been watching me through the glass doors. Like usual, I attract all the pervs. Phoenix and Sydney aren't that different after all. A thick charcoal wave swoops across his forehead and his gray eyes are only softened by the warm hues of his tanned skin.

"Hello, Shay." Sam's voice lacks emotion. He is Mary's opposite.

"G'day Mr. Forester," I fake a smile.

"I thought that I saw you from across the baggage claim. The agency only gave us this one picture." He pulls out a school picture of me and his tone brightens. My jaw unclenches. Maybe he isn't a perv after all.

"Have you seen your luggage yet, sweetie?" Mary hovers over the bags gliding around the carousel.

I wait for Sam to respond then realize she's talking to me. I can't remember the last time anyone called me sweetie.

"I think that's my bag over there," I say then point to a small navy duffle with a surfboard tag. Sam waits for it to come back around then lifts it from the carousel with ease.

"You only have one bag?" Mary's eyes widen. "We've got some serious shopping to do."

I try to hide the grimace on my lips. At the rock gym, where I worked back in Sydney, I made just enough money each month to cover the essentials. On the rare occasions when I had a little extra, I splurged on my favorite coconut and honey surfboard wax— that was my idea of shopping.

"So, you like to surf?" Mary touches the luggage tag bouncing up and down over Sam's shoulder as he leads us to the lift. I nod my head yes.

"I love the beach but you couldn't pay me to get in the water. I'm slightly terrified of sharks. It's a shame too because Sam and I travel to some pretty amazing places." Sam winces, almost as if he's in pain.

"Sam travels for business. He's an investment broker. I go with him from time to time but we've never been to Australia. Is this your first trip out of the country?"

"I traveled to New Zealand but I don't remember very much, I was really young."

"Did you take the trip with Ingrid?"

My head cocks involuntarily. "You know Ingrid?" I ask, taken aback.

"No," Mary shakes her head, "we read about her in your file the exchange program gave us." Pangs of worry wave through my mind. What other information did the program make available to the Foresters?

"I was with my parents and sister when we visited New Zealand. I started living with Ingrid four years ago." I'd become a master of avoiding the follow up question. I knew if I answered concisely and gave just enough information it would quench any curiosity.

"Wait," Mary freezes, "we need to take an airport selfie. Sam, take a picture of us, here use this." Mary thrusts a fancy black cell phone into Sam's hand and coaxes us to squeeze together while he effortlessly extends his arm and takes the picture. Mary examines the image and once it's deemed acceptable, she hands the phone to me.

"This is for you. We've already programed our numbers into it. Sam and I will feel better knowing we have a way to connect with you. Call or send messages back home as often as you'd like. Oh, and do you mind sending me that picture?"

"Sure," I say then stare at the image of the three of us on the screen. I don't fit in at all. They are like beautiful seashells and I am a craggy rock, rough and jagged.

"Thank you," I turn the phone over in my hand. "I don't know what to say." Unsettled, I wonder when and how I will find the strings attached to their generosity. In my experience, there are always strings. Gifts are never given "just because" and undeserved kindness is always the currency for turning a blind eye. I try to shrug off my cynicism and compose my first text message to Ingrid.

Shay: Hey Ing, I made it here safely. You can reach me at this # They gave me a phone! This is Shay btw.

Dozens of saguaro cactus, arms bending in all directions, cast monster-like shadows over me in the backseat. A deep purple streak follows the sun and slides through tufts of pink and orange clouds. The lavender-gray sky falls in on us from all sides. It's a dreamy sky, like the ones found in fairy

9

tales and lullabies. I blink slowly and my eyes beckon me to sleep. The phone resting in my hand buzzes me awake.

Ingrid: A new phone, lucky you. Glad you made it safe. Remember stay up as late as you can tonight to beat the jet lag and don't do anything I wouldn't do— seriously don't! :) Call me tomorrow.

I smile at the phone, feeling like it's the anchor I need to hold my former life in place. I tuck it into my pocket as Sam pulls up to a little yellow house. It is exactly what I pictured my American home to be. The house is one story, painted a pale shade of yellow and surrounded by a white fence. There is a small patch of grass near a porch with a white wooden swing. A set of wind chimes hangs near a planter overflowing with Bougainvillea and an American flag. I release my seat belt and gather my belongings.

"This will only take a minute. I need to run into my studio," Mary says then points to the yellow house. "Sit tight and I'll be right back." She hugs a manila folder to her chest and walks to the front door. I lean back nonchalantly and re-buckle my seatbelt.

"Our house is about fifteen minutes from here," Sam pauses, "we live in Paradise Valley." He tries to keep the conversation going but isn't as skilled as his wife. "Our son, Jake, is finishing his final year at Camelback Prep, the same school you will be attending," he motions behind us. "It's about five miles down the road."

Minutes pass and we quietly look out the windows until Mary opens the car door. "I'm so sorry," she says and locks eyes with Sam, "that took a little longer than I expected."

"Everything okay, dear?"

"Everything is fine; just a struggling patient," she says then sighs.

"I've been an Art Therapist for about fifteen years. With graduation around the corner, I knew my time with Jake was limited," Mary's voice cracks, "so I took a sabbatical. But just because I'm not currently seeing patients doesn't mean their problems stop."

We drive for about five minutes and Sam turns onto a dimly lit road at the foot of a small mountain; its silhouette looks like the back of a camel. Each switch advances us higher into the night as blankets of twinkling lights tuck in the city below.

At an iron gate Sam clicks a button and it opens slowly.

"Home sweet home."

Displayed at the end of the driveway, a sand colored house, less like a home and more like a hotel, spreads out in both directions. It is easily the biggest house I've ever seen. Sam parks in front of a massive marble archway that leads to an oversized wood and iron door.

I stare, gobsmacked, until I realize I am the only one left inside the car. I push the car door open and my eyes meet a shiny powder-blue sports car, proudly displayed in a large glass garage. It looks like a life-size version of little boy's packaged toy car.

Sam steps into my line of sight. "No matter what he says, Jake isn't allowed near the Spyder."

CHAPTER THREE

THEN

SAM PACES TOWARD THE GARAGE. "WHAT HE MEANS, IS that Jake is always trying to come up with reasons to drive the Porsche," Mary says, softening the blow, "the Porsche is very special to Sam." She glances at her husband as he pushes against one of the giant glass panels until he's satisfied it is secure.

Mary takes my hand and ushers me through the massive front door, "Welcome home, Shay." Inside, an atrium fills the center of an oversized lobby. Three towering fig trees berth near a moss covered fountain trickling with water. Branches sweep high in all directions, cascading over the banister of one of two identical staircases. Each staircase is a tidal wave of white marble that launches up and around the atrium. They are connected by a landing which overlooks the botanical oasis.

An old wooden birdcage hangs from the lowest limb of the tallest tree. It houses a pair of orange canaries while a large yellow parrot perches freely on the pinnacle of the fountain.

"Let me show you to your room." Mary ascends the left staircase and I follow. The sound of flowing water drowns out my anxiety.

"That's Baby, our parrot." The yellow bird hops to a closer limb and ruffles its feathers. "She's a sweet old bird."

"Hello, Baby!" the bird squawks.

"Hello, Baby," I say, unsure how to converse with a bird.

"Polly hates crackers!" the bird says and I laugh.

"I apologize in advance if she says something inappropriate," Mary's eyes narrow but her lips curve into a smile. "Jake and Sam taught her a handful of phrases over the years."

Opposite the atrium, a huge living room sprawls out below. Crystal chandeliers move ever so slightly, dancing light onto the exterior wall made entirely of glass. Two sitting areas face a marble fireplace on the North wall and another overlooks the city to the West.

Down a wide marble hallway, Mary leads me past a sculpture showcased in a small alcove and then another dressed in light atop a pedestal. Canvases streaked with vibrant colors cover the walls. The second floor feels like a museum. Mary, the curator, names select pieces along with the artist that created them as we pass. I point out a smaller watercolor painting of the barrel of a breaking wave.

"What is that one called?"

"Broken Echo. I painted it after our trip to Costa Rica last year," Mary says proudly.

"You painted that? Wow, it's amazing."

"Thank you," she says then stops at the first open door; the three before had been closed. "And here we are, your room. I hope you like it." Mary follows me in.

Bigger than Ingrid's entire flat, the room is like a small house. A white four-poster bed with white linens and blue and turquoise striped pillows, is centered on a teal wall. The exterior wall, made of windows, is hidden by white plantation shutters. An enormous bathroom with a spa tub and fireplace is behind one door and another leads to a wardrobe of the same size. I walk into the wardrobe lined with empty shelves and cabinets. I almost laugh out loud realizing the contents of my entire bag will fill up three, maybe four, shelves. In the middle, a yellow velvet couch backs up to a royal blue antique bureau. Both pieces center on a huge floor to ceiling mirror.

I set my duffle on the floor and my backpack falls off my shoulder. I place it near the mirrored wall then examine the set of black bags sagging under my eyes. Disheartened, I reapply some concealer, mascara and lip balm. Wishing I had made a better first impression, I exit the closet. Mary is sitting on the edge of the bed, studying her phone. She looks up only when I stand directly in front of her.

"Is there anything I can get you, anything you need?" she asks as she puts her phone in her pocket and pats the bed next to her.

"I don't think so," I say then awkwardly sit.

"I am so glad you are here. Finally, another girl in the house!" the woman's eyes brim with tears and she fans her face trying to ward them off. I squirm and refuse to make eye contact not knowing what to do with this woman and all of her feelings.

"I'm such a softie. That's what the guys say." Mary smirks. "They're right though." A sheepish smile forms on her lips and she pulls me into another awkward hug.

"Mary?" Sam calls from the hallway halting the overdose of Mary's affection.

"Settle in," she says then squeezes my hand and stands. "You can meet Jake and see the rest of the house in a little bit." She pats my leg then vanishes out the door.

Back in the wardrobe, I retrieve my backpack and fall into the oversized yellow sofa. The unexpected accommodations leave me feeling small and insignificant and the effort Mary puts forth to make me feel special only births more guilt. I don't deserve this. The Exchange program made a mistake.

I rummage through my backpack and remove my turquoise folder. I search the tabs corresponding with the research I'd done once I'd been accepted into the program and locate the tab labeled California Beaches. I thumb through the pictures overcome with an ache for the salty waters of my beloved Pacific. "Six months," I say aloud then sigh. "I can do anything for six months."

I pull a blank sheet of paper from the back of the folder and begin to write:

Mary Forester is very kind and will hug you until you suffocate.

Sam Forester is an Investment Broker. I think he's having an affair with his car.

I hear a rap on my door and hastily tuck the piece of paper into the front pocket of the folder then place it back into my bag. I am about to open the bedroom door when I hear Mary talking, "I understand you're worried but I'm afraid you are scaring her."

Not wanting to hear the rest of the private conversation, I cough then open the door. In the hallway, Mary frowns at Sam though her countenance lifts when she sees me.

"Ready to see the rest of the house?" she takes my hand, without waiting for an answer.

We continue down the marble hallway past three enormous paintings of the San Francisco Peaks mountain range then stop at the next door.

Two Lacrosse sticks center on a gray wall over the headboard of a large bed.

"This is Jake's room." Small black pillows are piled haphazardly atop a gray and black striped duvet. On the opposite wall is a framed jersey of a sports team I'd never heard of.

Mary rushes past the bed to a pile of clothes in the corner. "Boys will be boys."

"Have you heard from Jake?" Sam asks, with an icy edge in his voice.

Arms laden with dirty clothes, Mary walks into the wardrobe then returns phone in her hand.

"He just sent a text message. Practice ran late." Mary puts her hand on Sam's chest. "He'll be home soon," she soothes then smiles at me.

We continue down the hall and Mary names the rooms behind each closed door. It seems strange that so many doors are left unopened. Maybe the Exchange Program included the two petty theft infractions in my file and the Foresters were just trying to protect their stuff. Whatever the reason, I don't dare say anything for fear of Sam's reaction. At the end of the hall, we arrive at a final open door. The room lights up as Mary steps through.

Pieces of exercise equipment are arranged strategically on the hardwood floors. It is the same size as my bedroom but with mirrored walls it looks twice as big.

"The gym is sound proof so use it whenever you'd like and feel free to crank up the music," she says and points to the built in sound system.

"Most of the time it's empty but I imagine we might find you in here quite often. I read that you worked at a gym back in Sydney?"

"Yes, I worked out their everyday back home," I reply, taking an inventory of what information was offered to the Foresters. My past has a way of never staying in the past.

Across the hall from Jake's room, Sam opens a door and enters. He slides his finger up a dimmer switch illuminating a small theater room covered in gray fabric. Black leather recliners, arranged in rows, sit on three descending tiers. At the bottom, a sofa with a connecting chaise focuses on a giant, white screen framed in red silk.

"The media room is Jake's domain. You might have to kick him out when you want to watch TV. He comes in here to study."

"So watching Stranger Things counts as studying?" Sam chides coolly then checks his phone again.

17

We backtrack down the hallway, stopping on the landing, which overlooks the atrium.

"Shay, you look exhausted. We should let you rest. Do you remember which room is yours?" Mary waves down the hallway.

I am tempted to retreat but remember Ingrid's text and force myself to continue. "I'm okay," I say trying to sound convincing.

"You sure?" Mary asks, and I nod yes. "Then let's go downstairs and get you a snack. You must be starving."

We head down the right staircase and make our way back to the atrium. Then Mary leads us down a short hallway that opens into an enormous kitchen and dining room.

"This is where I slave and toil." Mary says. Her grin is contagious. Even Sam's lips turn up slightly when he looks at his wife.

Shiny steel appliances reflect the soft grey-colored walls. A white-washed wood island, in the center of the room, is covered in gray and white marble with four stools on one side.

"Help yourself to anything in the cabinets, pantry, fridge."

I look to each place as she names them and silently worry that my surrogate parents can sense my apprehension. It is in my DNA to keep people at arms length and now, like a stray animal, I've been invited inside. I wonder if they trust me as little as I trust them.

We follow Sam past the dining room table which is adorned with more place settings than I can count, and enter into the great room we viewed from the second floor landing. Sam opens a door made of windows that leads to a covered patio outside. Navy and white striped sofas surround three circular pits filled with shimmering black rocks. As we walk by, each pit spits out a set of electric blue flames. I step toward the colored fire and warm my hands. I didn't expect the desert to be so cold.

"Let's sit for a minute," Mary says and hands me a blanket as if anticipating the need.

"This is just a formality but we wanted to go over some house rules," I nod as Sam speaks. Though stern, his voice has regained some of the warmth I experienced at the airport.

"Just so we're all on the same page," Mary says supportively.

"The same rules we set for Jake will apply to you. Curfew is at 10:30 on weeknights and 12:30 on weekends. Since you don't have a driver's license, we will provide you with transportation. Jake will drive you to and from school except on the days he has practice. On those days Mary will pick you up."

"As you probably know, the legal drinking age in the U.S. is twenty-one," Mary states.

"That won't be a problem," I interrupt, "I mean, I don't drink."

Sam nods dubiously and I know he must have read my file too.

Behind Mary, a shadow appears near the wall of glass and the door to the patio opens.

"You're late," Sam says, without turning around.

Jake steps into the shifting shadows of the fire. Black hair sticks out in all directions from under his baseball cap. A fitted white t-shirt exaggerates his broad shoulders and toned chest.

"Practice ran late. Mom didn't tell you?" his eyes burn blue like the flames. He pulls his hat off and twists the brim tight in his hands. Jaw clenched, a strand of black falls into his eyes until he swipes it away.

19

"Dad's giving you a hard time. Come over here and meet Shay."

I hear my name and look away, realizing that I'd been staring at Jake. He steps toward me and I stand then try to unwrap myself from the blanket.

"G'day," I wave, not knowing what to do with my hand. It is a terrible decision.

"Hey," he says in a monotone voice. We lock eyes for a millisecond but then he looks away uninterested.

"Jake's been playing Lacrosse for a couple years now. He has a scholarship to play at San Diego State University. We will be taking a trip to San Diego in a couple weeks so he can visit the campus again before the semester starts in the fall."

A calm washes over me. The ocean had been the only constant in my life. The salty waters of the South Pacific were my only refuge. It swallowed my sorrows on my worst days and strengthened my resolve on my best. Long ago, I'd given up hope that I would ever love a person as much as I loved the sea. With the exception of Ingrid, most people came and went, each taking a piece of me. The ocean never took anything. Paddling out early every morning on my board to catch a wave, the foamy water restored me.

At the end of his mother's introduction, Jake leans down and kisses her cheek then turns toward the door.

"Night," he says over his shoulder and walks inside.

"He's tired from practice," Mary says and shrugs as disappointment tightens Sam's jaw.

Mary walks over to the pool and dips her fingers into the water and I follow.

"It's heated," she says in a sing-song voice, trying to change the subject. "You can go for a swim whenever you'd like. Come check out the pool house."

I peek inside.

"There's a game room, if you ever feel like playing bumper pool or pinball," she says and closes the door then leads us back to the main house. I follow her inside and up the marble steps.

"One last thing…" Mary says and stops at the second story landing just as the yellow parrot squawks and flaps its wings.

"Baby, you scared me!" Mary pulls her hands to her chest. Once she regains her composure she continues, "Sometimes, there are coyotes and wild pigs in the yard early in the morning. Jake saw a bobcat a couple weeks ago; so if you here strange noises…"

"Spider. Spider. Spider!" Baby squawks.

Mary laughs nervously. "I've never heard her say that. There are insects in the desert, but none inside the house, I promise," she stutters and takes my hand, "and any strange noises you hear are nothing to worry about either." She gives my hand a gentle squeeze.

"Good night, Baby," I say turning my attention to the yellow bird.

"Don't go near the spider!" Baby squawks.

Mary's face loses all color. She drops my hand.

"Sam must have taught her that," she says and forces a laugh. "He sure loves that car." She clears her throat then hugs me goodnight and speed-walks toward her bedroom.

I pass by Mary's painting of the barrel wave on the way to my room and smile. Even though my head aches and my legs are like wet noodles, the promised trip to the ocean renews me. I breathe in the first long silence of the day and turn the handle to my bedroom door. Suddenly, the peel of an electric guitar sweeps down the long corridor, erasing the quiet. Light spills out from Jake's room, followed by more loud music. Wearing only a pair of cotton shorts and runners, Jake steps into the hall, his phone at his ear. Funny, you don't look buggered, mate. The lights in the gym flicker on. Jake turns to close the door behind him and I panic. Unsure if he can see me, I fling open my door and jump through. With a loud thud, it shuts behind me and I fall onto the bed reaching for the nearest pillow to stifle my laughter.

CHAPTER FOUR

NOW

I DART PAST SAM, HEAVE OPEN THE FRONT DOOR AND RUN through, all while focusing on the iron gate at the end of the stone driveway. It begins to close and a string of curse words flow from my lips as a burst of panic jolts my legs into a full sprint.

At the gate, I turn my body sideways and shimmy through the closing gap. A half-smile hijacks my lips when I hear the metal clink together behind me. I refuse to look over my shoulder; they don't deserve a second glance. Instead, I plow forward, bounding down the switchbacks of the small mountain—running away had always been the easy part. The last time I ran was before I moved in with Ingrid. I walked in on my caregiver Mrs. Newton pashing Liam, the oldest orphan in her house. She threatened to tell my caseworker that I stole her car if I shared their secret. I knew if someone was trying to control you because of their own lack of self-control, it was time to go. So I ran then, and today was no different. The Foresters were trying to control future events but were unsuccessful. But, unlike Mrs. Newton, I had no idea what the Foresters wanted from me. Why had they included me in their elaborate scheme to save Jake?

At the bottom of the mountain, I crouch next to a metal bench to catch my breath. The neighborhood is quiet and peaceful and my body relaxes with each exhale. In the stillness, the memory of what I'd seen overtakes me. I try to blink the image away but the two frightened figures, bound and gagged, stare back at me, pleading for their lives.

The approaching bus lets out a growl and the terrified couple disappears as I focus on my incoming freedom. I look over my shoulder then escape up the black rubber steps once I'm satisfied that I'm not being followed. I hunker down low in the back of the bus then reach for my bag resting at my feet. The middle pocket unzips with ease and I cast a shadow over the black-framed glasses. The translucent lenses turn milky white and a faint blue tint renders where the glass meet the frames. I lean in, examining glossy, pastel circles that form in the middle of each lens. They grow in size, expanding outward until each looks like an oil slick. The shadow of my hand shifts and the pigments follow. I flutter my fingers and the colors dance under my spell. My thumb unintentionally swipes the left side of the frames and a low frequency hum replaces the watercolor display. The vibration intensifies and the lenses gloss over, emitting shiny charcoal ripples from the center of each lens. I remember Sam's words, that the glasses would explain everything, and my curiosity conquers my fear. With both hands, I pick up the frames. My fingers tremble uncontrollably as I place them on the bridge of my nose. Eyes wide open, I watch the methodic black tides wash over the inside of the lenses until the tremors subside and darkness surrounds me.

The bus switches gears and I hear a woman's voice. Instinctively, I dip the glasses down and look around the bus, but all the seats are empty. Convinced I am alone, I move the lenses back into place. I close my eyes and surrender to the black void. A long silence disappoints and I concede with a sigh. When I breathe in again, a sweet citrus scent fills the air.

"I will never get used to this," I hear Mary's voice. I try to touch the glasses but can't move. I'm no longer sitting on the bus but at a small table in Mary's bedroom, overlooking the city lights. In the window's reflection, I see Mary sitting in a chair, wearing the glasses. Next to her, Sam examines an identical pair of pulsating glasses. My heart speeds up, as I form solutions in my head. Have I gone back in time? Is this how they travel?

"Welcome to your first Adaptation Sequence. It's our way of updating you, our past-selves, of our missions." I hear Mary's voice, but oddly it feels as though my mouth is moving. It's as if I'm silently reciting the words she speaks. "Each time you use the glasses, you'll live through my experiences. This is a virtual diary of our journey to save Jake." I look for my own reflection in the window next to Mary and it hits me like a rogue wave, I'm a prisoner in Mary Forester's body. I try to open my mouth to scream but instead Mary's voice emerges. "I must warn you, many things you encounter will be hard to stomach—"

"Try living through them," Sam says but Mary shushes him.

"You will be fully immersed in my experience, so if ever you're overwhelmed, blink your eyes three times and the vision will subside."

25

One, two, three blinks; I waste no time in regaining my freedom. I feel for the smooth frames. They take form under my fingertips and I rip them from my face.

CHAPTER FIVE

THEN

MARY SLIDES INTO THE DRIVER'S SEAT AND REVS THE engine of the Mercedes. Over my shoulder, colored boxes and bags litter the backseat. I'd been kindly forced into countless fitting rooms while Mary, along with a dozen different sales clerks, ushered in an ungodly number of outfits and accessories for me to try on. At the last store we visited, Mary liked one of the outfits so much she insisted that I wear it home. So now I sit pretty in the passenger seat, donning a new pair of jeans, black ankle boots and a baby blue cashmere sweater. I can't ignore that the price tags on those items alone exceed a couple months' worth of wages at the rock gym. I know a "thank you" on the way out the door of the last shop isn't adequate, so I quietly fret and plot a way to repay my would-be mum for her generosity.

"You look tired. I hope I didn't wear you out," she says then backs out of the parking space.

"I didn't sleep well. I had some strange dreams last night."

Mary's eyes perk up as I muffle a yawn.

"Next time you dream you should write about it. I journal my dreams."

"I'll have to try that sometime," I say. Afraid the jet lag has finally caught up with me, I'm unsure if Mary is serious or joking.

"It might just be my background in art therapy but I've found dream journaling to be very helpful. It can help you to see struggles in your past and anxieties in your future. Sometimes, when I don't have the words, I paint my dreams." Mary moves her sunglasses down the bridge of her nose. "Sorry, I'm treating you like a patient. Thank you for shopping with me today."

"Thank you, for everything," I say but my words are too small.

Down the driveway, the car pulls into the first of the three garage bays. Mary inches forward into the space and I catch a glimpse of Sam's beloved powder-blue Spyder, in the light of day. The engine stops and Mary's eyes seem to pierce a hole through the back of my head. She puts her hand over mine and continues the conversation.

"Shopping for a girl is so much more fun," Mary says then grins. "This is how it must feel to have a daughter." My heart races at panic attack speed. I fumble to release my seat belt and leap out of the vehicle. Mary, completely unaware of the cataclysmic impact of her words, gathers packages from the backseat while I fight the intense desire to haul ass down the driveway and through the iron gate. I take in a deep breath and my fingers find their place, tracing my tattoo. A calm settles over me and I

28

loop a bundle of shopping bags around my wrist. It had been a long time since I'd been anyone's daughter.

———

A stack of silver trays abuts a box of neatly folded vanilla-colored linens on the kitchen counter. Partially opened flower boxes, containing orange tulips, spread out across the dining table next to a basket of candles and a bin of collapsed paper lanterns. Two men in black slacks and white, pressed shirts unpack the supplies while I lug shopping bags and boxes to my room.

"Shay, sweetheart, I still have a few things to do to prepare for the party tonight. You should go on upstairs and relax."

"Party?" I say, trying to sound calm.

"Just a little gathering, so you can get to know some of your new classmates. Go rest. Sam will bring up the last of the packages." Mary waves at a dozen bags and boxes arranged neatly near the pantry door. I was fairly convinced I'd gotten them all.

"Are you sure I can't help?"

"No silly, you're the guest of honor," Mary says then refocuses her energy to the flowers on the table.

"She's got it under control." Sam winks at his wife then grabs an armful of bags.

It isn't the party details that concern me but my newly acquired title. What does a guest of honor do anyway? I reach my room and search for my running shoes. Running was the best way to clear my head. I quickly change into a sports tank and pair of running shorts then sweep my hair back into a messy bun. I pause for a moment in the doorway and run back to my wardrobe, remembering the chilled water in the mini fridge. Once I'm confident that I haven't forgotten anything else, I jog into the hallway.

"Whoa!"

I look up just in time to collide into the chiseled chest of the dark-haired boy from the room next door.

"Sorry, Jake. You right, mate?"

"It's cool," he says and picks up his hat; a casualty of the collision.

"I'll try to watch where I'm going next time," I say, then let out a nervous laugh. I instantly hate myself.

His silence conveys his indifference.

Too embarrassed to see if he is still standing in the hallway, I jog straight ahead into the gym without looking back. The room brightens and I let out a deep sigh then shut the door. Bloody fantastic! Well done Shay. Well done! My eyes roll as I look at myself in the mirror. I force my legs to sprint the first four miles as retribution for the hallway mishap.

Fatigue finds me halfway through the fifth mile but I push on until I finish six. I drag myself back to my room and after a quick shower, plop down and fall asleep on my bed. A tap on the door wakes me.

"Should I leave these here?"

Through a groggy haze, I identify Jake's voice. I'd forgotten to close my door, a habit of living with only girls the past four years. I shoot up onto my feet, but the overwhelming feeling that I might faint forces me back down. Eyes pinched closed, I brace myself on the bed until the sensation passes. As I regain composure, I reluctantly open my eyes. In the doorway, Jake holds at least twenty shopping bags in his arms.

"Uh, are you okay?" he says and looks at me as if I am from a different planet. A flash of terror shoots through me, as I remember I'd fallen asleep right after my shower. Slowly, I reach around my body. The touch of cashmere puts me at ease.

"Yes, that's fine, I'm fine." My head jostles as the words scramble from my lips.

Jake approaches slowly and places the bags near me on the bed. I wonder if my befuddled mind is playing tricks on me because he looks different. His light blue linen shirt appears white until I see it near his eyes. Slightly wrinkled, it's left untucked from his fitted jeans. His black hair is slicked back with hair gel or water from a recent shower, I can't decide. As he releases the last bag from his hand, his coconut after shave tickles my nose. It reminds me of my coconut and honey surfboard wax and a wave of sadness hits me as I long for the ocean.

"Thank you," I say in a hoarse whisper.

"Yup," he replies and the scent of coconut follows him out the doorway.

I rise slowly and close the door behind him. At a complete loss for time, I grab my cell phone, more worried about the task at hand than another embarrassing encounter with Jake. After all, the guest of honor can't be late.

CHAPTER SIX

.

THEN

ON THE PATIO, A GENTLE BREEZE, MADE WARM BY numerous petrol heaters, whirls around locks of my already frizzed hair. Wrangling the strands together, I tuck them nervously behind my ear. Another gust weaves through the hanging paper lanterns overhead. They cast long shadows over bouquets of orange tulips atop ivory tablecloths. At one of the tables, Jake talks with a couple of girls; the taller one leans in and whispers something in his ear. His upper lip curves and points to a dimple on his left cheek. It is the first time I've seen him truly smile.

The only dark-skinned girl sitting at the table stands and walks over to me.

"You must be Shay. I'm Erin."

I nod then smile.

Short and slim, Erin wears a pair of fitted jeans with a blousy lavender top. A jeweled clip pins her short black hair into place. I can't tell if she is wearing makeup or if her face is just naturally beautiful.

"My parents have been best friends with Mary and Sam since before I was born," Erin says as Mary makes her way to us through a mob of girls huddled near Jake's table.

"Erin, did you meet Shay?"

"Yes, I just introduced myself," she replies, as if following orders.

"Great, but sweetie, your mom is looking for you; she found your cell phone."

"Are you serious? I thought I lost it. It was nice to meet you," Erin says then dashes off.

"Let me introduce you to some of Jake's friends. You ready?" Mary says.

I will my lips to smile and my head to nod yes, but I'm not ready. The circumstances thrust upon me in the last few days were bloody overwhelming. Living with the Foresters was like existing in a different reality.

Sets of eyes from each table watch me as I move around the room with Mary and I imagine myself as a slimy, gelatinous blob-fish; ugly and awkward, swimming with the sharks.

"Most of these boys are on Jake's LaCrosse team." Mary waves her hands over the group sitting at the table with Jake. She names each one until a girl in a white silk dress pulls her into an embrace.

"Shay, this is Taylor, Jake's… friend." Mary stumbles over the words.

33

Blonde hair cascades in layers over the girl's shoulders and the longest piece tucks into the crook of her arm as she extends her hand to me.

"You couldn't have ended up with a nicer family," Taylor says but her seemingly sincere brown eyes mismatch her sly smile. "Hopefully we'll have some classes together. Oh, I just remembered, I need to get the math homework from Jake. Excuse me."

Taylor glides in next to Jake. The random girl sitting on his left sulks and rolls her eyes as Jake wraps his arms around the waist of the beautiful girl in white.

"The woes of young love," Mary says and puts her hands over her heart. "Jake broke up with Taylor a while back. I don't think she's gotten over it, poor thing." It seems the opposite to me but I mind my own business and follow Mary, a natural-born hostess, as she initiates exchanges between me and almost every guest before dessert is even served.

Exhausted, I'm finally left to piece together a plate of food from the buffet table and mingle on my own. I'm about to take a bite of a prawn from the skewer in my hand when the clinking of a glass makes me pause. On the other side of the room, Mary gently taps a fork against a lifted glass, "Shay, sweetheart, come on over here."

A hush falls across the room and I am frozen in place. What the bloody hell is she doing?

"Thank you all for coming. Tonight is a special night for the Forester family. It is my pleasure to introduce to you our newest member. All the way from Sydney, Australia, Shay Conrad."

A soft applause waves through the patio, spurring a bright red glow onto my cheeks. All eyes are on me and there is no escape.

"If you haven't met Shay, please take a minute to do so. She has some great stories from the land down under," Mary says in her best Australian accent and Jake murmurs something under his breath while Taylor grins in amusement.

Mary's speech ends and conversations resume. I abandon my plate of food and search for the best exit route. A tap on my shoulder foils my plan.

"I hear you like to climb." An attractive blonde-haired boy towers over me. I can't understand why I hadn't seen him until now, since he's easily the tallest person in the room.

"Aye, you like to climb?"

"Everyday," he says then runs his fingers through a tumble of flaxen waves. His brown eyes make me feel at home for the first time.

"There are some great places to climb around here." He looks the part of a climber; tanned, lean muscular arms and calloused hands. "I have a rock wall at my house. You should come by sometime."

"You have your own wall?" my eyes widen and I try to act cool.

"I have practice until five tomorrow. You could come over after. I can pick you up." His lips turn up into a smile and his fingers surf through the waves in his hair again.

"Sure," I say then I remember all the new rules governing me. "Wait, I should check with Mr. and Mrs. Forester to make sure it's okay."

"You can text me later…"

"Okay."

"Can I have your phone?"

I hand it over and he types in his name and number then passes it back to me.

"Grady," I say his name aloud as I read it. "I'll text you later." Avoiding a chance to ruin the moment, I turn and search for Mary. When I look up, Jake passes only centimeters in front of me. My stomach twists and I walk in the opposite direction, thankful I'd avoided a repeat collision.

I find Mary absorbed in conversation with a mate near one of the fire pits. I stand at a distance, not wanting to be rude, and wait for a lull. Nonchalantly, I turn back toward Grady who's now talking to Jake. They're mates?

"Shay, I'd like you to meet my best friend Jane," Mary says as she waves me over.

Jane extends her hand, then pulls me into a hug. I can see why she and Mary are best mates.

"Jane is Erin's mom." Instantly I see the resemblance except Jane is shorter with darker skin but just as beautiful.

"Does Shay know about the San Diego trip, Mary?" Jane asks and I nod my head.

"It's going to be fun. Are you sure you can't come?" Mary glooms.

"Rick mentioned he and Cassie were going to drive over for the weekend." Jane says then scrunches her nose. "Rick is Erin's father, my ex-husband." she relays, then gives a little wink.

"You know I had to extend an offer for them to stay at the beach house…" Mary says with a pout on her lips. "Cassie is letting us stay at Greystone Lodge over spring break. Besides, I thought you two were getting along?"

Jane shrugs her shoulders, "We are, I guess. It's just hard being a single parent. I miss out on so much of Erin's life. Ever since Rick announced his engagement to Cassie at Erin's 18th birthday party—which was a pretty tacky thing to do by the way—things haven't been the same."

"I think I'm going to get something to drink," I say excusing myself. Uncomfortable with the turn in conversation, I head for the kitchen. Surrounded by the wait staff, I get a glass of water then take short sips and avoid the other party-goers for as long as I can. My sense of utopia is lost when Jake's deep voice drifts down the hallway.

"My mom just wants us to be nice to her; you didn't have to ask her out."

I stop and turn then get as close as possible without being detected. I see Jake but Grady has his back to me. Both are laughing.

"Seriously, you don't have to take on the charity case from down-under. Some nerd from Calculus class will sweep her off her Aussie feet in no time." More laughter.

Anger bubbles up and I take a step forward, ready to walk directly into Jake's line of sight. Three years ago, maybe even two, I wouldn't have paused; I would've gone looking for the fight. I breathe in and step backward, allowing my newly acquired self-control to prevail, then opt for a different route away from the party.

Alone on the patio, I breathe a sigh of relief for the first time all night. A few guests remain, talking and laughing inside, but outside peace hovers around me. High overhead, the amber colored moon casts puddles of gold onto the tops of boulders and high-reaching saguaros. I sink into the calm, letting small gusts of wind swirl up and down my arms. For a moment, I swear I taste the salt from the sea on my lips. I pull in a deep breath through my nose and try to find the taste again but come up empty. My eyes squint as I look out over the city. Dark except the glimmering lights, I imagine them as boats in Sydney Harbour and for a moment I'm home. From darkness to bright white, my view is suddenly obstructed. I open my eyes to Taylor standing in front of me.

"I hope you enjoyed the party."

"I did, thank you."

"You must feel kind of outnumbered. Most of us have known each other since preschool." Is she trying to make me feel bad?

"It's hard for outsiders to fit in. Don't worry, you'll find your place," she says and I know immediately what she is saying. I might not be from around here but I am fluent in the universal language of mean-girl.

"I was looking for you." Jake soothes until he sees me. "Let's go inside."

"Let me know if you need anything." She attempts a side hug as inauthentic as the smile perched on her lips and turns and walks into Jake's open arms.

Mary greets them at the door. She hugs Taylor then whispers something into her ear. "It's no problem, glad I could help," Taylor says loudly, then winks at me and walks back inside. Back home, I avoided proper Toffs like her.

"Are you having a good time?" Mary asks then sits and drapes her arm around my shoulders.

I try to muster some sincerity into a smile.

"Grady said you're going to hang out at his house tomorrow after practice; that should be fun."

"Oh, I don't know, maybe." I shrug my shoulders as my mind searches for an excuse.

"You should go. Grady is a great guy. He and Jake have been best friends since the second grade." Perfect, they seem quite the pair and I'll do my best to avoid them both.

I stifle a fake yawn, looking for a way out of the conversation. Thankfully, Mary takes the bait and dismisses me.

Back in my room, I use my phone to take a picture of the pile of boxes and shopping bags then send it to Ingrid.

Ingrid: Shay went shopping???

Shay: Mary went shopping.

Ingrid: Wow! Generous!

Shay: It's bananas here. I met a guy who has a climbing wall at his house.

Ingrid: You are never going to want to come home.

I think about texting Ingrid how I'm really feeling but I don't want to be a burden. She sacrificed so much for me to come here. The least I can do is pretend.

I pull the turquoise folder from my bag and begin to write. The events of the night strengthened my resolve.

No matter the outcome of each day I am here for me, no one else.

CHAPTER SEVEN

THEN

"ARE YOU READY YET?" JAKE HOVERS WITH HIS BACKPACK snug over his shoulders.

My first bite of porridge is still milling around inside my mouth and I am unable to reply. Obviously, I am not ready. What a knob. Luckily, Sam begins a semi-formal interrogation concerning Jake's plans after practice. It buys me a couple minutes to inhale my bowl of hot cereal and orange juice. Jake sees my progress and takes advantage of the lull in his father's questioning. He dodges his mother's open arms and heads for the door. I grab my bag and scurry out of the kitchen after him. Lacking Jake's knack for dodging his mum, I fall prey to yet another one of Mary's awkward embraces.

"Jake is going to show you where you need to go. Okay, sweetie?"

My frustration swells. The faith Mary has in her son and his ability to keep his word is disheartening. I'd been privy to Mary's keen intuition at the party. The woman had an uncanny skill of identifying and solving problems before anyone was aware of them. I don't understand why this amazing, generous woman, has such a blind spot when it comes to her own son.

I walk briskly to the passenger side door of the silver ute as Jake revs the engine impatiently. The bass reverberates through the cab and my hands shake as I pull the door open. Loud music escapes in all directions and the porridge in my belly turns over. Walking and riding public buses were my preferred methods of transportation. I rarely asked mates for a lift. Anyone with my tragic history would understand.

A space no wider than an arm's length separates us in the cab but his indifference proves me invisible. He peels out of the driveway and one of my hands grips the leather armrest while the other involuntarily traces the tattoo on my wrist. Each vibration reminds me that my life is in his hands. He makes a hard left. My eyes squeeze shut and I swallow a scream. The ute jerks to a stop. I open my eyes slowly, hoping it's over, then sigh, seeing we arrived at the school intact. Jake grabs his backpack and exits the ute in silence then walks toward one of the tan-colored buildings across the lot. The cab door shuts behind me and Jake glances back. His head drops and his pace slows. I finally catch up as he steps from the asphalt to the sidewalk.

"Where's your schedule?" he says, then waits for me to respond. "Where is your list of classes?" he starts again slower and louder, his impatience pours over each syllable. "Can I see it?"

I pull a piece of paper from my pocket and hand it to him. He scans it quickly then hands it back.

"Your first two classes are in that building over there. You have lunch in there and the next class you have with me, in the building over there." he points to each structure. "Your last two classes are on the second floor of the gray building behind this one," he says searching for a sign that I understand so his obligation will be over. I try to digest his words and slowly nod.

"If you can't remember, someone in the school office can help you."

In other words if you can't find a class, ask someone who cares.

"I have to go. If I'm late to Statistics again, I'll get detention and miss practice."

I barely hear him as he jogs in the other direction.

I set out to find my first class, unwilling to let his blatant disregard shred my confidence. Surprisingly, Jake's instructions are spot on. I step through the door of my first class and a handful of students are clustered together in chairs at the front.

"Shay!" a voice shouts, from behind.

In a pair of jeans and white t-shirt, Grady approaches. So much for trying to avoid him. There is something comforting in his sweet smile and lanky physique. I hate myself for hoping he that actually cares.

"Are we still on, after practice?"

"It's okay if you're too busy. I'm sure I'll have heaps of homework," I stutter and an amused grin spreads over his lips.

"Oh wait, I am busy," he says.

"No worries, we'll climb some other time," I try to hide my relief.

"I'm busy because I have plans, with you." He smiles.

"Sweet! I'm stoked," I say trying to sound stoked."

"I invited Jake too, but he has other plans."

I'm sure he doesn't, I think to myself and I can barely keep from smirking.

We talk about climbing until class starts. Warm and comforting, Grady is like a cozy blanket on a dreary day. The more I listen to him, the more I like him. I want so much to believe the best and that I'm not just an obligatory pet project. After class, I quickly sneak out behind Grady who is discussing an assignment with another mate and find my next class. Once it's over I head for the library.

Near a tall shelf full of dusty books in the back corner, I unfurl my brown lunch sack, stealthy like a ninja, trying not to draw attention. I'd walked by the cafeteria but couldn't convince my feet to move inside. In Sydney, students typically ate outside. I figured the library, in all its quiet solidarity, was my best option. I peek inside the lunch bag Mary packed. I can't remember the last time anyone made me lunch. Apple slices, peach yogurt, and avocado toast hide under a folded napkin. On the napkin, a handwritten note:

Wishing you a fantastic first day!

Love, Mary

I wonder if Jake's lunch has a napkin with a similar inscription. My thoughts are interrupted by a girl walking past me. She's the first person

I'd seen since sitting down in the furthest corner of the school's library. Seconds later the girl walks by again, this time with a stack of books in her arms. She stops and stares, confused.

"Shay, is that you?"

Embarrassed, I realize I met her but I don't remember her name.

"I'm Erin, Jane's daughter, we met the other night at the Foresters' party."

I nod, mouth full.

"Are you eating your lunch in the library?"

My face turns pink.

"Come on, pack up your stuff," Erin grunts as she shifts the books in her arms. "I need to check these books out then we are going to eat lunch together, in the *cafeteria*," she emphasizes the last word.

Reluctantly, I pack my bag and follow Erin's instructions.

"How do you like living with the Foresters?"

We stop at Erin's locker, to drop off her load of books.

"Mary and Sam are really great, so generous," I say, omitting anything about their imp of a son.

Erin notices. "Jake is the closest thing I have to a brother. He is a spoiled pain in the butt." She slams her locker shut. "But deep down," she pauses, "okay, really deep down, he has a good heart." Her eyes are apologetic.

The cafeteria looks like a giant greenhouse, with windows on all sides. Even the ceiling is glass but instead of fostering the growth of flowers and herbs, teenagers grow wild. At a crowded table, I sit next to Erin, wishing

44

I was actually surrounded by plants instead of people. When I look up, Grady's smiling brown eyes stare back.

"I was wondering where you were. How's your day been?"

"This is Shay," Erin interrupts and introduces me to the others before I can answer.

"Why did you choose Arizona?" Taylor says coolly.

"It's not like she gets to pick," Erin pipes in.

"You didn't get to pick did you?"

I shake my head no.

"Figures, who would pick Arizona?" Erin says.

"It's beautiful so far," I reply.

"Wait until summer," Erin says.

Jake leans his head back toward Erin, his arm holding tight around Taylor. He doesn't think I can see him as he points to me then mouths the words "What the hell?"

Erin rolls her eyes and turns back toward me.

"So are you excited for the trip to San Diego?"

"Yes, very."

"You're going to San Diego? When?" Grady interjects.

"Next month," Erin answers for me. "Jake needs to tour San Diego State again."

Jake turns his head, hearing his name.

"I was just telling Grady that you are going to Cali in a couple weeks."

"We should all go. I haven't been in months," Grady says and stares at me. "During the summer we practically live at our beach house in La Jolla."

"Because Arizona summers suck." Taylor chimes in.

"Erin's family owns the house next door to my mine." Grady's fist taps Erin's.

"Actually, it's my mom's beach house now, since the divorce. I haven't been allowed to go back without adult supervision since spring break. Who knew filling a hot tub with chocolate pudding would cause so many problems?" Erin shrugs her shoulders with a devilish grin.

"We'll have to stay at your house, Grady," Erin says, still grinning.

"I'm staying with you too." Jake turns to Grady.

"Sure, as long as you get your dad to let you drive the Spyder over!"

"Yeah, I'll be sure to ask him when I get home," he says then kisses Taylor on the neck.

CHAPTER EIGHT

THEN

GRADY'S CHALKED HAND REACHES FOR THE NEXT HOLD. Already three stories up, he's about to reach the top and he's not even fatigued.

"You coming?" I barely hear the question over the music bouncing from the walls to the floor where I sit.

I force myself onto my feet and within seconds I tie my harness into the safety line and begin to climb. Five times up the wall, trying to match Grady's pace, has worn me out. I resist the temptation to move over to an easier section and follow his path. Halfway up, I rest. Grady rappels himself down next to my hold.

"Tired?"

I nod, sending beads of sweat down the bridge of my nose.

"That overhang is a beast and the holds are so far apart. Did you space them like that on purpose?"

"I like a challenge. How often do you climb back in Sydney?"

"Almost everyday. I work at a rock gym back home." I reach for the next hold.

"I started climbing to strengthen my core and upper body in hopes of becoming a better surfer. It worked so I applied for a part-time job."

"So which do you like more, climbing or surfing?"

"Surfing is my passion. There's something cathartic about the ocean."

"Food is my passion. Are you ready for a break? I'm hungry."

"Sure. Can I make it to the top first?" I look up.

"I don't know, can you?" Grady smirks and I take it as a personal challenge.

He finds a hold and climbs above me. Wet with sweat, his biceps show their strength as he shifts his weight from one arm to the other, pulling himself up to the next hold, using only his upper body. Mirroring his gait, I reach the top a minute behind him.

"Shay, most of the guys on the Lacrosse team couldn't do what you just did."

My face glistens red with perspiration and pride.

"Crap, I didn't realize it was so late. We've gotta go, I'm babysitting my sister tonight." Grady eyes the wall clock on the other side of the room.

We rappel back down and I hear dogs barking along with a child giggling.

"Sorry, Jimena. We lost track of time." He addresses a woman with dark hair and eyes who is holding the hand of a little girl wearing blonde pigtails and a pink dress. Three small dogs circle and jump around her, licking her face and whapping her legs with their tails.

"Hey, you!" he calls out. Before he can shimmy out of his harness, the three dogs run loops around his legs and the little girl follows.

"Shay, this is my sister Lucy. Lucy, this is my friend Shay."

She hides behind her brother's legs; one big brown eye peers around his kneecap.

"Do you have brothers or sisters?" Grady asks while he attends to Lucy.

"No," I say too quickly. Grady looks up but I kneel down next to Lucy.

"G'day."

The child slowly emerges as the three small dogs whirl around me, whining for the same attention.

"This is Whitman and Tennyson." Grady points to the pair of yapping black Chihuahuas. "And this big boy is Cheese Steak." Grady scratches the English Bulldog behind the ears.

"Cheese Steak?"

"It was his given name at the shelter. I started volunteering there a couple years ago and it helped me decide that I wanted to be a vet. Sometime, I'll take you by and we can play with the puppies."

"Puppies!" Lucy hollers excitedly.

"Don't worry Lucy, you can come too." The little girl claps her hands together.

"How old are you?"

Not making a sound, she holds up four small fingers.

"Mr. Grady, your dinner is ready upstairs."

"Thank you, Jimena."

"Are you hungry?" he asks Lucy then turns to me.

"I don't want to intrude."

Grady sneers. "Lucy, is it okay if Shay eats dinner with us?" She nods her head yes.

I concede. "Okay, I'll stay."

Lucy takes hold of her brother's hand then reaches for my mine.

The touch of the little girl's hand reminds me of my own sister at that age. Flashes of teddy bear picnics and tea parties overwhelm me, sending a sorrowful ache across my chest.

"You okay?" Grady's eyes hold sincere concern. I cast the painful memories aside.

"Just hungry," I say with a smile.

———

"Shay, is that you?" The smell of garlic and onions meets me at the front door, masking the smell of my own sweat.

Bugger all, I forgot to ask Mary if I could eat with Grady. I walk slowly toward the kitchen trying to concoct an apology.

Mary and Sam sit around the marble island while Jake hovers over the stove, spooning another helping onto his plate.

"Do you want some more, Mom?"

"It was so good but I'm stuffed, honey. Thank you."

"Shay, are you hungry? Jake made his famous tamale pie."

"I'm sorry, I forgot to call you. I had tea," I pause realizing that doesn't mean the same thing in America, "I mean I ate dinner at Grady's house." I wince.

"We figured you'd eat over there. Jimena makes an excellent fettuccine al pesto. Did you have fun climbing?"

"Heaps. His wall is impressive. A month ago, he added another five meters to an overhang at the top."

"Jake, have you seen the new addition?" Mary asks, trying to invite her son into the conversation.

"Sure. We raced a couple times to see who could make it to the top first, but he climbs the thing everyday and is about a foot taller than me."

"He beat me every time too," I admit.

"Yeah, but you're a girl." With his back turned to me, I can only imagine his smug grin.

"I could beat you." I regret the words the second I say them.

"Good luck with that, Sydney," he says, then turns to face me.

It wasn't the first time Jake had referred to me by the name of my hometown, but this time it wasn't because he'd forgotten my name. He was purposely mocking me. Although insecurity had woven itself into almost every facet of my life, my strength and agility never fell victim to my self-doubt. Backed into a corner, his arrogance incensed my competitive nature. Without a rock wall to prove myself, I unleashed with the first words that came to my lips. "Jake, Grady wanted me to tell you that his parents said you could stay at their beach house when we go to San Diego, but you have to drive. He said you offered to drive the Porsche?"

I ignore Jake's glare and head up toward my room to take a shower.

It was a low blow but I knew what I was doing. As much as I didn't like playing dirty, Jake had it coming.

CHAPTER NINE

NOW

THE BUS SLOWS TO A STOP AND THE GLASSES SLIDE OFF the seat and onto the floor. My right foot hovers above, ready to strike. I yearn to crush them, to be done with all of this; however, things have changed and I'm realizing that it's not as easy to runaway this time. I reach down to where the frames are humming and I notice a new passenger looking on from across the aisle. I scoop them up and toss them into my bag in one fluid motion. I need a place where I can use the glasses without prying eyes; somewhere the Foresters wouldn't think to look. My shoulders deflate. Where do you hide from people who have all the time in the world to look for you?

I see a sign advertising a 3-D movie marathon at a nearby cinema and know it's my best option. I demand to get off the bus and start walking the few blocks to the theater. I make good time and swing the door open to enter. A bee buzzes near my ear and before I can swat it away a strange panic freezes me into place. A vision of bees swarming around my feet plays out in my mind. Moisture beads across my forehead and my heart races. I can't discern if it's a dream or a memory. Either way, it doesn't belong to me. I close my eyes and hear Mary whisper, "Moses, I'm allergic to bees."

"Good." I instantly recognize the gruff voice of the Asian bloke who held Mary and Sam's clones captive at the house. "Use it as motivation to stand perfectly still. Your body's response to fear is to flinch, if you move during the dig you could hurt yourself or worse... Just don't move okay?"

Moses holds a large piece of honeycomb out toward Mary's chest. A dozen bees land on her shoulders and arms then take turns buzzing her head. Her body tenses and I feel the raw honey drip down her legs. She squeezes her eyes shut as a bee burrows down into the neck of her jumper. I blink so I can be released from Mary's body but I realize I'm not wearing the glasses. I feel a hand on my shoulder.

"Miss, are you okay?" A woman dressed in an usher costume opens the door for me. I feign a smile and walk through, trying to shake the memory away but I can't avoid the fact that Mary's experiences are infiltrating my own memories.

I shove my frustration away and pull my wallet from the front pouch of my gray backpack. The black and white photo we took in the picture booth falls to the floor. Just looking at him makes my heart hurt. I tuck it away and redirect my energy into blending in with a crowd of people. The group moves toward screen 10 and I find it easy to appear like I belong, a gift from my days of living on the streets.

The lights begin to dim and I find a seat in the back left corner. A sick feeling starts in the pit of my stomach. I have no control over what is being downloaded onto my brain; it's evident by my new memories. I move the glasses into place. This is my punishment for all my years of insobriety and recklessness. Or maybe I just hate myself that much. Who in their right mind would subject themselves to this? The movie begins and I wait to be injected into Mary's past.

"What you are about to see is necessary for you to understand the sacrifices we've made to save Jake."

Diffused sunlight bounces from the water to the clouds, causing Mary's eyes to squint into slits. It takes a second to adjust to the brightness. I hear waves crashing nearby and a peace settles over me; the type of peace only the ocean brings.

Facing the sea, a couple dozen people sit quietly in white chairs adorned with small bouquets of teal and lavender hydrangeas. I look down at the long purple gown hugging Mary's hips as Sam loops his arm through hers and walks down the rose petal aisle.

Offshore, a large sailboat carves through small white-capped waves. The bow of a cellist glides over its strings, scoring a soundtrack for the vessel.

"Son, take your mother's arm." Jake comes up from behind and Mary gently squeezes Jake's forearm with her hand. Her lips turn into a half-smile and for a moment I feel like they are my own. We sit together in the front row beside Erin and a quiet whisper weaves through the waiting crowd.

The wedding march begins as the sun burns a hole through the remaining clouds, shining bright white rays into the sea.

"Your dad looks so handsome," Mary whispers into Erin's ear. Near a wooden archway, a tall pale man, dressed in a tan linen suit, stands next to the minister. His eyes scan the small stairway leading down the aisle. The cellist finishes the anthem but the bride has yet to make an appearance. The musician beckons her by starting the procession again.

Erin turns to Mary, "Where's Cassie?" Eyebrows raised, I see her unspoken hopes of cancelled nuptials. Her wishes are dashed as a tall slender blonde, dressed in ivory, floats down the stone staircase.

Cassie's bare feet meet the aisle laden with white rose petals and the guests stand and turn to honor her. Her face is veiled in antique lace that falls to the waist of her fitted gown. In lieu of flowers, a small silver necklace with a large smooth gray stone pendant dangles from her hands. She brings it to her lips then gently kisses the stone and places it on the only empty seat in the first row next to Jake.

"There is a time for everything and a season for every activity under the heavens;" the Minister pauses, "a time to be born and a time to die, a time to plant and a time to uproot, a time to kill and a time to heal, a time to tear down and a time to build, a time to weep and a time to laugh, a time to mourn and a time to dance." He looks up from the text.

"Today we celebrate, we dance, we laugh; rejoicing with one another on this beautiful day. However, days aren't always like this. Some days are full of sorrow. But without those sad days, how would we know the sweetness of ones like these? It is with this scripture in mind, the bride has asked that we take a moment to remember a very important guest who could not be here today."

Cassie turns from Rick and addresses her guests.

"Two years ago I lost the love of my life."

Sam glances at Mary and she shrugs her shoulders.

"My sweet little boy was the life of the party. He was funny and caring and I miss him every minute of every day." She clears her throat and continues. "I never thought I could love again or have hope again. Fate proved me wrong."

Rick wipes a stray tear from Cassie's cheek and she steps into his embrace. The crowd is silent and the couple turns toward their guests.

"I share this day with all of you and with my beloved son. I love you, Stone."

Erin puts a hand on Mary's shoulder. "Dad never said anything about Cassie having a son."

Mary reaches for Jake's hand. His fingers are tough and calloused from years of Lacrosse. Unaffected, Jake looks at his phone. She squeezes tighter and her eyes blur with tears. He drops her hand and moves his arm around her shoulders and pulls her close, sending a wave of warmth through her chest. A lump forms in her throat and then in my own.

Darkness falls in around me and I wonder if I've been released from Mary's past. A voice ascends from the floor underneath me.

"Hopelessness and despair are words you attach to tragedy." Mary's voice is hollow. "Jake's death was…" her voice cracks, "Jake's death *is*, words that don't exist. Manipulating time so that it won't happen again is a terrifying privilege; with each attempt, we are stalked by the darkness that awaits the moment we fail. Cassie gives me hope while making me feel utterly hopeless all at the same time."

Mary's shifting reflection appears by candlelight in the glass wall of the Foresters' home. It's dark out on the patio and there's a low hum of people talking in hushed voices. Dressed in black, Mary dabs her reddened eyes with a handkerchief and she begins to spin. Round and round she turns until I start to feel sick and she falls to the floor. When she stands to her feet she is dressed in gold sequins. I can't differentiate her shiny dress from the dancing sparklers around her. A crowd begins a countdown and I hear her voice. "A new year has come." She stares at herself in the glass wall. "3-2-1..." The floor falls out from under her feet and her body begins to plummet. Classical music wafts through the air around us. A barrage of instruments bounces off of what seems like the walls of a dark tunnel. The distortion of sound and movement makes Mary's stomach queasy. It feels like we are sliding down a water slide. Near the bottom, Mary lands softly in a chair next to Cassie at the kitchen table. "Do you want to see Jake again?" Cassie asks, fidgeting with the spoon in her teacup.

Mary's body stiffens and her head cocks. "What kind of a sick question is that?" Mary storms out of the house but stops as she faces the empty glass garage.

She walks slowly back inside but the house has disappeared and Mary is left standing in front of her art studio. I note the address: 2652 Biltmore Avenue.

"Cassie isn't crazy or cruel; she is the key. She suggests I document my dreams."

My own memory emerges and I recall receiving the same advice from Mary.

"More accurately, Cassie wants me to write out my nightmares, stressing the importance of dream documentation as a way of healing. She says, 'Dreams are like subconscious connections to the future and the past.' I think I'll try painting them instead."

A large paintbrush appears in Mary's hand. The smooth wood handle moves back and forth, streaking powder blue paint onto an empty white canvas. Mary trades in for a smaller brush and dips it in black. She swirls and slices through the blue, splattering black dots all over the piece.

A sudden, blinding flash of light erases everything in Mary's sight. It takes a moment for Mary's eyes to readjust. The canvas comes into focus and not far in the distance the wrecked Porsche Spyder is illuminated. Mangled and twisted, it smells like gasoline. The vision dims, leaving an overwhelming stench of burnt rubber in the darkness. Mary's heart pounds hard in her chest.

Another burst of light; the paintbrush slips from her hand and her jaw clenches. Tears sting her eyes and she plunges both of her hands into a bucket of cold paint. Her hands smear red streaks all over the canvas with force. I blink my eyes.

In a fast flicker, the car reappears. Next to it, two bodies lay lifeless. I blink my eyes again. A final blaze burns the inside of my lids. I blink one more time, refusing to see what Mary saw and a blanket of darkness covers me as I tear the glasses from my face.

CHAPTER TEN

THEN

"WHY ARE WE GOING THE LONG WAY?" CONTEMPT POURS from Jake's lips. In the backseat, my head hangs low as I silently take the blame for his anger. His dagger-like stares and backhanded comments are my punishment for instigating the shouting match between him and his parents over the Spyder.

I explained myself to Grady over the phone, apologizing for using him as a pawn in my attempt to knock Jake down a peg. Unfazed, Grady thought it comical that I put Jake in his place but warned me to watch my back. Apparently Jake was a sore loser and his defeat always warranted revenge. I had taken Grady's advice and spent most of the last two weeks at his house, avoiding Jake as much as possible.

"Your mother decided on this route before we left. She had a feeling there would be traffic on the 10," Sam replies calmly.

"Perfect." Jake closes his eyes and puts his earphones over his ears.

I occupy my time with calculus, worried what Jake might do if I drift off to sleep. After solving the last problem on the page, I allow my eyes to rest and give my mind permission to think about Grady. Ever since he laced his fingers through mine at the zoo last weekend, I dreamed of how it would feel to rest my head against his chest and feel his lips on mine. I look at my hands, remembering how his thumbs strummed the inside of my palms when I asked Lucy which animal was her favorite.

———

Long way or not, we make good time from the arid desert to the balmy coast. I lower my window and the salty sea air spills into the backseat. The air is different than what I'm used to, less moisture and more brine, but I welcome it just the same. I take in a deep drag and hold it in my lungs, relishing the flavor and aroma before letting it go.

Seeing the beach changes everyone's mood. Even Jake smiles and offers to make dinner. On the way to the house we stop by a street market to get fresh prawns and scallops. Ten minutes later we arrive at the Sea Glass house: the Foresters' ultra-modern, three-story beach house, comprised of more windows than I can count.

"I told you he'd come around," Sam says and Mary shrugs as Jake carries two brown paper sacks to the kitchen.

"I have the perfect place for you." Mary leads me down a hallway near the back of the house. She opens a door into a small apartment with its own bathroom and kitchenette. There's a door that opens to a private patio overlooking the ocean.

"This is for me?" I ask and Mary nods. I can't help myself and hug her. She holds me for a second too long and I let go.

"Wetsuits and surfboards are in the garage." Mary chokes on her words. "Let's go back to the kitchen and see if Jake needs any help." I obey.

A boisterous laugh wafts in from outside. Through the glass door, a beautiful blonde in tight gray jeans and yellow platform heels stands next to a tall, pale bloke with receding pepper hair and a partially-buttoned red, Hawaiian shirt. They seem oddly paired.

"Shay, these are our friends, Rick and his wife, Cassie," Mary states and for a moment I think she is kidding. Cassie looks slightly older than me and could be the man's daughter. "Rick is Erin's dad."

"Nice to meet you," I say while quickly replacing the surprised look on my face with a smile. Cassie refuses to make eye contact but forces a grin while clutching the stone pendant dangling around her neck.

"Rick and Cassie were married here in San Diego about seven months ago. Their reception was held right here."

"Congratulations," I say politely.

"Did Sam show you to your room upstairs?" Mary asks, turning to Cassie.

"He did. Thanks again for letting us stay with you," Cassie replies cordially.

"No problem. Thank you for letting us stay at Greystone next month."

"You will be our very first guests," Cassie states proudly.

"I hope you're hungry, Jake is making dinner," Sam interjects and Mary stares with pride at her son through the kitchen window.

"I can always eat." The older bloke touches his belly then loops a hairy arm around his wife, pulling her close.

Feeling awkward, I look down at the patio floor and notice the word Echo tattooed above Cassie's left ankle. It reminds me of Mary's barrel wave and I'm instantly glad to be near the sea.

"Hey, Mar. I was just asking Sam why you didn't drive the Spyder over. That machine is meant to be driven, not just looked at."

"Butt out." Cassie gives her husband the evil eye and smacks his shoulder.

"I offered to drive it over." Jake walks through the patio door with a sly smile and a saucepan. I look down, refusing to meet Jake's intent stare. "But the old man didn't think it was such a good idea."

"Someday, Son, you will understand. You will have something precious and you won't want anything to happen to it." Sam's jaw clenches.

"It's a car," Jake says repulsed, then walks back inside.

"I wasn't talking about the car," Sam mutters under his breath.

The small party moves inside as everyone searches for a seat around the table.

"We didn't get to eat lunch," Rick says, trying to lighten the mood. "We got stuck behind a five-car pileup on the 10."

"I guess you were right, Mom. Not taking the 10 was a good idea." Jake places a bowl of pasta in the middle of the table.

"What did you say? Did you say *I* was right?" She purses her lips at her son and makes kissing sounds.

I close the glass patio door and find a chair but Jake blocks me. He leans in close and whispers. "I've made something special just for you, Sydney. I hope you like it." He eyes the frying pan on the stove.

He's bluffing.

I sit next to Mary at the table. There's no way he could have added something special for me without giving it to the others.

"Cassie, how's the camera shop fairing these days?" Sam asks.

"Cassie manages a photography studio and camera shop," Mary interjects.

"I have many new clients since I added a new online editing course and a studio lighting workshop." I look up and Cassie is staring intently at me.

"Shay, honey, aren't you hungry? You haven't touched your food." Mary sounds concerned and Cassie looks away.

"I reckon I might be a little car sick," I say, chucking a sickie. "I'm sorry, Jake. I know you went to so much trouble." I grin.

"Go lay down sweetheart, you look tired."

I walk slowly down the hallway, milking it with each step.

An hour later Mary knocks on my door. "How are you feeling?" she says, holding a sleeve of crackers.

"A little better. I know it's game night, but would you mind if I went to bed early?"

"A bit of rest will do you good. You need to save your energy for surfing in the morning." Mary always seems one step ahead, like she knows what I'm thinking.

"Sleep well, sweetheart." She squeezes my hand then shuts the door. I have grown fond of Mary. The constant barrage of hugs and hand-holding were strange at first but now I almost look forward to them. It has been such a long time since anyone had mothered me. Ingrid had tried, but she was more like a sister than a mum. I grab my phone from the table and text Ingrid.

Shay: Ingrid! Guess who's going surfing tomorrow?

I wait for a response but receive a message from Grady instead.

Grady: Erin and I just pulled up to my house in La Jolla. Lunch tomorrow?

I hop up from the bed and open the door hoping to find Mary nearby.

"Feeling better?" Jake asks dryly as he walks into the kitchen.

"Much better. Thank you." I sneer.

Seeing that Mary isn't in the kitchen or dining room, I go back to my room and pick up my cell phone, readying my reply to Grady. Murmuring voices prompt me to look through my window onto my private patio. Huddled together, Cassie examines Mary's left forearm. Focused, the two women don't notice I've opened the door.

"It's healing nicely. I got a scar the first time." Cassie shifts her jumper, revealing a pink and white tuft of raised skin, the size of a lime, on her bare shoulder.

"Me too," Mary shakes her head, annoyed, and points to her knee. "I've been using a knee bandage and now I have to figure out how to cover this one," she says, delicately touching the small pink welt on her arm.

"What does Sam suggest?"

"Long sleeves," Mary quips.

"Sounds like Sam."

Suddenly, a gust of sea air takes hold of the door, slamming it open. Startled, Mary lowers her sleeve and walks over.

"Shay, is everything okay?"

"Yes, everything is brilliant," I hesitate. "I was looking for you. Grady and Erin were wondering…"

"If you could go to lunch and the beach tomorrow?" Mary interrupts. "Jake already asked. It's fine with me."

"Okay, thanks," I pause. "Good night." I shut the door carefully. Their voices go quiet and all is still. I peer out the window. Without a word, Cassie's face twists with anger and she points to my door then storms off into the sand. The exchange wasn't meant for me to see. I feel guilty that I didn't shut the door right away. But why was Cassie so angry that I saw their scars? I climb into bed trying to forget the awkward encounter and focus on the waves that await me in the morning.

CHAPTER ELEVEN

THEN

A COUPLE OF LOCALS PADDLE OUT ALONGSIDE ME AT dawn. The swells are small but clean and easy to ride. Wave by wave, all my worries and doubts crash to the shore, shattering into a million pieces. The water seeps into my pores, pulsing salt through my veins, embalming every part of me until I feel whole again.

Pangs churn in my stomach, reminding me I haven't eaten. I ride a final wave in and shuffle through the sand toward the boardwalk. I pull my wetsuit down to my waist and wrap a towel around my shoulders. Content, I lean against the patio wall watching the sea gulls scream as they dive for fish, haloed by the sun searing through the clouds. Smells of bacon waft up behind me and my hunger pangs return. I shimmy my wet suit down the rest of the way, trying to keep my togs in place knowing with my luck I would bare all just as Grady, or worse, Jake walked by.

The ocean disappears when I walk into the kitchen. The aroma of hotcakes and syrup replace the salty air. Two covered silver platters hover over warmers and the card next to the first platter has my name on it. I lift the lid just as the music from Jake's room gets louder. The bass pounds and my stomach twists in knots. I turn to escape, food in hand—I'm too late. Jake stares at me coldly.

"G'day," I say, trying to keep up some sort of civility.

"My parents went out. I'm going out with Grady. We are hanging out with you and Erin at the beach later." He fakes a smile, grabs his food then slams the door behind him.

"Righto, can't wait."

———

At the small pizza shop near the boardwalk, Grady and I sit across the table from Jake and Erin.

"What's the plan?" Erin asks, looking expectantly at the boys.

"Eat delicious pizza." Jake scoops up a huge slice using both hands.

"And after that?"

"Ride the roller coaster and puke up all the pizza." Jake opens his mouth revealing pieces of partially chewed pizza.

"Pass." Erin grimaces.

"We were thinking we could play a friendly game of miniature golf," Grady states, then nods at Jake.

"Great," Erin sighs, "what's the bet?" she says then frowns.

"Can't we suggest a fun activity without our motives being called into question?" Grady sports the same frown.

"Um, no," Erin replies with her hands on her hips.

"Loser has to ride the Ferris wheel with a stranger; in a speedo," Jake says, unfazed by Erin's accusation.

"Gross, but okay." Erin raises a slice of pizza in the air, "I guess we're playing Mini-golf!" she says then takes a bite.

———

"So you really have never been miniature golfing?" Erin asks. "They do have miniature golf in Australia, right?"

"Yes, they have putt-putt golf."

"But do they have glow-in-the-dark miniature golf?" Grady points to the sign hanging above them. I shrug my shoulders.

"I'll keep score." Jake grabs a scorecard that glows white in his hand.

"*Erin* will keep score," Grady commands and loosens the scorecard from Jake's grip. "I'm not losing today because you cheat." He passes the scorecard over to Erin.

"I'd be happy to be scorekeeper. Which one of you boneheads wants to wear a speedo?" Grinning, she pencils in our names.

"I haven't been mini-golfing in a long time," Grady says in a loud voice.

"Nice try, hustler. You and what's her face, what's the name of the girl you dated last month?"

"Daphne," Erin blurts out.

"Yes, Daphne. You and Daphne went mini-golfing last month. I know this because she posted a million pictures of how you were 'teaching her to how to putt,'" Jake makes his fingers into air quotes. "How is Daphne by the way?" Jake looks pointedly at Grady then at me.

"She's good," Erin chimes in, "after she broke up with Grady, she started dating a really hot guy at that Catholic school in Arcadia." She fans herself, then looks at Grady. "Sorry, G."

"No need to be sorry. She moved on and so have I." He turns his gaze to me and I fidget with my zipper.

"Can we play already?" Jake says impatiently. "The world needs to experience Grady in a Speedo."

"Go ahead, Jake, you're up first," Erin calls out.

Jake drops the glowing ball between his feet. Crouching down, he studies the lines of the hole then positions the ball in a divot on the neon green turf. With a slight tap, the ball rolls up and over two small green hills. It rests just shy of a miniature neon Volkswagen bus.

Grady shakes his head. "Amateur."

"Shay, you're up," Erin says, looking at the scorecard.

"Do what Jake did, just better." Grady laughs.

"Good luck," Jake says, insincerely.

I place my neon yellow ball in the middle divot on the glowing green turf and grip my club. Grady comes up from behind. With his arms around me, he moves my hands, realigning them to grip the inside of the club.

"Try that," he says then steps away.

"Thanks, that feels better."

"Shoot me now." Jake groans.

I tap the ball. It soars over the small hills, and bumps into Jake's ball, then rebounds into the hole.

"Hole in one!" Excited, Grady picks me up and twirls me around.

———

Grady points to a storefront window displaying men's bathers. "One stroke. It must feel pretty crappy to lose by one stroke, huh Jake?"

"I get to pick the ding-aling-sling." Erin runs past Jake toward the store.

"No way," Jake yells, shaking his head.

"It's either me or Grady." Erin shrugs, jogging backwards.

Grady's eyes go wide and hopeful. "I'm sure I could find a great one."

"Erin it is." Jake points at Erin then closes his eyes.

"Can I at least come with you so you get the right size?" Jake asks.

"Taylor already told me, you're an extra small." Erin chortles at her own joke.

"You can come inside but *we* are choosing the budgie smuggler. Shay, isn't that what you called it? It's way better when Shay says it with her Australian accent."

"Wait, *we*?" Jake says, confused.

Erin points to herself, then to me. "*We*."

"I'll stay out here," he concedes.

"Suit yourself," Erin says.

"Ha, did you hear that, suit yourself?" Grady grins. "Bet you wish you could suit yourself."

"Shut up, G."

After scouring the entire store, Erin and I emerge with a tiny black bag.

"Jake it is with deep regret and a queasy stomach that I give you this."
She hands Jake the bag.

"What are you waiting for? Go put it on, big boy." Grady pats Jake's
butt.

The bag dangles loosely from Jake's fingers as he walks into the public
bathroom.

"How much do you want to bet he flushes it?" Grady asks.

"He better not, Shay found the perfect one."

"This should be good." Grady rubs his hands together in anticipation.

"Here he comes." Erin pats Grady's shoulder then squeals in delight.

Jake struts confidently through a small crowd of tourists who whisper
and point as he passes by.

"Is that…"

"The Australian flag," I finish Grady's sentence. "Aye mate, it is," I say
with pride.

"Jake, you wear Australia well," Erin says. Jake nods at Grady and they
laugh at some unspoken joke.

"Nice choice, Sydney." Jake's voice is void of hostility, for once, and I
smile.

"The girls picked the speedo, now I get to pick the stranger." Grady
turns from side to side, scanning the amusement park.

"I can't decide between the aging body-builder in the white bikini or the
homeless man licking the park bench."

"Both are good choices for completely different reasons," Erin agrees.

"I think I'll go with muscles." Grady walks over to the woman flexing her wrinkly, bronzed quads to the amazement of passers by. He points to Jake and soon both are walking back together.

"Jake, this is Carla. Carla, Jake." The two awkwardly shake hands. "Carla's agreed to be your Ferris wheel friend for today."

"G'day, mate," the woman says, lifting her eyebrows at Jake's swimmers and Erin bursts into a fit of laughter.

"Ready?" Jake asks, trying to get the bet squared away.

"Wait, Jake. Can I get a quick pic?" Erin pulls her phone from her pocket and takes a picture. "Thanks," she smiles coyly.

The Ferris wheel is empty except for the blue cart that Jake and the muscle woman, Carla, occupy. After a few times around, Grady bribes the operator to stop their cart at the top for a couple minutes.

When they come back down, the barely-clothed couple exit the cart. Carla hugs Jake then walks past Grady.

"Thanks again, Carla. You made his day!" Grady calls after the woman, who smiles then goes back to her storefront.

"That was nice," Jake says as he approaches Grady, "she told me I reminded her of her son."

"Ah, that's so sweet." Erin cocks her head to one side.

"Then she kissed me."

"Ugh!"

"It wasn't so bad. Though her tongue was surprisingly weak for a body so muscular."

"I think I might throw up." Erin's hands cover her mouth and I burst out laughing.

72

"Can I go change now?" Jake asks.

"Unless you and Carla want to have another go at it?" Grady smirks.

"I'm good."

Jake walks toward the bathroom and Erin snaps another photo.

"You any good at darts?" Grady asks then points to a large wall of balloons encased by hanging stuffed monkeys.

"I wouldn't end up in a speedo, if that's what you're asking."

Grady grins and follows me to the booth.

The bloke behind the counter gives me eight darts. I pop six balloons in a row and just barely miss the last two. Impressed, the man awards me one of the bigger monkeys holding a partially peeled banana. Up next, Grady manages to pop four. The bloke hands him a small stuffed banana and I laugh.

"Nice banana!" A fully clothed Jake emerges and grabs Grady by the shoulders.

"Actually, Jake, it's for you. The carnie in the booth asked me to give it to you. He saw you wearing the speedo earlier and felt bad." Grady offers the banana and Jake punches him hard in the arm.

"Some things never change," Erin says, leaning toward me.

"Did you get a banana too?" Jake asks, nodding at me.

I lift the large monkey in the air and he laughs. "How does it feel to lose to a girl, Grady?"

I lower the monkey and try not to scowl.

"Roller coaster time." Erin points to the small wooden coaster.

I pull Grady aside. "Do you mind if I sit this one out?"

"There's no one in line. Let's go." Jake pulls Grady's arm.

"You and Erin go. Shay and I are going to chill out on the beach."

"Grady, this is your favorite ride." Jake looks at Grady then at me.

"Go," I encourage him.

"I'm good." Grady looks down at me and smiles and Jake rolls his eyes then jogs over to the coaster.

"Tell me about Australia."

"What do you want to know?"

"Where's your favorite place?"

"The beach where I surf every morning." I take a deep breath in and look out over the water, secretly wishing I was there.

"It reminds me a lot of this place."

"Who do you surf with?"

"Most mornings I go alone."

"Would you like some company in the morning?" He takes my hand in his. "I could meet you at the beach tomorrow."

"That would be nice," I say and then we sit quietly watching the waves.

"Dude, there was no one in line. We rode two times forward and a third time in reverse. You totally missed out." Jake picks up a volleyball near a net on the beach and throws it hard at Grady's chest.

"You game?"

"Sure! Loser has to…"

"No bets. We are playing for fun or I'm not playing," Erin interrupts.

"Okay, Mom," Jake says sarcastically.

"Erin, you're with me. Grady, you get Sydney." Jake moves to the other side of the empty net and pulls off his t-shirt.

74

"Jake Forester, when did you get a six-pack?" Erin steps toward her teammate and touches his abs. "You are cut." Jake smiles and nods at Grady.

"See Grady, I told you."

"You're right. I didn't believe you at first." Grady shakes his head.

"What?" Erin furrows her eyebrows.

"Go ahead Grady, take your shirt off. She won't say anything to you." Grady strips off his shirt and Erin looks confused.

"Erin Angela Brooks, you have a problem and this is your intervention." Grady moves under the net to Erin's side. "We know you are in love… with Jake's abs." Both boys nod their heads. "Every time Jake takes off his shirt, you touch his chest or comment on his abs."

"Gross, Jake is like my brother. I am not in love with his abs."

"Erin, my eyes are up here." Jake holds a serious tone as his finger travels from his flexed six-pack to his eyes. I try not to laugh.

"See, even Shay is laughing because she's seen you do it." Grady points to me and I shake my head in protest.

"There's more to me than all this." Jake moves his hands over his stomach. "I'm a person and I have feelings."

"The first step to recovery is admitting you have a problem, Ernie," Grady chimes in.

"I hate you guys," she says laughing, "and Grady, if you start calling me Ernie again I will punch you in the balls."

"When you're ready to talk about it," Jake motions to Erin, "we'll be here for you, okay Ernie?" Erin bolts toward him, arms flailing, punching the air wildly. Jake holds one arm out and gingerly scoops her up, pinning her arms to her sides.

"Put me down." She struggles to get loose.

"Are you ready to behave?" Jake sounds like Sam.

"Yes," Erin says then goes limp in his arms.

"Great, let's play." He sets Erin upright on the sand then begins to volley back and forth with Grady until the ball flies out of bounds into a surging wave.

"Got it!" Jake runs toward the surf. Not to be outdone, Grady follows. Knee deep in cold foamy water, Jake reaches for the ball, his fingertips, like the legs of a spider, try to spin the ball closer. On the opposite side, Grady forces the ball into deeper water.

"This could take a while. Those two are secretly in love with each other." Erin smiles. "In love with his abs..." Erin closes her eyes and shakes her head.

I turn back toward the net and notice a woman watching us from the boardwalk. In a blue sundress and a floppy sun hat, she leans against the concrete ledge.

"Erin, isn't that your step-mum?" I say and Erin turns to look.

"Yes," she sighs, "Quick, pretend you don't see her. I don't feel like talking to her right now."

"I thought you liked her?" I ask as we turn in the opposite direction.

"I do. But sometimes she can be really weird and intense. She's only five years older than me but she acts like she's forty. The other day I was joking around and I told her that Jake and I were dating and she freaked out. My mom says that a lot of crazy stuff has happened to her and sometimes she's a bit paranoid but, oh crap, she's coming over. Just smile and compliment her shoes, you'll be fine." Erin waves as Cassie gets closer.

"I'm glad I found you. Your dad and I were wondering if you and Grady wanted to join us for dinner tonight? We were thinking about the seafood place on the water in La Jolla." Wide-eyed, Erin looks over at the boys partially soaking wet and covered in seaweed.

"Sure, but don't you need a reservation for that place. My mom tried to get a table there a couple months ago and they were booked solid for the entire month."

"Our reservation is for 6:30. I have connections." Cassie winks.

"Grady, how does E.B.'s Seafood on the water in La Jolla sound for dinner?" Erin calls over to Grady.

"Great. My parents will be jealous."

"Jake, your mom wants you and Shay to have dinner with them at the beach house tonight," Cassie says.

"Of course she does." Jake frowns.

"Grady, I'll see you later. I'm sleeping at your place tonight." Jake sounds desperate.

"Are we still planning on hot-tubbing with the girls?" Grady's tone is hopeful and Erin looks at her step-mum.

"Do what you want. I only asked you to dinner." Cassie smirks then walks to where Rick is sitting in a parked car.

"Before we leave, we need to get a picture of the four of us in the photo booth." Erin points to a small blue booth near the arcade. Both boys complain but follow Erin obediently over to the blue box.

Jake and Grady pout and sit on the small bench. Frowns turn to smiles as they encourage us to sit on their soaking wet, sand-covered laps.

"Awesome, it's going to look like I peed my pants." Erin looks down disappointed, then puts a few dollar bills into the machine. "Normal picture first, okay boys?"

"Yea, yea, normal picture first," Jake repeats.

"Okay, everyone smile."

Following Erin's directions, I smile and the camera flashes.

The picture pops up on the screen in front of us. Both Erin and I are smiling while the boys pretend to be asleep.

"Come on guys. One nice one, ready?"

The camera flashes. Again, both Erin and I are smiling but Jake is holding the stuffed monkey up in place of his face and Grady uses the banana as his smile.

"I smiled." Grady points to the image when he notices Erin's frown.

"I give up." Erin waves her hands in disgust. "Do whatever you want."

The camera flashes a third time. The picture shows Erin screaming as Jake tries to lick her nose, while I smile as Grady kisses my cheek.

"Eew, Jake, gross!"

"One nice one, I promise." Jake tries to convince Erin.

"I'll believe it when I see it."

The camera flashes and projects the final image onto the screen. Keeping his promise, Jake is perfectly posed. He and Erin look like cover models on a magazine, while Grady and I ignore the camera and smile at each another. Grady tears the last two black and white pictures from the photo strip.

"Do you mind if I keep this one?" He points to the picture of him kissing my cheek.

"As long as I can keep this one." I admire the small picture then tuck it safely into my purse.

CHAPTER TWELVE

THEN

THE FOUR OF US PILE INTO GRADY'S UTE AND MARY AND Sam wave as we pull away. Jake moans. "I couldn't get out of there quick enough. My mom wanted to know every detail of the day and this one kept answering all her questions." Jake motions to me then makes his hand into the shape of a gun and points it at his temple.

"I told you Jake, the closer it gets to graduation, the more they smother. It's like they know the end is near," Erin pipes in. "My mom hasn't stopped texting me all weekend since I'm missing weekly brunch with her tomorrow. It's one week people!"

"I'd be mad at you for missing brunch! Brunch is by far the best meal," Grady says, eyes smiling.

Encouraged by Erin's shared misery, Jake continues, "Every night after practice, my mom comes up to my room and asks me about my day, then kisses me on the forehead. Every. Single. Night! Lately my dad has been coming with her. I'm graduating from High School, not dying!"

Glad to be hidden in the shadows of the back seat, the conversation makes me uncomfortable. There are many nights that I long for what they think is a nuisance.

"Your parents must be amazing to let you travel across the globe months before graduation?" Erin says and turns toward me.

I'd mapped out the answer to this specific question weeks ago, now lost in my own thoughts, I'm caught off guard.

"I don't live with them."

"Who do you live with? Are you one of those emancipated minors? That would be awesome." Erin asks and answers her own question.

"No, it's not. I mean, no, I don't live by myself. I've been living with a woman named Ingrid for the past four years," I say stammering, mad that I didn't stick to the script.

Grady breaks the silence. "Mom or not, this Ingrid seems pretty cool if she let you spend six months away from home. She must be pretty trusting."

I smile, partly because it's taken Ingrid years to trust me, but also because of Grady's attempt to make things less awkward.

The conversation shifts as Grady pulls into the driveway of his family's ivory beach house.

"My house is the one next door." Erin points to a house as tall as the three massive palm trees swaying next to it.

We walk out to the backyard. Beyond the pool, faint sounds of breaking waves echo below. At the edge of the black abyss I listen, eyes closed, reminding me of the nights I camped out on the beach. Even when I was homeless, you could always find me near the sea.

"This is one of my favorite places." Grady moves in close next to me.

"Even in the dark it's beautiful," I say.

"Sure is."

I feel his eyes on me and a warmth spreads over my arms and chest, trickling down my hands to my fingertips.

"I could stay here all night listening to the waves."

"I think you should." His hand wraps around mine.

"As lovely as that sounds, I still need to change." I hold up my togs in the other hand.

He reluctantly lets go. "Hurry back."

In the kitchen, Erin points out the nearest bathroom where I can change. Down the hallway, I locate the third door on the left. I turn the handle and the door swings open on its own, nearly hitting me in face. Jake walks past me wearing a pair of board shorts and a towel over one shoulder. He stops in the middle of the hall and faces me.

"Hanging out here, with *my* friends, doesn't change anything." He turns back around and continues down the hall.

What is his problem?

I take my time changing; the venom of Jake's words still sting me and I hate that I let him wound me.

Grady and Jake are already soaking in the hot tub when I walk outside. Insecurity hits as I see Erin inch her way into the water. Looking the part of cute cheerleader with a barely there bikini and perfect hair, I cringe. I know how my wavy hair revolts when taunted by the wet sea air. I strip off my towel like an unwanted bandaid and melt into the water as fast as I can without scalding myself. I untwist the straps of my bikini top and meet Grady's eyes.

"How was the seafood restaurant?" I ask.

"So good!" Erin replies.

"Pretty tasty," he winks. "Are we going surfing in the morning?"

"Yes!" I nod my head as I reply.

"I hear the waves are supposed to pretty solid tomorrow."

"Oh yeah, Grady, how would you know? You've been surfing how many times in your life?" Jake turns from Erin.

Grady responds with a tidal wave of water aimed directly at Jake.

Jake wipes his face then tries unsuccessfully to dunk Grady who has a huge height advantage.

"Boy! Boys! Seriously, you are getting my hair wet." Erin tries to shield her head with her small arms. Finally giving up, she moves to a nearby chair and covers herself with a beach towel.

A truce ensues and Jake jumps out and grabs a towel next to Erin. He asks her a question about her dog and they become submersed in their own conversation. Grady moves in close and takes my hand in his.

"Are you cold?" he says, seeing his own breath in the air.

I shake my head right as Jake shouts, "Now!"

"Now!" Grady repeats.

Jake hurls Erin over his shoulder, subduing her small frame with one arm. Kicking and screaming, she is helpless in his grip. His sly, childlike smile causes me to grin.

"Jake! I don't want to get wet. I'm telling your mom!"

"What? Did you say you want to get wet?"

Before I have time to laugh, Grady's arms pull me down into the bubbling water. I pretend to struggle and Grady responds, holding me tighter. Both our heads dip under the water.

Erin emerges and wipes her eyes. "I didn't want to get wet," she says then splashes water in Jake's face.

"I'm sorry Ernie, I thought you wanted to be close to my abs." Jake flexes then hops out of the water and begins toweling off.

"Going somewhere?" Grady says.

"Taylor's picking me up in five minutes."

"Taylor is here, in San Diego?" Erin asks.

"She's staying at her aunt's this weekend, in Coronado." Jake's smile takes over his entire face.

"That's convenient," Grady says.

"As far as Mary and Sam are concerned I'm staying here tonight. Cover for me Grady?"

The mischievous grin on his face turns to a snarl as Jake's eyes meet mine.

"At least wait until morning to tell my parents, okay Sydney." The irritation in his voice cuts through the air like a knife that deflates the mood.

"Sure thing, mate," I mumble, hating how he makes me feel. I don't care what he does as long as he leaves me alone.

"Shay, we should probably get going too. Grady, where are the truck keys?" Erin asks. Since Jake had convinced his parents to let him spend a night at Grady's house, Erin offered to stay at the Foresters' beach house with me.

"On the counter."

"I'm going to get changed," Erin says and shoves Jake as she walks past him. "I can touch your abs whenever I want." It's her way of easing the tension.

The ocean air hits my shoulders and Grady wraps his arms around me.

"Jake is a good guy, you just have to get to know him."

"I highly doubt that will ever happen." I rest my head on his shoulder.

"Can I tell you something?" his voice is serious.

"Sure."

"I really like you."

"You do?"

"Yes."

I refuse to look at him, afraid he might kiss me. I thought I'd be ready but I'm not. In the past I would've thought it juvenile to go out of my way to avoid a little kiss. But back then, giving myself away made me feel special and wanted. It had taken four long years to figure out who I was and how to love myself again. Now, sitting here with Grady, I'm so afraid of giving too much and losing myself again. With all my flaws and insecurities, I don't know if I am strong enough to be my own person with Grady. I want to believe I am but that isn't enough. Not yet.

"Can I take you out on a proper date when we get back to Phoenix?" he asks as his lips touch my forehead.

"I'd like that," I reply, hoping to be ready by then. I really want to be ready.

Erin and I arrive back at the Foresters' beach house. Mary opens the front door, wrapped in her bathrobe.

"Did you girls have fun?"

Erin nods and relays how Jake dunked her in the hot tub, then says goodnight and follows me back to my room.

"Are Mary and Cassie good mates?" I ask.

"They weren't in the beginning, because of my mom. Mary and Mom have been best friends for as long as I can remember. I think there is this unwritten rule that you can't get too close to your best friend's ex-husband's new wife." Erin slurs the words together then laughs.

"But things changed after the wedding. I don't know if Mary felt bad for her since she didn't have many friends, but they have been getting a lot closer. They are together all the time. I know it pisses my mom off but she won't say anything. Speaking of pissed, Jake was convinced you were going to tell his parents about his meet-up with Taylor," Erin changes the subject, "but I knew you wouldn't say anything."

"I don't understand. What is his problem?"

"He has been in a major funk ever since his parents made him break things off with Taylor. They thought they were getting too serious, making him lose sight of important things like his classes and Lacrosse. He's always suspected there was more to it, like they had something against her."

"How long were they together?"

"Not long, a couple months, maybe?"

86

"The way Mary tells it, it was his decision to break up with Taylor. I didn't know."

"How could you have known? It's not like Jake knocks on your door late at night, wanting to talk. He doesn't do that, does he?"

"Yes, every night, sometimes he doesn't even knock!" I laugh and throw a pillow at her.

"There is someone who has been asking about you a lot lately."

I blush.

"I've known Grady since the third grade. You can't go wrong with that one."

CHAPTER THIRTEEN

THEN

I TAKE MY CUSTOMARY PLACE NEXT TO JAKE IN THE BACK-seat. Mary and Sam had insisted I come along for the tour of the university. Jake, not even attempting to hide his disappointment, glares at me the whole way there.

"Are you ready to meet with Coach Rawlings?" Mary asks, light-hearted, from the front seat.

"Yes, I'm ready," he replies flatly.

"Son, you know first impressions are very important," Sam pipes in.

"Yes, I know," he says and his teeth clench.

"Do you have plans to go to college when you get back home, Shay?" Sam asks and Mary shifts in her seat then clears her throat as if the question makes her uncomfortable.

"I begin classes in July at a Uni in Sydney."

"What will you study?" Mary's question feels coerced.

"Sports medicine," I say, ignoring the awkward vibe coming from the front seat. Jake looks at me, his sulk softens.

"Jake is interested in sports medicine too," Mary says, a little more at ease.

"We have about a half hour to kill before we need to be at the athletic complex." Sam pulls into a parking space near a large, white building with red Mexican tile. I open the car door and notice my cellphone under the seat in front of me. I don't understand how it ended up there but pick it up and shove it in my backpack then shut the car door.

"The bookstore is over this way. Let's check it out." Mary walks toward a large two-story building. It looks more like a department store than a bookstore.

"We'll meet back here in ten minutes." Sam looks at his watch.

I follow Mary to the clothing section. She holds up three university sweatshirts.

"Which one do you like best?"

"The crimson one with black letters," I answer.

"I think all three would look good on you," she says and tosses the lot over her shoulder.

The same expression was on her face when we were on the shopping spree a few days after I arrived. It's like her only mission in life is to make me happy.

"I reckon I'll use the bathroom before we go." I sought an escape, knowing Mary would purchase half the store for me if I didn't walk away.

"Okay, I'll meet you up front."

I find the loo and enter one of the many empty stalls. I unzip my bag and locate my phone near the top, except it isn't my phone after all. I turn the small black device over in my hand and two thin red beams of light float high above the black base. The beams move around each other quickly then more slowly, never intersecting. It's mesmerizing.

"Shay, sweetheart, are you in here?" Mary pushes open the restroom door.

"I found another shirt for you."

"Brilliant, I'll be right..." but before I finish my sentence the entire room brightens with a flash of white light.

"Shay, honey? Are you okay?" Mary shuffles to my occupied stall.

I shimmy up my trousers and open the door. The device trembles in my other hand.

"I found this under the seat in the car. I thought it was my cell phone so I tossed it into my bag. Do you know what it is?"

Mary looks shocked but before she can answer, a loud knock comes from outside the ladies' room door.

"Mary and Shay, if you're in there, we need to go," Sam's voice commands from the other side.

"Give us a minute," Mary shouts back.

"This belongs to Cassie. She's been looking for it. She will be so glad you found it." Mary takes the smooth rectangular device from my cradled hands, and slides it into her handbag.

"What is it?" I ask again.

"Some new camera Rick gave her for her birthday. It's all the rage in Japan, I guess. I'll return it to her when we get back to Phoenix."

"Let's go, ladies!" Sam shouts.

We file out of the restroom.

"What took you so long?"

"We'll talk about it later," Mary says in a hushed voice and Sam walks to the front of the store.

"We are going to be late," Jake scolds his mother and ignores me completely.

Father and son jog toward what looks like an Athletic center. A man with a whistle around his neck waits at the entrance.

"Coach, I'm sorry we're late," Sam says, shaking the man's hand.

"Coach Rawlings, you remember, Jake." Jake extends his hand.

"Jake, we are excited to see what you'll bring to our team this fall. Let's take a look around." The coach walks us through the gym and shows Jake his assigned locker. He introduces Jake to one of the mentors who will meet with him weekly to discuss classes and schedule tutoring. Jealousy creeps up on me. Does he even have the capacity to truly appreciate all of this?

The coach leads us out to the Lacrosse field next to the baseball stadium.

"Can you see it, Jake? Can you see yourself playing on that field?" Pride oozes from Sam's voice.

"I can," Mary interrupts, eyes watering, "we will be back here in a couple months to watch you play your first game."

"To watch you win your first game," Sam corrects and takes Mary's hand then points to the scoreboard.

The red lights displayed on the scoreboard trigger thoughts of the black device now resting in Mary's handbag. I've never seen a camera like that. There was no view-finder or lens and it didn't produce an image. Mary is lying, but why?

———

I can barely eat another bite. Not wanting to seem rude, I move the white fish around my plate with my fork. A yawn escapes my lips and I try to muffle it with my hand.

"Are you tired?" Mary asks, concerned.

"I had some really weird dreams last night."

Her eyes perk up.

"Too bad I can't remember anything about them or I would have written them down," I add, remembering Mary's strange fascination with dreams.

"My step-mom tells me to write down my dreams all the time too," Erin says. "Hey Mary, is Cassie stopping by later?"

"She and your dad drove back to Phoenix this morning. I thought she told you."

"She probably sent me a text," Erin says.

"By the way, I was talking to your mom last night on the phone, did Cassie really buy beer for you and your friends a couple weeks ago?" Mary asks.

"My mom told you that?" Erin shakes her head. "Cassie let me drink one of Dad's beers when I spent the night with them last week. Most everything Cassie does makes Mom mad. She still talks about how pissed she was when Cassie and Dad announced their engagement at my birthday party. I didn't care. I was waiting for the party to end so I could go out dancing."

"I remember that night." Mary smirks. "After the party, Jake tried to convince me to let you both go to the club on Mill."

"Jake bet me hundred bucks he could convince you," Erin added.

"Sounds about right." Mary grins but her eyes look sad.

"Mary, I thought you said Cassie and my dad drove home. Why is she sitting over there?" Erin points to the bar. "I hope everything is okay."

"You girls stay here. I'll be right back." Mary walks over to the blonde sitting with her back to us, gulping down a pint.

My curiosity gets the better of me. "I'm going to find the bathroom. I'll be right back," I say and excuse myself.

Down a small paneled hallway, I pretend to wait in line for the single toilet. I can see Mary from where I stand.

"What are you doing here?" Mary looks angry.

I move closer and hear the women arguing at the bar.

"What does it look like, I'm having a drink." Cassie lifts her empty glass.

"You need to get back to Phoenix," Mary demands.

"I checked in, everything is fine there. I couldn't leave."

"Why couldn't you leave? What's so important?"

"I saw Taylor driving over to Grady's beach house last night."

"What? Are you sure?" There is marked panic in Mary's voice.

"Yes. I followed them and made sure nothing happened." Relief settles over Mary's face.

"Shay found this today in the truck." Mary pulls the small device from her pocket and hands it to Cassie. "I tried to explain but I think she knew that I was lying."

Cassie puts the slender black box in her front pocket. "I had to make sure I wasn't followed, Mary," Cassie says with attitude.

"I know," Mary replies, her voice calm, "thank you."

It makes no sense. Why is Mary so concerned with Jake and Taylor and why did she allow Cassie to spy on them? The conversation reminds me of when I heard them talking about their scars on the patio. I walk back to my seat at the table and try to appear at peace but new questions keep firing over and over in my mind.

CHAPTER FOURTEEN

NOW

THE NEXT 3-D MOVIE BEGINS AMIDST CHEERS FROM THE audience. My eyes close and I focus on the warmth of the buzzing frames on my face.

When my eyes reopen, I am in Mary's body, sitting in Jake's room. Dirty socks hang from the desk lamp and his hats and shoes are strewn across the floor like someone tossed the place. Cassie sits on the edge of the bed next to Mary near a pile of twisted bed sheets.

"It won't be easy." Cassie's eyebrows lower. "There are tons of hoops to jump through but if you want to see him again there is a way."

Mary buries her face into a grass-stained t-shirt in her hands and a cocktail of stale sweat, coconut, and freshly cut grass overwhelms me. The room blurs with her tears and I feel Cassie's hand on her back as Mary heaves forward into a sob. "I'll set up a meeting with my contact in the morning."

When Mary opens her eyes again we are walking in the desert. She is following Sam in a single file line, on a trail that weaves between knits of brambly bushes and low-lying cactus. It reminds me of the Walkabout trip I took in Grammar School to the Bush in year three.

"Step directly into each other's footsteps." I hear a bloke call from the front. "The jumping cholla will strike if you get too close." I try to look around to gain some understanding of where we are but Mary is fixated on Sam's feet. "If you hear a rattlesnake, make no sudden movements. I don't have any anti-venom and we're hours away from a hospital." A stick snaps behind Mary and she jumps then turns around. Moses is pulling on a limb, trying to free himself and the ladder he carries from the encroaching thicket. She turns back and jogs to catch up to the group, who've stopped at a narrow clearing extending to a large derelict metal tower.

"Welcome to the birthplace of time travel." The man in charge stretches his arms toward the tower and Sam lifts a cynical brow at Mary.

"Anything for Jake... you promised," she whispers and Sam's eyes close.

Cassie leans in, "I know Mr. Bradley is a little over the top but trust me, you'll want to see what's in that tower."

"Moses, lead us to the promised land," Mr. Bradley calls over his shoulder.

The Asian man emerges with a snarl; it's quite obvious he doesn't appreciate Mr. Bradley's jest. He leads the group to the left side of the structure. Mary looks up. There's a "No Trespassing" sign that seems unnecessary. It's impossible to reach the first set of rusted rungs welded inside the middle of the tower without Moses' ladder.

"Is it safe?" Mary asks as Moses moves his ladder in place and holds it steady.

"Probably not," he states without remorse. "Bradley," he calls and motions to the ladder.

Mr. Bradley removes his tweed jacket and drapes it across Moses' shoulder then unclips his cufflinks and drops then into the front pocket of Moses' shirt. "Moses, you are a true prince." He winks and pats Moses on the shoulder then ascends up the ladder. Moses does something with his hands and though I've never seen the gesture I know exactly what it means. Cassie follows Mr. Bradley, and Mary follows.

At the top, a gentle breeze rustles through Mary's hair as she turns the circumference of the tower. The sun is setting in the West, leaving purple-gray ink blots over the desert floor to the east. Due south, an airstrip made of red dirt extends at least a kilometer in length.

"Let's get started." Mr. Bradley motions Mary and Sam to a pair of thick metal chairs near a panel of exposed wires. Sam sits and pockets Mary's hand in his.

Mr. Bradley leans against an open filing cabinet. "The Aviator's Historical Society was formed in 1951. Founder Arthur Stevens dedicated his life to educating young and old through hands-on interactions with historical artifacts," Mr. Bradley's fingers fumble the old newspaper clipping as he reads. He looks up from the text. "What the article doesn't tell you is that he acquired these artifacts during his travels through time. When he couldn't authenticate his antiquities or the means by which he acquired them, Stevens was labeled a fraud and in 1969 The Aviator's Historical Society dissolved. However, a new secret collective emerged: The Echo Initiative."

Mr. Bradley moves a metal stool. Behind it is a defunct radio whose tangled innards lay exposed on a stained counter.

"The goal of the Echo Initiative is much like Arthur Stevens's Aviator's Society, to learn from the past. But the Initiative's methods take nothing from the past except knowledge for the future. We are avowed silent observers. We operate solely by the donations and fees of members and require a first dig fee of $100,000, which will cover your initial trip."

Sam stands up. "Excuse me, Mr. Bradley, I mean no disrespect but it's time for us to go." He pulls Mary to her feet. "It sounds like you're asking for money to fund a bogus science experiment. I appreciate your zeal for the exploration of new technologies but not at the expense of my grieving wife who came here hoping to see her son one last time." Sam walks toward the ladder in the center of the floor. He pulls Mary along with him. "I told you this was a waste of time," he says under his breath.

"This is my favorite part," Mr. Bradley says with an obnoxious grin. Mary looks at Cassie and she is grinning too. Sam ignores their bemusement and continues to the gaping hole in the floor near the set of rusty rungs. His foot moves to the first wrung but it hovers in mid-air. He tries to force it to the ground but an invisible force holds it in place. He shifts all of his weight to the hovering foot and it looks like he is levitating mid-air.

"Okay Moses, that's enough," Bradley commands.

"Thank God," a voice grunts and a ripple of air shifts under Sam causing him to fall to the ground. Mary rushes to Sam's aid but he is transfixed on Cassie who is tapping the air with her fingers; it looks like vapors from a lit barbecue.

"Come, try it. It doesn't hurt," she suggests.

Mary stands then pulls Sam to his feet. Hesitantly, she reaches out. A wet, sticky substance molds around the tips of her fingers.

"Ouch!" a low voice bellows. Mary pulls her hand away and takes a step back.

"Quit it, Moses," Cassie reprimands then lifts her hands. "Help me find the seam." An invisible force moves Cassie's hand out in front of her and stops about a meter and half from the ground.

"Got it." She tugs and a tuft of black hair pops through. Cassie pulls again and Moses's face is exposed.

"What is this? What is he... wearing?" Sam asks.

"It is a suit that, when activated, allows fluidity of movement through exacted holes made in space and time," Mr. Bradley states.

"It's a self contained time machine: a time travel suit," Cassie explains.

"It's amazing technology for sure." Sam touches the suit again. "But time travel? Really?"

"You need more proof?" Mr. Bradley looks around the room, "Moses, the radio."

Cassie reseals the suit over Moses's face then calls out a series of commands. "Commence dig in 3, 2, 1." A violent surge of wind whirls through the tower. A second later, Cassie moves her hands in place and pulls the seam open. "I think that's a new record."

"I don't understand. How is this supposed to prove the existence of time travel?"

"Look," Cassie commands and points to the counter behind them. The busted radio is completely fixed.

"Good as new. Try it, it works," Moses states proudly.

"How do we know you didn't just switch them out in that suit of yours while we were fixated on the wind?"

"You don't." Moses says.

"And you won't until you try it for yourself." Cassie says.

"Faith in the unseen," Bradley pipes in. "People will always be skeptical. Ultimately, that's why dear Arthur Stevens was deemed a fraud and forced underground. His goal changed from the education of the masses to influencing a few; from bringing history to the people to taking a select number to the history. Sadly, most people have no interest in historical events. They say they do, but really they are so self-involved, the only past they want to revisit is their own."

"Okay, so what if we decide to take you at your word. What then?" Sam says.

"If a verbal agreement to participate is initiated, then it's the job of your Actuator," Bradley waves to Cassie, "and your Digger," he motions to Moses, whose face appears floating in the center of the room, "to educate you and vet you so that all parties enter into the binding agreement knowing what's at stake."

"For now, all you need to know is that I will coordinate all your travel plans and seek approval from the Initiative on your behalf," Cassie says.

"And Moses will be your pilot, flight attendant, and tour guide," Bradley chides and Moses's floating eyes roll upward.

"In the coming weeks, you will be asked to participate in several rigorous physical and psychological tests. After your evaluations, if you are green-lit for travel, formal training will commence. Your Actuator," Cassie bows her head, "is responsible for you both. I want to be clear, the primary goal of the Initiative has always been to allow others to see the past, first hand, in order to create a better future. If you follow the rules and keep your Actuator informed, you will be afforded the amazing opportunity of seeing your son. But if you veer off page and tread in dangerous waters, this offer rescinds and your chances of a happy reunion disappear forever. The past is etched in stone; it cannot be changed. It's like an echo, if you yell 'Hello,' the echo will always return. 'Hello,' never 'Goodbye.' There are no broken echoes."

"No broken echoes," Mary repeats.

Bradley, Cassie, and Moses exit the tower and Mary leans over and whispers into Sam's ear, "Something isn't adding up. If there are no broken echoes then how did Moses fix the radio?"

"I'm not sure, "Sam says, "but I am going to make it my mission to find out."

CHAPTER FIFTEEN

THEN

OUTSIDE THE GYMNASIUM, I SEND A TEXT MESSAGE TO Mary, asking if I can stay after school to lift weights with Grady after his LaCrosse practice. Ever since Mary and Sam found out about Jake's rendezvous with Taylor in San Diego, Jake and I have both been put on house arrest. Mary messages back, agreeing to the plan as long as Jake brings me straight home afterward. I know Mary is using me as Jake's punishment and though satisfying, I know it will only create more tension between us.

I find Jake talking to Grady near the door to the men's locker room and take advantage of Grady's presence, knowing Jake might handle the news better if others are around.

"Jake, Grady asked me to lift weights with him after practice. Your mum said it was okay as long as you bring me home." He closes his eyes and sighs.

"Sure, whatever. I have no life now."

"Thanks J." Grady slaps Jake on the back. "Shay, I will meet you in the weight room in about an hour." Grady grins and walks into the locker room after Jake.

I sit on the benches in the gymnasium and pull out my English homework. Quickly opting for a more comfortable place to sit, I move to a floor mat under the scoreboard. The men's locker room door opens. I can't see anyone but recognize the deep voice.

"She is here to ruin my life." Irritation streams through Jake's words. No one responds and I realize he is on his cell phone.

"Taylor, I'm not overreacting. Now they're telling me I can't go to Mexico. Yes, I'm serious! They're making me go to the Grand Canyon for two weeks. Of course she is going."

"Forester get your butt out on the field!" a voice booms through the doorway of the locker room.

"I gotta go. I'll call you after practice."

The door opens and closes behind Jake. I try to study but it's almost impossible focus. An hour later, Grady walks through the locker room door. His smile makes everything worth it.

"You ready?" I gather my things while nodding my head.

"Why can't you drive yourself home?" Grady asks.

"I don't have a driving license… and I've never driven a car." I look down, embarrassed.

"Your dad never taught you to drive?"

I shake my head.

"Not even in a parking lot or around the block?"

"Nope."

"Let's go." Grady tugs at my arm.

"Wait, we're leaving? What about lifting? What about Jake?"

"Don't worry about Jake. I'm going to teach you how to drive."

A wave of panic overwhelms me. "That's really not a good idea." I stop walking. "I really don't want to, Grady. I'll hit something or hurt someone."

"You won't. Trust me. I won't let you." He takes my hand and I reluctantly follow. I feel sick. I never wanted to learn to drive but trying to explain to Grady why is not an option.

Grady opens the driver's side door of his black Jaguar and I slide in over the leather seat. He jogs to the other side of the car and sits next to me.

"The first thing you are going to do is fasten your seat belt and adjust your mirrors." A subtle tremor moves through my hands and I follow his instructions.

"This car is slightly harder to drive because it requires you to manually switch gears. But, if you can drive this, you can drive anything."

I heed each command, putting the car in neutral then pressing the clutch pedal to the floor before starting the engine. Though Grady is an excellent teacher, I am distracted. Fear courses through me as the car moves around the empty lot. I see my parents in the front seat and my sister in the back as they pull out of the driveway and never return.

"Are you sure you have never driven a car?" The sweet sound of his voice calms me. I change gears and force a smile.

"You never talk about your parents or where you lived before Ingrid, why is that?" My eyes are glued to the asphalt in front of me and I pull into a parking space and put the car in park.

"I prefer to leave the past where it belongs, in the past." I remove the keys from the ignition and peace pours over me.

"If you ever want to talk about it, I'm here."

"Thank you." My voice holds more emotion than I anticipated. Grady takes my hand in his.

"And Jake isn't mad at you. He's mad at his parents. He will figure that out soon enough." Even though Jake wasn't the cause of my emotional lapse during the lesson, I play along, marveling at Grady's empathy.

"It would be nice if he could figure it out soon." I close my eyes and let out a long sigh. Grady's lips brush against mine. He kisses me softly, then pulls back, grinning.

"I was going to wait until Friday to kiss you, since it will be our first official date but you're too beautiful and those lips..." He gently grazes my bottom lip with his thumb.

"I'm glad you didn't wait."

A knock on the window makes me jump. Jake stands, arms crossed, with a look of disgust on his face.

"Don't worry about Jake, I kicked his butt in second grade and I can do it again."

———

From my window, I watch Grady pull up in his Jaguar. In a denim shirt and gray shorts, I've never seen him look so good. I check my reflection in the mirror one last time and apply some lip balm then walk through the door. A loud burst of laughter fills the hallway.

"Oh look, Jake, it's our best friend Shay." Taylor's voice sounds like she found a frightened bunny.

"I wonder whose day she's about to ruin?" Jake asks.

"Be careful Jake, she might tell your parents I drove over here to see you." Taylor gasps. "Oh wait, no, she already did that when we were in San Diego."

I follow the sound of the doorbell downstairs.

"Hey gorgeous!" Grady says as I let him in the front door. Behind me, Jake and Taylor mock his words. I try to smile.

"What's that all about?"

"Mary and Sam are gone for the night so Jake invited Taylor over. He thinks I was the one who told his parents they hooked up when we were in San Diego. I didn't but he doesn't believe me. It's his mission to make my life a living hell."

I shut the front door and walk toward the passenger side door.

"Where do you think you're going?" Grady says. He opens the driver's side and points at the steering wheel.

"You're going to make me drive on our first date?" I protest, still uneasy.

"It's a short distance, I promise, and you need practice."

Down the hill, I turn out of the Foresters' neighborhood. My palms are sweaty and my breathing is fast. I feel like I might pass out.

"Turn onto the dirt road. There, on the right."

I follow Grady's directions, wishing we were already there. The afterglow of the sun setting behind the mountains relaxes me. Deep purple hues in the sky leave a silky lavender layer that darkens as the night descends.

"Park here, we'll walk the rest of the way."

He opens my door then grabs a basket from the backseat. He leads the way to an oversized patchwork quilt spread out over the desert floor. Dozens of small, lit candles surround the blanket along with a couple small throw pillows. I sit in the middle of the blanket then realize the candles are arranged in the shape of a heart.

"I don't know what to say. I think this might be the nicest thing anyone has ever done for me."

Grady beams and moves closer to me on the blanket. "Are you hungry? I have sandwiches and chocolate-covered strawberries." He rummages through the basket. "I almost forgot; these are for you." He hands me a small bouquet of red and pink roses hidden under one of the pillows.

The fragrance of the flowers fills my nose and transports me back to my darkest day at the funeral home. My stomach turns at the familiar aroma. Flowering wreaths lined the walls of the melancholy room, each bouquet tainted with varying amounts of grief.

"Thank you. They're beautiful." I fake a smile and place the flowers behind me. "I would love a sandwich."

"I was going to bring my guitar but I thought it might get in the way." He pulls me close and kisses my cheek. "So I brought this instead." He removes a ukulele from the basket. "I hope you don't mind. Can I play you a song I wrote?" His fingers begin to strum the tiny strings.

"Sure," I say and he begins to sing.

"I know a girl from a far away place,
She has the most beautiful face.
Her laugh is so sweet and quite contagious.
It might sound absurd and completely outrageous,
But I've already given her my foolish heart,
Please pretty baby, don't go and break it apart."

As I listen to the lyrics, my head spins. Grady went out of his way to make me feel special but I can't help but wonder what would happen if he knew the real me. Would he put forth as much of an effort? Was I worth it? My past was littered with the consequences of my poor choices and I'd worked hard to reclaim confidence and self-discipline but that didn't stop grief from sneaking up on me. It often sliced open old battle wounds, letting the blood of my former life spill onto the floor of the new. I liked Grady way too much to let him experience my carnage.

His voice continues on, soft and smooth, as the sun dips low behind the mountains and the darkness pours in around us. The only light is from the flickering of the surrounding candles.

He ends with one last pluck of a string then leans over and kisses me. It wouldn't be such a bad thing to get lost in Grady.

"I wish you were going to Mexico with us over Spring break. I am going to miss this face," he says and caresses my cheek.

"I am going to miss you more. I have to spend the next two weeks with Jake at the Grand Canyon. One of us might die out there."

He laughs and I kiss his lips again.

CHAPTER SIXTEEN

NOW

"IF THERE ARE NO BROKEN ECHOES, THEN HOW DID MOSES fix the radio in the air tower?" Mary asks as she pours a cup of tea. Through Mary's eyes I see Cassie sitting at the kitchen table next to her.

"Okay, I'm going to let you in on a little secret,"Cassie says, "Mr. Bradley is full of crap. His name isn't even Bradley, it's Stevens, Arthur Stevens." Cassie steeps her tea.

"Wait, Mr. Bradley is Arthur Stevens?" Mary places a plate of chocolate biscuits on the table and Cassie nods. "The same Arthur Stevens who founded the first secret time travel society in 1951?"

"He goes by Steven Bradley now, but yes."

"How is that even possible? He looks thirty not ninety."

"Let's just say time-travelers like Bradley, have their ways of blending in."

"What do you mean like Bradley?"

"Others refer to him as an Enforcer. Supposedly, Bradley created the Echo Initiative to stop rogue time travelers from changing the past."

"So wait, the past can be changed?" I feel a tingling sensation radiate through Mary's chest and down her arms.

"Technically, yes."

"What about 'There are no broken echoes'?" Mary creates quotations with her fingers.

"That's propaganda the Initiative feeds to newcomers to limit the risks of changes made to the past and the future. The fabric of space and time is woven together like a beautiful tapestry, cut some strings here and there and it might not unravel but in time, holes are inevitable." Cassie looks at the clock on her phone. "It's time to go. Are you ready?"

"As ready as I'll ever be," Mary says and I feel her chest tighten.

———

"Communication check, final gear inspection, then dig." Mary's voice shakes.

"Mar, cover your face, it's time."

She obeys and a voice speaks into her ear.

"Mary, check one, two. Repeat."

"One. Two. Over." Mary replies with less hesitation.

Moses' face floats over to where we stand.

"Make sure all your skin is covered," he says, pulling the filmy substance over Sam's eyes then rolling his fingers over the seams. The transparent film seals in place. He moves to Mary and repeats the same steps. The suit blurs her vision and removes most of the light. All I can make out are hazy shadows beside and in front of us.

"We begin in 30 seconds. Drop your hands please," Moses commands, moving to the other side of Sam.

Mary squeezes Sam's hand, long and hard, then drops it and takes a deep breath in.

"After my count, remain perfectly still or you'll be sorry. And 5, 4, 3, 2, 1."

A loud beep sounds and an eerie breeze surges up from behind, causing Mary's suit to ripple.

"See you on the other side," Moses says, almost laughing as the radio cuts out, replacing his voice with classical music. The music bounces off of the suit and back into Mary's ears. I focus on the distraction, visualizing the piano keys as moving points on a rolling wave. A gush of air hits Mary from the front and her body tenses but I continue to focus on losing myself in the melody of the nearby wave I've created. Far off, a popping noise shoots between the notes. Like claps of thunder, they crack in the distance then rumble closer. A fast-moving shadow darts in front of us. Did Sam or Moses move? No one is supposed to move. A gush of air punches the front of the suit. Mary gasps and I lose my breath. The popping returns, this time encircling Mary. Each pop causes her stiff body to jolt in disobedience. The classical music is now long gone. Loud clicks like the cocking of a twelve-gun salute sound in stale air, heavy with the smell of steel and mortar. The odor seeps through the suit and presses in. A chilling moment of silence holds and, for just a moment, all is calm. Mary breathes deeply. Click. Click. Boom. Sounds of guns cocking then firing circle around Mary's face. I know they aren't really guns and that terrifies me even more. Something tugs at the flaps covering her eyes and pulls them from her face. A searing light floods in, blinding me until the flaps gel themselves back into place. Overcome with fear and unable to separate my reality from hers, I try to scream but my efforts are in vain. I have no voice during Mary's visions. Everything goes black. Is it over? Please, let it be over. I blink invisible tears. Smells of burnt flesh saturate the air. I want to search through the darkness for Sam or Moses but Mary won't move. Memories flash before me of Mary standing completely still, allowing the bees to fly around her head, revealing the purpose of the evaluation.

A new loneliness pushes in on me, convincing me that I've never truly experienced the word. I long for the comfort of someone, anyone. The smell of seared flesh makes me feel like Mary might vomit. Mary's legs begin to shake, they almost buckle and she tries to catch herself. Before she rights herself, the floor disappears. Mary looks up and all the air escapes from her lungs into a horrible scream. For the first time, I feel sorry for the woman and all she has subjected her body and mind to so that she can spend a few extra moments with her dead son. Through the darkness I see Jake standing in front of her, smiling. I try to smile back but Mary is unwilling. Tears blur her eyes and we continue to fall through time. Jake's smiling face flashes before her every time she opens her eyes. I can almost feel his arms around Mary's shoulders as her feet plunge into a cold pool of water. Her body submerges completely. The suit ripples up and down and presses in against her on all sides. It starts as a heaviness, then turns painful, like a frantic crowd pushing through a small doorway. It is hard to breathe. Panic sets in as Mary tries to withstand the increasing, crushing force. Her feet kick in rebellion, struggling to find the air to fill her lungs. Unable to fight any longer, her body goes limp. I feel lightheaded, like I am falling into a deep sleep, until Mary's feet crash hard into a surface below. With one last burst of resolve, Mary tries to springboard herself upward out of the murky abyss but it tightens its grip around her feet. It holds her at the bottom until she gives up the struggle. As Mary's resistance wanes, the pressure subsides and she regains her bearings. I realize she is standing upright. Piano music sings, once again, in her ears as she pants for air. In the distance, a blood curdling scream gets louder and louder, until it fills the air above us. Mary's scream finally catches up.

"Easy as bees," Moses says with a laugh in Mary's ear.

"Easy as bees," Mary repeats breathlessly.

She closes her eyes and when they reopen, she is next to Sam in the back seat of a rusty old jeep. I feel Sam's arm pulled taut around her shoulders and his hand on her leg. The car is quiet except for the beat Moses taps out onto the steering wheel. He pulls up to the curb and Mary's pulse quickens. Sam adjusts his ball cap then opens the door.

"Wait." Mary grabs his arm and Sam sits back down and faces her. She presses at his fake mustache. In the reflection of his aviator sunglasses I see Mary in a short blonde wig and oversized purple sunglasses. Sam tucks a strand of yellow behind her ear.

"It's time," he says gently.

"I don't know if I can do this." Her body feels as if it's weighted down and anchored to the seat.

Sam pulls her close and I can feel his heart beating fast. "We have come too far. We need to do this." He lifts her sunglasses. "I need to do this." Mary nods her head and follows Sam across the ripped leather seat and out the door.

"Don't do anything I wouldn't do!" Moses calls out. Sam nods and shuts the door. They watch Moses until he is out of sight then trudge through freshly cut grass to a set of bleachers.

The sun beats down and Sam swipes a bead of sweat from his forehead as they climb to the middle section of the bleachers. As soon as they sit, the players pour onto the field and Mary grabs Sam's hand. I track Jake and I can tell Mary does the same. He is easy to spot, with strands of black hair poking out from under his helmet. A stray tear slides down Mary's cheek from under her sunglasses. Out of the corner of Mary's eye, I can see Sam watching Jake. His eyes are glued to his son. My heart aches or maybe it's Mary's heart but it feels like my own. I think Mary might pass out. Each one of her breaths feels like it is being forced from her lungs. Mary leans into Sam and grips his arm then brings his hands to her lips and everything fades around us, like a dream. All the players disappear from the field, except for Jake, who follows his pre-game warm up.

"I'm so sorry," Sam whispers and a tremendous pain pours over Mary's chest.

"We love you, son. We were supposed to protect you and we failed. We are so very sorry." Mary puts her arms around her husband and they hold each other. She blinks and when her eyes open, the quiet is erased and the other players appear. The crowd cheers around us as Jake scores, seconds before the game ends. He flashes a smile at the second row where his present-day parents cheer wildly. A grimace covers Mary's lips as she observes her past self.

"Look at us," she says with disgust. "We took it all for granted. We assumed he would grow up. As if it was promised," she snarls. "I can't do this." Mary stands. "I'm sorry. We need to go."

Sam nods and leads us down the metal risers and helps Mary over the last bench. Something in the distance catches Mary's attention. She doesn't look down but out toward the parking lot. I can tell by the goosebumps on her arms and the hair standing on the back of her neck that she sees it; the powder-blue sports car parked in the gravel lot. Mary's shoulders begin to shake and her hands ball into fists. Distracted, she misses the last step and we fall hard to the ground. Pain radiates around her shoulder and knee. A commotion ensues around us and Sam leans down to help.

"Ma'am, are you okay?"

Mary's eyes remain closed but we both know the voice. It is deep and gentle with a hint of mischief, like he's just finished laughing. I feel Jake's hand then see his face when Mary opens her eyes. He gently helps her to her feet.

"Thank you, Son," Sam says in an exaggerated deep voice and pats Jake's shoulder.

Unable to speak, Mary smiles. A euphoric glaze covers her eyes and her entire body feels warm, like she's submerged in a hot bath. We watch as Jake runs back out onto the field with his teammates.

Mary hobbles toward the parking lot and her bliss is undone when her eyes slide over to the Spyder. Moses is leaning against the hood, his arms are folded across his chest. He doesn't look happy.

"Sam, I'm sorry. I saw the car and I missed my step. Do you think Moses saw me touch him?" Mary whispers, slightly hysterical, as they near their Digger.

"I don't think so," Sam says but his voice sounds less confident.

"I want to destroy it, Sam!" Mary's hushed voice trembles. "I want to destroy the Spyder!"

Sam pulls her tight and whispers, "Me, too."

A wide smile camps on her lips.

———

Cassie pulls the flap open and as Mary moves the translucent suit away from her face. I can see they are back in the desert at the air control tower.

"How'd it go? Did you see Jake?"

"Yes, we saw him," Mary nods and begins to cry, "but I did something wrong."

"What do you mean you did something wrong? What did you do?"

"I fell when I saw the Porsche and Jake helped me up." Mary chokes on the words. "It was the best moment of my life." I can tell she is reliving the experience as she speaks. "But I'm pretty sure Moses saw us. I don't have to tell you what will happen if he reports back to the Echo Initiative. We will lose everything, our house, our savings; but worse, we will never see Jake again."

Cassie motions around her then puts a finger to her lips. "Don't say another word," she whispers, "write down the address to your art studio. Meet me there tomorrow morning at 8."

Mary scribbles out the address on a gum wrapper, 2552 Biltmore Avenue, then slips it to Cassie. Mary closes her eyes and when they reopen, she is standing at the door of the quaint yellow studio. I can see the house number over her shoulder: 2552. I repeat it over and over then make it into a song so I'll remember, knowing it's the next place I'll visit when the vision is finished.

Cassie arrives and the two sit on a teal sofa surrounded by walls of art.

"I want to destroy the car." Mary's whole body shakes. "I know I shouldn't say things like that, especially to you, but what does it even matter now? I'm never going to see him again. Moses saw everything." Mary barely finishes before a sob catches in her throat.

"Moses won't say a word."

"How can you be sure?"

"Because, he's been helping me. We've been trying to save Stone for the past year."

"Why didn't you tell me all of this before my dig?"

"Changing fate isn't easy. The timing has to be perfect and, more than that, you must go undetected since members of The Initiative are always watching. We were making progress but came across some outlying circumstances that had to be addressed first. I think someone else was in the house when Stone died."

"Someone from The Initiative?"

"I'm not sure but this will help me find out." Cassie pulls out a small black box that looks like a cell phone; the same device I found in San Diego.

"Moses discovered this new technology. It can detect time-travel activity within a twenty-five mile radius, in the last forty-eight hours. The next time I travel back to see Stone, I'm taking it with me."

"I really wish you would have just told me all this to begin with."

"I had to keep up appearances with Bradley and the Echo Initiative. Also I wanted to know how passionate you were to change things. If you don't truly want it, it will never happen."

"Sam and I will do anything to get our son back."

CHAPTER SEVENTEEN

THEN

ICY AIR HIDES IN THE SHADOWS OF THE LARGE ORANGE boulders on the hiking trail Sam chose, a couple of kilometers from the Grand Canyon. Jake's florescent green windbreaker takes turns from swishing with his body to flapping against the wind. He flashes a smug smile and pushes ahead; the increasing distance between us only inspires his arrogance. The burden of my heavy pack holds me back and I'm tempted to ditch my gear; but the allure of rappelling down from the first plateau is worth the extra effort.

"Go home, Sydney."

I hear him but don't reply. Insults will only encourage his pace. My footing secures on the next boulder and I use my legs to hoist up onto another large flat rock that looks like a surfboard. Fiery red cliffs, illuminated by the sun in the distance and pinpricked with tall pines, ascend high against the cerulean blue sky. The red rocks remind me of home and my steps slow as I surrender to the views. The moment passes and I refocus my energy. When I can't locate Jake and his obnoxious neon-green jacket, I begin to panic.

I keep moving and finally find him, off the trail, attempting to climb a dangerously steep vertical, fifteen meters to my left. His easy-to-spot, neon green shell has been turned inside out so that the gray lining of his jacket camouflages him against the rock. What a wanker.

A smile forms on my lips as I entertain thoughts of out-climbing him to the top of the steep cliff but my nagging common sense overrules my desire for victory. I stay the course and continue to hike the trail. A mocking laugh bounces from boulder to boulder behind me. Tosser.

Almost to the top, I make good time, though I fear it isn't good enough. I dread the thought of seeing him beyond the next boulder, chest puffed out, gloating one minute then forgetting me the next.

My eyes brighten when I scan the peak and I'm alone. I strut around, smirking with delight then remove my pack. I lean against a tree and impatiently wait for the arrival of the arrogant jackass with his tail between his legs. "How's it feel to be defeated by a girl?" I say to myself.

Thirst sets in and I pull my water bottle from my pack. I twist the cap and hear what sounds like a moan. I twist again; another moan.

"Jake?"

I walk over to the ledge. I don't understand. Why is he on his back? Is he taking a break? I don't appreciate his humor.

"Too tired to climb the rest of the way, mate?"

He turns his head and blood pools around his eye from a deep cut over his brow.

Instinct grabs me. I scan the path for help—Mary and Sam stopped a while back—there's no one around.

In my bag by the large tree, I find a line and secure it around the trunk. I tie myself into one end of the rope then tie in an extra harness to the other end. I lay flat on my stomach, hang half of my body over the edge and call out.

"Jake, can you hear me?"

His body moves toward the sound of my voice and he yells in pain.

"Don't move!" I shout, trying to mask the alarm in my voice.

He refuses my instruction and turns onto his side then curses. His leg begins to slip off the edge and dangles dangerously over the next plateau; another twenty meter drop.

"Don't move! I'm lowering a rope."

"Where's my dad?"

"He's not here." The words catch in my throat. I take in a deep breath and calm myself by making a plan. "Every time you move, you risk falling further. We can't wait for your parents. I've anchored myself to a tree and I'm lowering a rope."

"There is no way you will be able to lift me out of here."

His arrogance forges its way through the pain, proving that even in crisis he is a total knob.

I lower the rope. He takes hold of the harness then stops moving. "Jake? Open your eyes! I can't tell if you are okay! Open your eyes!"

"I'm wonderful, Sydney. Best spring break ever! Soon you will be joining me because there's no way in hell you will be able to get me out of here."

I ignore his sarcasm and watch him slowly slide the harness up over his chest. He shouts obscenities until he finally gets it into place around his waist.

"Did you tighten the harness?"

"Yes, Sydney. I'm not a moron."

"I'm just asking because I'm up here and you're down there." I say it loud enough for him to hear.

I pull the rope taut and he yells in pain as his body shifts.

"Ready, mate?" It is a question more for myself than for him.

"Just a second. My leg," he stops, pain hanging in his voice, "this is harder than it…"

My body suddenly jerks backward as Jake's weight leaves the rope. I scream then shout his name.

"I'm here! I'm okay! There was extra slack in the rope."

I close my eyes and rock back on my knees. My heart, a hummingbird in my chest, is the only sound I hear in the quiet. I secure my backpack then take the rope in my hands.

"Change of plans. I'm coming down to you."

Before he can argue, I lean backward and angle my body away from the rock then effortlessly rappel down to Jake.

I crouch over him, assessing the damage. "Does anything else hurt besides your leg?"

"My shoulder." He grabs his right shoulder.

"What about your back or neck?"

He lifts his head and shakes it no, satisfying any doubts of a neck injury.

"Can you sit up?"

He answers with a grimace, and slowly pulls his body up toward me. His body shakes as he grips my hand to brace himself. Once steady, I hand him my water bottle. "Drink."

I pull my long-sleeve, gray T-shirt, over my head, exposing my bralette that matches my pale white skin. I wait for a slew of lewd comments. Surprisingly, he stays silent.

"Take this and tie it around your head; over your eye brow." I hand him the shirt. He doesn't move.

"Never mind, let me do it." I take the shirt from his hands and mop the excess blood from his forehead. Jake remains absolutely still and I'm afraid he is going into shock. I secure the shirt around his head with a tight knot then double check the harness straps around his chest. I tie him into the other line and add a pulley and brake.

"It will be easier if you use your good leg to keep from banging into the cliff and use your hands to steady yourself on the line."

He listens.

"Ready?" I don't wait for a malicious answer. On my feet, I reach high overhead and pull the rope hanging above me. With all my weight, I bring it down to the ground. Jake groans and his body lifts. Pull by pull, I manage to raise him about halfway to the top then stop to rest.

"You okay, Sydney? I can try to climb the rest of the way."

His sincerity catches me off guard.

"Just give me a minute." I try to hide my fatigue. The minute passes and I fake confidence.

"Ready?" I call to him loudly, to cover the doubt in my voice.

"You can do this," he says, void of sarcasm.

"You have about ten more feet until I can get a good grip and pull myself up near the ledge. Ten feet, you got this."

Compelled to move, I pull the rope and rein in my fears with each new grip. My arms begin to tremble then shake beyond my control.

"Two more feet." Jake responds to the tremors pulsing up the rope. "You're doing great."

I heave once more, throwing my entire body toward the ground. The weight anchored to me vanishes.

"Jake?" I try to yell but collapse near the blood-stained rocks. Breathing heavily, one of my hands covers my face while the other traces the tattoo on my wrist.

"Shay, are you okay? Are you hurt?" Sam appears from atop the ledge next to Jake, whose makeshift bandage is now soaked through with blood. I hear the worry in Sam's voice and my body responds. I wipe tears from my cheeks and rise to my feet, brushing the dirt from my daks. Methodically, I tie myself into the line and begin to climb. My arms are on fire but I climb through the pain. Sam's hands meet me at the top and pull me up and away from the ledge. I catch my breath then busy myself by gathering my gear. I can't look at Jake. I know if I look, I will see the blank look of indifference on his face. After all the physical and mental exhaustion he put me through, I can't stand the thought of being ignored. It is quiet for a long time as Sam inspects Jake's injuries.

"Dude, Shay, you're an ox!" Jake's blue eyes are warm with admiration.

Caught off guard, I grin then go back to repacking my gear, knowing it is his way of saying thank you.

"Are you sure you're okay?" Sam asks again.

"I'm fine. I'll be sore tomorrow." I grip my biceps and they tremble but I realize that I am shirtless and shivering. Jake responds, tossing me his jacket.

The three of us start back down the mountain, Jake hobbling on one foot between his dad and me. Down the trail, Mary sees us and runs.

"What happened? Are you okay?" Frantically, she touches his face and forehead.

"He's okay!" Sam's hand finds her shoulder and she calms almost instantly. I'd heard of couples that could finish each other's sentences but this was different. Sam's touch relayed something more; something Mary understood even before his words. It was eerie.

"I'm fine. I lost my hold when I was climbing off-trail. Good thing this beast was here." Jake nods at me. "She hoisted me up."

Mary takes my face in her hands. "You saved him?" she chokes on the words and tears spill onto her cheeks. "Are *you* okay?"

"I'm fine, just tired." My eyes react to Mary's tears by flooding with water and I look away, pretending to wipe my brow.

"What were you thinking? You aren't invincible!" Mary redirects her focus to Jake. "Something could have happened to you."

"He's okay Mary," Sam says and she nods in agreement. We begin the long, slow trek down the trail.

"This time," Mary mumbles, "he's okay. This time."

CHAPTER EIGHTEEN

THEN

THE MERCEDES MOVES DEEP INTO THE WOODS AND RAYS of light cast white and gold streaks over the forest floor. The sun shines ribbons at the end of a long, gravel road, highlighting a large, stone house with wooden archways and picture windows. Behind it, a lake, the color of the sea, peaks out on both sides.

"Welcome to Greystone Lodge, our home away from home…" Mary turns to me, "for the next two blissful weeks." Her introduction reminds me of my first days on Camelback Mountain almost three months ago.

I gather my bags at my feet and a single crutch shifts between us as Jake adjusts the sling around his arm. He was ordered to stay off the sprained ankle for at least a week, while the shoulder was fine once it was popped back into place. The sling was prescribed to appease Mary but the seven stitches over his eyebrow were necessary. They had already lent to his use of the phrase, "You should see the other guy."

Jake wobbles through the back hallway and I pass by, choosing a room with a balcony overlooking snow-capped mountains covered in dusty-white pine trees at the North end of the lake. I open the doors to the terrace, shrug my shoulders and laugh.

"What's so funny?"

Five or so meters to my right, Jake stands on an identical balcony. Leaning on his crutch, one hand holds his phone high in the air.

"It's beautiful."

"You're right, that is funny," he scrunches his nose, confused, then refocuses on his phone. "Not a single bar," he shakes his head, "not one." He concedes and puts his phone back in his pocket then looks out over the lake.

"I wish they were double diamonds," he nods to the snow-covered mountains. "I guess it wouldn't matter now," he looks down at his swollen ankle. "Do you ski?"

"Snow ski? No. I've never even seen snow until today." I speak in the direction of the mountains, as if paying them a compliment.

"You've never seen snow?" Jake cocks his head in disbelief. "Doesn't it snow in Australia?"

"In some places but not where I lived. I grew up on a surfboard not a snowboard."

"I saw you surfing in San Diego." I replay our trip and try to remember a time he would've seen me.

"You're pretty good." Is it the painkillers talking or is he actually being kind?

"I'm in the water every morning, before school. Have you ever been?"

"Surfing? A couple times but I suck at it."

I smile, picturing Jake face-planting into the ocean.

"How old were you when you started?"

"My dad taught me when I was four. I'm getting cold, Jake. I'm going to go inside."

I turn around and shut the doors behind me. Just because I'm no longer invisible doesn't mean we are mates now. I reach for the gray jumper in my bag and my arms scream with pain as I pull it slowly over my head. A moment later, I hear someone shuffling in the hallway outside my open door.

"Bad news, it's not just cell service, there's no internet either." Jake leans against my doorframe. Mary had said we were going to rough it in the woods. This must be what she meant.

"What are we going to do out here for two weeks?" he bows his head, defeated.

"Someone told me you're really good at rock climbing." I say.

———

"What are we doing tomorrow?" The aroma of Jake's latest culinary dish, chicken and dumplings, hangs heavy in the air.

"You don't need to know everything, Son," Sam says, exasperated.

"Let's finish dinner before hashing out all the details," Mary suggests.

"You know the doctor said I needed to rest my ankle, so I was thinking we should go to a coffee shop in town and relax. You know, maybe go to a place with free Wi-Fi?" Jake tries to sound nonchalant.

"There will be plenty of time to rest your ankle tomorrow, although I doubt there will be Wi-Fi."

Jake slumps his shoulders at his father's response.

"Your father and I are confident you both will enjoy what we've got planned. It will be an early morning, so don't stay up too late." Mary spoke to us as if we both belonged to her and for the first time, I no longer found it uncomfortable. I had grown to like the idea of someone taking the time to dream up plans for my enjoyment and look out for my well-being.

I ask to be excused from the table then offer to do the dishes, but Mary shoos me away from the sink. I obey and plop down in the over-stuffed sofa near the fireplace. Jake follows, sitting across from me, spellbound by the flames.

"So, what's the plan for tonight?" he asks.

"Do you always need to be entertained?" Sam says with a slight edge in his voice.

"Your dad and I are going for a walk around the lake. Shay, you are welcome to join us but Jake, you should stay here and rest your ankle."

The thought of rehashing everything that happened on the trail with Mary and Sam doesn't hold much appeal. "I think I'll stay here."

"There's plenty of fun right there." Sam points to a shelf overflowing with games and movies. "When I was your age, we didn't even have…"

"Yeah, yeah, yeah, isn't it time for your walk?" Jake chimes in before his dad can finish.

Jake lists off ten or so movie titles then picks one I have never heard of. We watch the opening credits silently, on opposite ends of the sofa, and my mind wanders to Grady, wishing I was cuddled up in his arms.

"I blamed you." Jake turns to me.

"I told my parents I didn't want a foreign exchange student living with us my senior year of high school and they went ahead with it anyways."

I try to hide my shock at his candidness.

"They were already so overprotective, I didn't think it could get worse, but it did."

There wasn't a baseline for me to measure whether a parent was overprotective or not. I just assumed all parents were like the Foresters and that the Foresters were like all parents.

"But, I started thinking…" Jake pauses.

"Shocking." I smirk.

"Ha ha. No, but seriously, I realized that things started to change way before you got here. It was after they returned from their anniversary cruise to Costa Rica, that's when they started freaking out over everything."

"Erin told me they made you end things with Taylor, that must have been hard?"

"Yes, it sucked but it was getting better, until they found out about us meeting up in San Diego." Jake glares. "Thanks for that by the way."

"It wasn't me, I swear. I think Cassie saw the two of you together."

"It doesn't matter. It's not just Taylor. My dad developed this disturbing man-crush on his car. He used to drive it at least once a week, usually to take my mom out to dinner. The day after they returned from Costa Rica,

131

construction on the fourth garage bay was started and he hasn't driven it since. It's like a trophy locked away in a trophy case. Last year, he let me take it to the prom. This year, I wouldn't even dare ask him. He would bite my head off. You saw how mad he got when you told him Grady wanted me to drive it to San Diego."

I grin sheepishly. "I did do that. Sorry, mate. In my defense, you were being a total wanker."

Jake doesn't respond and I can tell he is still trying to make sense of it, trying to pinpoint what caused everything to change. My fingers trace the numbers on my wrist and I feel sorry for him. I know the exact moment my life capsized.

"Have you always lived with that woman, Hazel?"

His question catches me off guard and I realize he'd been listening when we were in Grady's ute in San Diego.

"Ingrid? No, I moved in with her when I was fourteen."

"Where did you live before that?"

"With a few other families and then on my own for a bit."

"What happened to your parents?"

I hold my wrist tight and fix my eyes on one of the large stones mortared into the fireplace.

"They died in a car accident the day before my 12th birthday." I don't move my gaze from the stone.

"Shay..."

It's weird to hear him use my actual name and how he says it, I know what's coming. Since the day of the accident, pity has followed me; it circles like a wake of vultures, waiting for my weaknesses to be revealed

132

then devouring me with its pathetic looks and condescending half-smiles. My past has always been my achilles heel. And now the standing I'd gained, by saving Jake, is obliterated with just a few words.

"Shay, you're badass. You know that, right?"

I look up. His face is absent of solace.

"Thanks?" I shrug my shoulders. Thankfully, my instincts were wrong and Jake is different. But I change the subject just the same.

"Who is that?" I ask. In a corner opposite the fireplace, a picture of a young child hangs on the wall.

"Cassie's son, Stone."

"She has a son?"

"Had a son, he died in a fire. Rick had this place built in honor of her kid. Erin refuses to come here, she says it creeps her out."

"That's awful. He's such a cute kid. He reminds me of my sister at that age, red hair and blue eyes."

"You have a sister?"

"Had a sister; she died in the accident too." Jake is quiet as he processes my words.

"So, Ingrid…" He says her name slowly making sure he has it right.

"Did she adopt you?"

I'm amused at his interest.

"Never officially. By the time we both decided it was something we wanted, I was seventeen and it seemed silly.

"What is she like?"

"Really strict. She's always afraid I'm going to start drinking again."

133

"Shay is a party girl?" Jake asks, pretending to take a drag from a joint. I pull my recovery chip from my pocket and flip it through the air in his direction.

"A has-been party girl."

He examines the chip.

"What about you? I've seen your mates and heard about the parties you go to."

He tosses the coin back. "Second semester of my sophomore year was a blur. I was put on academic probation after I showed up to school drunk. It wasn't until I was benched for three games that I decided if it didn't make me a better athlete, I wasn't interested."

"But, you were totally bombed out at the desert party a few weeks ago. Erin said she saw you."

"Sometimes its easier to let people think what they want to think."

"Even Taylor?"

"Especially Taylor, that girl drinks like a fish." He grins.

"So has Grady kissed you yet?" he intentionally changes the subject.

"He kept telling me how much he wanted to kiss you and I kept saying, 'Ew gross, but okay, just do it. What are you waiting for?'"

I roll my eyes and hate that my cheeks burn.

"You could do worse. All the girls like him. He's good at all that sensitive crap—flowers, chocolates and holding doors."

And there is the Jake I know. Why does he assume that because of some near death experience, he has the authority to give me his stamp of approval? I know that once we're back in the Valley, he'll return to being the same tosser I met the day I arrived.

"Well, that's unfortunate since I prefer seashells to roses and jellybeans to chocolate. Grady is ace but I'm not interested in anything serious. Besides, the exchange program frowns on dating anyway."

He smirks and I know he doesn't believe me, which is even more irritating.

"I'm knackered." I stretch and yawn the best I can on demand. "We have an early morning tomorrow. I'm going to bed."

"Night, Sydney," his voice taunts.

Jake is still Jake. Nothing's changed.

I walk to my door and stop. It sounds like someone is crying down the hall. Mary and Sam returned from their walk but I thought they went to bed. Around the corner, Mary's back is to me and she holds an oversized satellite phone to her ear.

"I don't think we can go through with this. It's too hard."

I barely understand Mary's words through her sobs.

"Cassie, it's too much. This just feels wrong." Mary puts her hands over her mouth then turns around. I jump back around the corner and open my bedroom door. I close it quickly behind me as my heart pounds in my chest.

A moment later, there's a knock on my door. I open it slowly.

"Is everything okay?" Sam asks, concern hanging on his face.

"Yes, I'm just getting ready for bed." I answer with a fake smile.

"Mary and I thought we heard someone crying. Did you hear anything?" Sam asks.

"Crying? No," I shrug, "I didn't hear anyone crying." I lie.

"Okay, goodnight then." Sam leaves and I close the door. It almost seems as if Mary sent Sam to see if I witnessed her sobbing in the hallway. I know they are hiding something but I have no clue what it is.

I jump into the shower, hoping the water will bring me some much needed clarity. It doesn't help—it's the wrong kind of water. I need the ocean, to paddle out on my board and ride a couple waves in. Everything makes sense in salt water.

CHAPTER NINETEEN

THEN

THE NEXT MORNING, I SNEAK DOWNSTAIRS AND GRAB some brekkie before the others are up. Excited for what the day holds, I try to put the awkward encounter of Mary's emotional phone call with Cassie out of my mind. I convince myself that Mary and Sam must have had a tiff and afterward Mary confided in Cassie.

I grab my slice of toast and reach for a mug. I notice a piece of paper wedged between the coffeemaker and Mary's handbag that reads: ECO-Star G888

It probably has something to do with the morning's adventures. Brekkie in hand, I go back to my room and then out onto my private patio. I place my plate and mug on the small coffee table then curl up with a blanket on an oversized deck chair. The sun peers over the mountains, beaming light through the boughs of the tallest pines. The only sounds come from birds singing to each other in the nearby trees. I take a sip from my steaming mug and close my eyes.

"You missed a great ending!"

Jake is looking out over the lake. A cornflower blanket, the same color as his eyes, is draped loosely around his shoulders.

"The guy was dead the whole time!" he shakes his head.

I nod, realizing he's referring to the movie we started the night before.

"Really? Dead the entire time?"

Jake doesn't reply and I look over and see him hanging over the railing of his balcony, the blue blanket in a pile at his feet. Bloody hell! Am I going to have to save him again today? He rights himself slightly then waves at me with one hand while the other holds a finger to his lips. Sensing my confusion, he looks up at me and mouths for me to come and see.

Without even thinking, I run though my room and down the hall. I open his door then sprint to the balcony and lean over the railing next to him. A magnificent black bear grazes directly below us.

Feeling a tug on my arm, Jake points out two cubs standing about twenty meters from their mother. One slowly stumbles over to the giant mum while the other stays behind.

Fascinated, we watch the cautious mother bear fill her belly with berries then lift her snout to sniff out the danger carried in the cold wind. I shudder as the frigid air laces through my hair. Slowly, Jake reaches down, using his crutch for balance, and grabs the corner of the blue blanket. Careful not to make a sound, he shimmies it up over his shoulders then hands the corner to me. I wrap it around my shoulders and hold it tight, cocooning us together with warmth.

One of the cubs pounces on top of the other and I can feel Jake trying not to laugh. I have never been so close to him and it's scary how comfortable it feels.

"Jake, you out here?" Sam's voice booms out onto the balcony.

"Shhh!" we both respond in unison.

Unable to hear the shushing, Sam continues to call out. He finds us huddled together outside.

He finally sees what has our attention and his eyes go big. "Sorry," he whispers.

Sensing danger, all three heads pop up. They run toward the far end of the lake. The mother first, then her two cubs, trying with all their might to match her pace.

"Sorry, I didn't mean to scare them off."

We turn from the railing and face Sam. Looking down, I am reminded that I'm still in my pajamas. I look over at Jake, who's in a t-shirt and boxer shorts, and I instantly drop the corner of the blanket.

"We are leaving in ten minutes."

Sam walks through Jake's room and I follow almost as fast as the mother bear. I shower and dress quickly, the whole time hoping Sam hadn't gotten the wrong impression. Surely he didn't think anything was going on between us, up until yesterday we hated each other.

———

Mary exaggerates a pout. "I can't believe I missed the bears."

"We've been driving forever. Are we almost there?" Jake whines, making the same pout face.

"This will far surpass any bear sighting, I promise." Sam ignores Jake and kisses his wife on the cheek. Mary smiles at him and puts her hand into his. They don't look like they're angry with each other. Maybe the phone call to Cassie helped. They must have made up.

Sam pulls off the main road then through an old wooden gate and down a dirt lane. Ten minutes later, he pulls into an abandoned field. He hops out of the Mercedes but leaves the engine running.

"They must be running a little late," Mary says right as a woman rides up on horseback and motions to Sam.

"Horses are not better than bears. Seriously, Mom?"

"Jake, we aren't riding horses today."

A methodic pounding sounds overhead. Blades of dry grass wave wildly and the trees dance in the wind as a black and gray helicopter lands about a 100 meters from the ute.

"Now, that's more like it." Jake grabs his crutch and jumps out of the Mercedes, onto his good ankle. Mary seems less enthused. Her face pales and her eyes fill with fear as she watches Jake limp toward the chopper.

"Mary, are you okay?"

She looks over at me and her expression shifts from fright to peace. A wave of calm fills her eyes. "I'm great. Are you ready?"

I ignore my gut feeling that Mary is once again hiding something and follow her toward the helicopter. I notice the number on the tail: ECO-Star G926. It's different than the one written on the notepad I saw this morning. Maybe the wrong chopper made Mary panic?

I sit next to Jake in the glass cockpit and place the radio over my ears then secure my seat belt. After a simple greeting from the pilot, we lift off the ground and ascend up into the blue. Red earth beneath our feet disappears into a lush green sea of trees, then stops abruptly as a canvas of orange rock veined with thin purple shadows spans as far as I can see. Tan and gray walls of stone rise up like chiseled ocean waves and the aircraft dips low like a surfer cutting in. We weave through a divide, and follow a teal river as it snakes through the orange walls. We dart up and over a white stone formation then land near one of the green banks of the turquoise river. Once we're cleared to exit, Jake and Sam find stones to skip into the rushing water while Mary stands on a boulder next to me.

"It's crazy, in minutes you can see the canyon from a completely different perspective. It doesn't seem so big from down here. A new point of view can change everything." She looks up at the surrounding ledges. Though they seem inspiring,

Mary's words weigh me down. This perspective isn't a new one for me. Walled in on all sides, swimming in the shadows, the bottom is where I've spent most of my life. But I vowed four years ago to do whatever I could to claw my way out.

In many ways, the Foresters seem like the magnificent canyon; a sight to behold from the top, but with secrets hiding deep in the trenches below. I so desperately want to know them better and to let them know me. I want to love them and be loved in return but what if, just like everything else, it all breaks apart? What if everything is already broken?

After a few minutes, the pilot motions us back to the helicopter.

"I'm sorry folks but we have to cut things short today. A chopper went off radar. We have been directed to report back to the airport while rescuers look for ECO-Star G888."

I recognize the number immediately. It's the same number that I found written on Mary's notepad this morning in the kitchen.

CHAPTER TWENTY

THEN

"YOU ALIVE IN THERE, SYDNEY?" JAKE'S MUFFLED VOICE calls through my door.

"Aye, mate. Come in."

"Okay, mate." His eyebrows raise and he walks in without his crutch.

"Look at you." It had been a little over a week since he sprained his ankle on the trail and it was healing quickly.

"I didn't want to wake you but I was getting worried."

"If you would let me go to bed at a normal hour, I wouldn't be so knackered."

Each night we stayed up later and later, playing games and watching movies. The night before last, we talked until 2 a.m. as I tried to explain that thongs are something you wear on your feet, not up your butt and that when an Aussie says 'let's root' they're asking to hook up, not cheer for the home team. Since that night, he's told me he's rooting for me at least five times. The most recent was tonight at dinner while I was I finishing my plate of spaghetti. He caught me off guard and I almost spit out my last bite of noodles. Mary and Sam couldn't understand what was so funny.

I had wanted to mention the note I'd seen in the kitchen but I didn't know how to bring it up. Hey Jake, by the way, I think your parents might be psychic. Yeah, that would go over really well.

I prop myself up against some pillows and pull my knees to my chest, to give Jake a place to sit. Maybe this will be a good time to bring it up in conversation. He picks up the magazine next to him on the bed and flips through the pages.

"I don't get all this stuff. 'The Best Way To Get a Man and Keep Him.' Maybe this'll work for you and Grady?" He squeezes his eyes shut and makes pashing sounds in the air and I chuck another magazine at his head.

He dodges the flying periodical and flips to the next page as if nothing happened.

"'Is Your Man Into His Own Looks More Than Yours?'" I read aloud, "Taylor needs to read this!" I point to the title on the magazine in my lap.

"You made that up. There is no way that's a title of an article."

"I did not and it is." I laugh then hug the magazine to my chest.

He lunges at me and wrestles the magazine from my hands then skims the subtitles and shakes his head.

"No, seriously Sydney, why travel all this way if you're not going to hook up with someone," he pauses then coughs out Grady's name.

"Did you really just ask me that?" My eyes roll. "What about new experiences, different cultures, seeing the world?"

"Yeah, but you'll have plenty of time to do that when you are old. My parents travel all the time. Why would you leave in the middle of your last year of high school?"

I shrug, not knowing how to answer. I'd already lived so much life in my eighteen years. So many of my years were filled with heartache and I knew there were no guarantees. If I waited to experience things later in life, I might not be given the chance.

"I felt like I owed it to myself to make great memories and I am far too adventurous to think all those memories are only in Australia."

"What's this?" he opens my turquoise folder and reads aloud the different sections as he flips through the pages.

"New York, been there. San Diego, been there. Grand Canyon, been there. The Skywalk! It's amazing. I'm sure the roads are closed now though, due to the snow. At least you got the helicopter tour of the Grand Canyon."

"I'm sure the helicopter tour is even better than the Skywalk." I suggest.

"No, the Skywalk is better." He grins and I throw a pillow at his face.

"Is this your family?" he holds up a picture, nestled in the pocket of the folder.

"Yes."

"Your sister looks a lot like you, same red hair."

"People always asked my mum if we were twins. It made me so mad since she was two years younger than me."

Jake thumbs to the next tab. "The Foresters!" I leap onto him, and try to pry the folder from his hands.

He shakes me off and laughs as if it's a game then begins to read.

"Mary Forester is kind and will hug you until you suffocate. She plays tennis and likes chocolate croissants. She is an Art Therapist and has a weird fascination with dreams. She always appears to be hiding something." Jake raises an eyebrow.

"You think she's hiding something? Hmm?" Amused, Jake continues. "Sam is an investment broker. I think he's having an affair with his car." Jake nods his head in agreement.

I hate that he's seeing my notes. They weren't intended for anyone else. He continues to read and I remember the words I penned in San Diego.

"Okay that's enough." I try again to tear the folder from his grip. "Seriously, give it back." I don't hide my irritation.

"Jake Forester plays Lacrosse and will be attending San Diego State University in September. Jake is by far the best looking guy at school..." He stops and looks at me; his eyes beam with delight. "Best looking guy at school?" He chides but I refuse to look at him.

"Can I please have my folder?"

He ignores me and continues, "at least that's what he would tell you. Jake is completely unaware of anyone but himself. He is indifferent to me except when his parents are around. I am referred to as a 'charity-case' and he blames me for his parents' lack of trust and harsh rules. I'm not sure why his mates like him but I never will." Jake stops and closes the folder.

"I wrote those things when we were in San Diego," I say quietly without looking up.

"No, I get it," he says then closes the folder and tosses it onto the bed. He walks out of the room without another word.

Obviously, he didn't get it.

———

Dinner is unusually quiet. Jake's seat is empty. Apparently, he asked Mary if he could eat in his room. Around the table, I avoid eye contact with Mary and Sam, not knowing if Jake shared what I had written with his parents. I scarf down my food then excuse myself.

I walk past Jake's door but can't muster the courage to knock. There's no use in trying now. He's already made up his mind. Pleading my case would only make things worse. I retreat to my room, curling up to a pillow on my bed. A knock on the door makes me rise, but when I open my door no one is there. I peek out into the hallway.

Mary opens Jake's door. She leans her head in and speaks through the crack. I can hear his voice but not his words. Mary's tone softens and my stomach turns to knots. I know he is relaying the awful things I wrote. I hear footsteps and Sam's angry voice breaks through the murmurs. I shut my door quietly, then change into my pajamas and pack my bags. Next door, voices fluctuate from rage to soft hums then back to silence. I know what is coming. They'll send me away, just like all the others.

CHAPTER TWENTY-ONE

THEN

THE NEXT MORNING, I WAKE UP EARLY AND TRY TO mentally prepare myself out on the balcony. It snowed through the night and I marvel at the amount of white blanketing the trees and ground. I'd already experienced so much; if this was where it ended, I was grateful for the time I had.

Inside, I wait for Mary, knowing she will be the one to deliver the bad news. Her ease with words and ability to comfort make her the perfect candidate. I am certain I will be on a flight back to Sydney within a day or so.

A knock on my door makes me rise, and I plaster a brave smile to my lips. I crack the door slowly, delaying the inevitable. Jake Forester stares at the floor, lifting his chin only when he begins to speak.

"I want to make things right, but I didn't know how."

Our eyes meet, and the look in his eyes hurts, rather than satisfies me.

"Last night after you went to bed, I talked to my parents and explained what an idiot I've been. So, we came up with a plan to make things right. We leave in twenty minutes."

Ashamed, I break his gaze. "But, I wrote all those horrible things."

"All those horrible things were true."

———

We pull off the main road into a partially plowed lot next to a ute fitted with a trailer. I get out and stretch my legs near a large drift of snow. It sparkles like a white-capped wave in the sunlight. My muscles are tight and the inside of my cheek is bloody and sore. I had bit it when the car slid off the road, even though Sam had painstakingly put snow chains on the Mercedes.

The fresh air unwinds my nerves. I allow my body to relax and stretch my arms high over my head. I lean to the right and, as I switch to the left, a snowball pelts my shoulder. I turn my head. Behind me Jake smiles mischievously with another snowball at the ready.

"Sydney, this is called a snowball."

Without turning my body around, I slowly gather a handful of snow from the nearby snow-drift.

"It is a ball made of…"

I turn and fire. Jake's chest explodes white before he can finish. Stunned, he brushes the powder from his jacket and with the back of his hand, wipes the residual ice from his face.

"Oh, it's on, Australia!"

He bends down and prepares his arsenal.

I scream and run for cover as balls of snow pummel me from head to foot.

"I surrender," I shout.

"Let me see your hands."

I move out into the open with my hands in the air. Vulnerable, my eyes squeeze shut and I wait for another strike.

"Truce?" he asks.

I blink my eyes open as his hand extends toward me.

"Truce."

I put my hand in his and give it a shake. He pulls me close and shoves a handful of snow down the back of my jacket. I squeal then dance around, trying to release the cold slush.

"No fair, you said truce." I frown.

"I'm sorry, Sydney. Truce? For real this time."

I scowl and he laughs.

"Come on, I promise."

Sam walks between us. "Jake I need your help." He motions over to a bloke standing near a tarp covered trailer. The man looks like he could be indigenous to Australia. Sam shakes hands then slyly places a huge wad of cash in the man's other hand. Jake helps two other Aboriginal-looking men untie the gray tarp from the trailer. Underneath are two huge machines that look like jet skis, but with snow skis attached to the bottom.

"There's no better way to experience snow." Mary grins.

"And there's no other way to get to where we are going without them." Jake says then winks.

The man hands Sam a paper map then tosses each of us one of the helmets dangling from his arms. Two other men move the giant sleds off the trailer as Sam studies the map in his hand.

"Let's go." Jake jumps onto one of the machines and motions me to join him.

I take a step and Sam moves next to Jake, holding the kill switch.

"Sorry, dude, you have to be eighteen." Sam shows his son a piece of folded white paper.

"In three months, I will be." Jake grabs for the dangling keys

"Rules are rules. Jake, you will ride with your mother. Shay you are with me."

"This is stupid, I've driven a snowmobile before."

"You can drive me," Mary says then looks to Sam for permission. He nods.

"We can't chance anything happening to Shay," Sam says and Mary looks away as Jake scoots into the seat in front of her.

We bolt through the snow, slicing through icy air. At first, my arms belt tightly around Sam's waist. I try to keep my eyes open, embarrassed that I am so frightened. But as the joyride continues, I begin to wish I could have a turn at the wheel. Grady would've been so proud.

"Everyone okay?" Sam says as we slide to a stop in a clearing.

"Do we have a little time to play?" Mary asks and Sam looks at his watch.

"Not a lot of time, but sure."

Mary jumps from the snowmobile. "Snowman contest starts now." She doesn't hesitate and begins to collect a large pile of snow.

I wait for Jake's protest but see him dart in the opposite direction, maneuvering a sheet of snow into a ball.

"Don't worry, Sydney. I'll show you how," he says over his shoulder sarcastically.

"I'll be right, mate." I pack the snow together and soon I have three small balls ready to stack on top of one another. Jake moves the bottom of his giant snowman next to the short stout couple his parents created, then carries the remaining top half with ease.

"Let me help you," he says.

Carefully, he picks up my three small lumps and places them next to his. He pulls the scarf from around my neck and puts it around his snowman then takes his hat and places it on the head of mine.

"The Forester snow family is complete." Jake's eyes meet mine and we lock arms.

I wonder if he knows what he's done? Probably not, since he is oblivious to most things. Being included and considered a part of the family means more than a fun day in the snow ever could. I'd never been invited in, no strings attached. Sure, I'd been welcomed into homes for the extra income or for the way it made a person appear philanthropic, but I'd never felt wanted or chosen. The closest thing to a family I had was Ingrid. Ingrid took me in, and loved and mentored me, but was often distracted by the numerous other girls who came through her revolving door.

"I captured myself quite well; I won, hands down." Jake moves next to his snowman.

"Drum roll please," Mary commands and both Jake and Sam beat their gloved hands against their legs. I follow their lead. "The winner of the snowman, excuse me, snow-person contest is…Dad." Mary squeezes Sam's shoulder.

"Rigged," Jake says through a loud cough.

Sam ignores his son and dips Mary in his arms and kisses her.

"Gross, get a room."

They pash a moment longer then Sam returns Mary to her feet.

"Before we go, let's get a family picture with our snowmen?" Mary prompts.

"I'll take it," I offer and Mary looks confused.

"Sweetheart, we need you in the picture."

Sam puts the camera on a large rock and sets a timer. A stray tear slides down my cheek but I wipe it away just before the camera clicks.

CHAPTER TWENTY-TWO

THEN

"WE NEED TO LEAVE SOON IF WE ARE GOING TO MAKE IT IN time." In true Forester style, there was always something more, another surprise hiding around the corner.

Sam hands me my helmet and the keys. "Your turn to drive, Shay. Stay close to Jake and you'll be fine." I hesitate but take the keys in my hand.

We race through the forest, dodging trees and boulders, until we hit an open road with an open gate. With sunset only a few hours away, I wonder if we will be returning to Greystone before dark or sleeping somewhere else for the night. Over a hilly road, we ascend up toward a large plateau. Covered in snow, it looks like a giant drop off. Sam motions for me to look ahead, beyond Jake and Mary's sled.

"Can you see it?" he shouts over the roar of the engine. I shake my head and shout no simultaneously.

"Over there." He points toward the edge of what looks like the Grand Canyon and a couple large buildings with a handful of snowmobiles in front. Attached to each machine is a tarp-covered sled. We pull in next to them and I finally see what Sam is talking about. A steel horseshoe-shaped bridge loops out over the snow-covered canyon.

"The Skywalk," the words escape my lips in a reverent whisper.

A maze of snow-packed walkways leads to the main building. Aboriginal men in snowsuits pass us carrying propane heaters and snow shovels.

At the entrance of the hovering bridge, thick glass rests on steal beams, creating a walkway high above the snowy canyon.

The first step out onto the glass is a bit intimidating. The reflection of clouds and blue sky makes me feel like I'm surfing on air. Mesmerized by the movement of my own feet, I don't look up when Jake calls my name. I shuffle over to the sound of his voice and kick his side when I find him lying on his stomach, face pressed to the glass.

"You've got to try this. It's amazing," he says as he taps the glass next to him.

I lie down and feel like I'm a soaring bird over the giant, snow-filled ravine.

"Best day ever," I say without thinking.

"What was that? Did you just say best day ever?" A glorious smile sits on his lips.

"What's your best day ever?" I chide. "Or worst day, if you like. You pick."

"Hmm?" he scratches his chin in exaggerated thought.

"Best day ever, hmm," he pauses for dramatic effect, "the Friday before Spring break. We were late for school and I didn't get detention, then at lunch…"

"Wait," I interrupt, "you didn't get detention? You were the one that made us late! I got detention. I cannot believe you didn't get detention."

"Hold on, it gets better," he says and holds a finger to my lips, "at lunch, the cafeteria served ham and pineapple pizza, which never happens. Also, there was fire drill during the chemistry test that I forgot to study for. Best day ever!" He winks then turns back toward the glass.

"What's your worst day?" he asks, laughing.

I knew dodging detention, Hawaiian pizza, and getting out of a test weren't what he'd truly consider his best day. In the same way I knew he wasn't really asking to hear about my worst day. It was just a silly game; a way to sidestep the real answers to the questions that, for me, were attached to real pain and heartache. I knew the game well. I was a master at crafting answers others wanted to hear. Maybe it was for that very reason I decided to ditch the game and unload my worst day on the boy whose life I saved. Maybe it was because I felt like he owed me, or maybe it was just because I was so tired of keeping it bottled up like a live grenade, pin pulled, ready for release. Jake, aloof to everything, would be the perfect bystander. My candidness would not evoke melancholy stares or sad follow-up questions. I doubt he'd even register what I was saying. I take in a breath of courage and begin.

"I slammed the front door in my sister's face because she was wearing my favorite necklace again and refused to give it back. I never understood why she liked it so much, since my name was engraved into it. Seeing it around her neck was the only reason I didn't get in the car. I heard the hum of the engine, and I knew they were pulling out of the driveway without me. I stomped so hard up the stairs, I was sure one of the floorboards would break. I pulled my bedroom door closed so hard that our family photo hanging in the hallway crashed to the floor. I flopped onto my bed and buried my face into my pillow and cried until I fell asleep. It all seems so foolish now."

"Wow, that is bad," he mocks me with an exaggerated frown but I continue.

"I must have been asleep for a while, because when I heard the knock at the front door the sun that usually floods through my front window in the afternoon was gone and my room was completely dark. I remember being so confused; it felt like I was still asleep. In a fog, I walked slowly down the stairs, my eyes sore and puffy from crying."

"How is this your worst day? Did you fall down the stairs? Please say you fell down the stairs."

I ignore him and go on. "I heard our next-door neighbor calling for me. I will never forget the way she said my name over and over. It was like she desperately needed me to answer the door but hoped I wouldn't. An eeriness hung on the hinges of the door as I swung it open. It was like there was something terrible waiting for me on the other side. Our neighbor, Mrs. Dillard, stood next to a police officer. Her face was splotchy and red. She held her hand out to me and I took it, not knowing what to do. I had never held her hand before. My sister was the one who would sit on her lap, holding her hand, waiting to be tickled when we were little. I was the one who sat in Mr. Dillard's boat that was parked between our houses. Some Saturdays, he would put me in the boat and let me play while Dad cut the grass. I'd put on the life saver and sit there, pretending I was surrounded by nothing but water."

Jake is silent and I wonder if he's fallen asleep. I focus on a stone jutting up through the snow.

"What did the officer say?" he asks quietly. With courage, I turn my head. His eyes find mine. They hold the same look of admiration as when I lifted him to safety on the hiking trail a week ago. Uncomfortable, I stare back into the canyon then reply.

"The officer asked if they could come inside. They followed me to the front room, where Mrs. Dillard sat with me on the small sofa. She sat close, so close I could feel her trembling. She smelled like lemons. I don't know why I remember that but I do."

I pause, trying to decide whether to go on or make an excuse and stop.

"What did the officer say?" he asks again.

"I could hardly hear his words through Mrs. Dillard's sobs. I remember he said, 'There has been an accident' and 'They didn't make it.' They told me that my sister, Alex, survived, but was in critical condition at the hospital. I didn't believe him at first. I thought it was some cruel joke they were playing on me, since I behaved so badly before they left. I kept waiting for the officer to say 'Just joking.' He never did."

"Were they hit by a drunk driver?" he asks and I shake my head no and try to swallow the sorrow damming in my throat.

"Their car was in the middle of the intersection when a ute ran a red light and hit the driver's side. Both my dad and the driver of the ute died instantly. At least, that's what the police report said. The autopsy report showed the driver was not under the influence, just negligent. A witness said my mum was conscious right after the impact and was asking for Alex and me but lost consciousness due to blood loss. Her left leg was severed at the hip. She died on the way to the hospital."

I turn over onto my back and look into the clouds, intentionally avoiding his eyes.

"Once it all set in, I demanded to see Alex. The thought of her all alone... since Mum and Dad weren't there." My voice catches in my throat. "Mrs. Dillard drove me over and we met Mr. Dillard in the lobby. I found out later Mr. Dillard had been called to the hospital to identify my parents' bodies as he was listed as next of kin. It explains why Mrs. Dillard had come over to the house with the police officer to tell me what had happened, and why Mr. Dillard looked so sick when I saw him standing there at the nurses' station. I often wish I hadn't known that he had seen them. To this day, the sadness and anguish in his eyes makes my imagination run wild. I'm convinced it would have been better if I saw them myself."

I forget where I am and I stare into the patchy blue above. It's easy to get lost in the torment of that day and the ones that followed.

"There is comfort knowing they weren't in pain when he saw them," I say. "Somedays, knowing that fact is the only way I find peace."

"What happened to Alex?"

"She died in my arms later that night; still wearing my necklace." I let out a small chuckle then wipe my eyes.

Jake lies still, absorbed in my words as I relive them. The silence collapses in on us and binds us together, side-by-side on the glass. He turns on his side and gently reaches for my hand. He holds it for a moment, then lets go, and turns back onto his stomach. Face to the floor, I exhale, grateful he didn't say anything. Words are so overrated.

A minute later, Mary lies down beside me and Sam next to Jake.

"So is it as great as you thought it would be? Jake mentioned that this was one of the places you really wanted to see."

"It's better than I imagined. Best day ever." I turn my head toward Jake, and his smile smashes against the glass.

"Excuse me," a tribesmen says as he trips over my feet. He carries a small table while another man follows, holding two folding chairs.

"I thought we could have an early dinner out here." Sam helps Mary to her feet.

"Sounds great, Dad." Jake gives a thumbs-up but stays facedown on the glass. He pulls me closer to him as he points out rocks shaped like different animals.

———

"I want to get a picture of you two before dinner." Mary pulls Sam's camera from her bag. "Go stand by the railing and pretend this is one of the most amazing experiences you've ever had." She motions to me then Jake.

He stands near the rail and pulls me close to where the sun is beginning its plunge below the mountain walls. He puts his arm around my shoulder and tugs me into his chest.

"You are freezing!" he says and rubs the length of my arms.

I try to make sense of it but can't. Had we genuinely become mates? He saw what I wrote. He knew how damaged I was.

Is this some sort of act of redemption? Now he feels like he has to pretend to care? I find some comfort in knowing everything will return to how it was, before I saved his life on the trail. Once we arrive back in Phoenix, Jake will go back to being Jake and I'll be invisible again.

CHAPTER TWENTY-THREE

NOW

I SING THE SONG I CREATED OVER AND OVER IN MY HEAD, 2552 Biltmore freaking Avenue. I recognize the small house instantly. The night I arrived in Phoenix, we had stopped by Mary's art studio: 2552 Biltmore Ave.

Around the side of the house, I jump the cinderblock wall and try to open the back door but it's locked. I find a bobby pin in my bag and wiggle it inside the lock. With a slight click the lock releases and the door opens. There are some perks to being a former delinquent.

I go room by room, making sure I am alone, beginning in the room with an easel. In the kitchen, there is no food in the cabinets, no dishes in the sink. The place is empty. Down a short hallway, I open a bedroom door. Shocking, more closed doors. Paintings cover the walls, floor to ceiling. A queen-size bed looks slept in, but there are no clothes in the wardrobe or toiletries in the adjoining bathroom.

I sit on the long, teal sofa trying to piece it all together. I pull the black frames from my bag and put them over my eyes. Moses comes into focus. He is dressing two twin-sized beds with crisp white linens. They are a stark contrast to the stained brown carpet and chipped mustard paint peeling from the walls. The nauseating smell of stale cigarettes mixes with mold and Mary's stomach turns.

"Moses, how did you find this place?" Mary asks.

"A friend," he replies.

"A friend, really?"

"Do you want the truth because I don't really think you want to know how I came upon this place."

Mary's brow furrows and she turns around. A cracked mirror catches her reflection. Her skin is pale and dark circles cradle her eyes.

"I could use some help." Moses says, without tact, and Mary helps him move one of the two hospital beds against the wall.

He places a small generator on the floor between them and a humidifier on the table. A green lamp casts a subtle glow over the room, muting the streaks of dirt caked into the pillows on the small sofa and chairs.

"Are we sure about this?" Mary says to Sam, her hands fidgeting with the bracelet on her wrist.

"We cannot let our past selves dictate our son's future. They must be taken out of the equation," Sam says unapologetically.

"He's right Mary," Moses chimes in.

"You will be careful with them, right?" Mary asks as Moses hangs two bags of saline from a coat rack.

"These aren't the first medically-induced comas I've successfully administered." Moses states, without remorse.

"Be ready to leave in two."

He secures another clear bag then unlocks the three deadbolts from the door and leaves. Mary nervously picks up her things and waits by the door next to Sam.

Moses returns and they follow closely behind him to a rusty, old, blue van. Mary sits in the middle row of seats. A roll of duct tape and two burlap sacks are placed on the seat beside her. Mary must have seen them too because a set of goosebumps run up her arms.

"Okay kids, you ready? It's showtime." Moses flashes an exuberant smile then puts the van in gear. Within minutes, they arrive at the Marina.

"Wait here." Moses jumps from the seat and sneaks behind a group of pylons near one of the docks.

"There, over there. The tender boats from the cruise ship." Sam points them out to Mary. The small boats motored in load after load of tourists to the port.

"Do you see Cassie?" Mary asks.

"There she is… and there we are." Mary's arms and legs tingle and her breathing becomes shallow. A black screen darkens her vision as I try to see beyond the windows of the van.

"Are you okay?" Sam touches her hand.

Mary closes her eyes tight for a moment. A picture of Jake flashes before me, and when Mary opens them again, the black screen is gone.

"I'm fine," she states with confidence. She watches as her and Sam's replicas approach Cassie with concerned looks on their faces. Moses returns to the van.

"They took the bait," he says with a smile and I realize that Cassie is the bait Moses is referring to.

"Ready?" he asks, handing Mary and Sam each a white rag.

Cassie opens the van door. "No, Rick isn't here..." Cassie says, but before she can finish, Moses forces the couple on holiday into the van. With strength and accuracy, Mary places the white rag over the mouth of her clone. Her eyes squint until the struggling mother lies motionless on the floor of the van.

"I'm sorry." Her heart pounds and the black screen reappears.

"We have to go," Sam commands.

Moses and Cassie strip the unconscious bodies of their clothes and belongings then hand them to Mary and Sam, who redress quickly. Not more than five minutes had passed when they step out of the van.

"Don't worry, we will take good care of them." Cassie motions to the naked couple lying, comatose, on the van floor. She hands Mary her handbag and identification then slides the van door closed.

"Now what?" Mary looks to Sam.

"We save our son."

CHAPTER TWENTY-FOUR

THEN

"THE NEXT HOLD IS ABOVE YOUR LEFT HAND," I INSTRUCT. Seeing Jake's arms tremble as he struggles to pull himself up on Grady's wall reminds me of the day on the trail.

"Hey Sydney, remember that one time you saved my life at the Grand Canyon?" he says and he must be thinking the same.

"Take your time, you two." Grady shouts from the top of the wall.

"How do you put up with his arrogance?" Jake grins then strains for the next hold.

"I've had a lot of practice. I live with a guy who's a real pain in the butt." I look down at Jake.

"Weird, I heard he's a helluva guy."

"Hella... something." I return my focus and continue climbing until I reach Grady at the top.

"It's so strange to hear him treat you like a human being." Grady tips his head toward Jake. "The impossible has happened; I think you're friends."

"Maybe?" I shrug my shoulders. "Or maybe he just feels like he owes me?" I'd decided not to tell Grady all the details of our Grand Canyon adventure. Especially how I told Jake about my darkest day.

"You giving up, mate?" I shout down to Jake, who's lowering himself to the ground.

"I'm done. You two deserve each other." Jake hollers back.

I look over at Grady. "I think I might go too."

"Are you sure you can't stay and watch a movie? Lucy asked if you were coming by for a tea party later. She'll be sad." Grady pouts.

"Tell Lucy I will come by next week for tea. I have a ton of studying to do, especially since I'm meeting you at Jaden's party later."

"I guess I can't complain, I'll see you again in a few hours," Grady concedes.

I didn't want to disappoint Grady but I craved some time to myself. I'd been hanging out with him nonstop since returning from the Grand Canyon and when I was home, Jake was making a habit of hanging out in my room. At first, it was just to say goodnight or ask about Grady. Then he started coming by to tell me about his day and all the "Taylor drama" that unfolded. I guess Grady was right, Jake and I had become mates, maybe even good mates.

"I'll see you soon." I kiss him lightly on the lips then leap backward and rappel down the wall. I find Jake and bribe him for a ride home.

We aren't home more than ten minutes and Jake walks through my door.

"Jane's downstairs looking for my mom. Have you seen her?" he asks.

"Your mum told me she was spending the day with Jane at the spa."

"Weird." Jake turns around and traipses down the hall. I follow and stop at the landing.

He meets Jane near the fountain. "I guess she's at the spa today," he says.

"I wish I was at the spa. I could really use a spa day." Jane replies.

"I'm sure she has her phone. Give her a call and see if you can join her." Jake suggests and Jane leaves.

Back in my room, I open the white shutters. Jane drives out past the iron gate just as Jake pulls his ute to the front of the house. I decide that I can't keep quiet anymore. I shut the blinds, put on my shoes and head downstairs. As I walk through the open front door, a dry sponge hits my shoulder.

"I know you want to help me wash my truck."

"How you can you tell?"

"I can see it in your eyes."

"Okay, but what do I get out of it?"

"A ride to school every morning in my truck." His dimple appears.

I kneel and pick up a sponge, wondering if I should dive right in and mention all the weird things I'd seen or ease into it. Lost in thought, I toss the sponge into the sudsy bucket splattering frothy foam all over the side of the ute.

"Hey, Hey. Sally deserves better than that. You're fired."

"Why do you call your ute Sally?"

"Every guy names his truck, and Sally here doesn't like to be soaped up without a good rinse first," he states, as if it were a renowned truth.

"Don't blame me, I've never washed a car before. I have no idea of the proper washing etiquette." He raises his eyebrows and motions me over to an empty bucket and garden hose.

"First, we rinse the truck with water from the hose. Do you think you can handle that?" I nod and hold the hose as he turns the tap.

"So, why is Sally getting the works? Do you have a hot date with Taylor after Jaden's party?"

"I am meeting up with Taylor, but that's not why I'm washing her. Grady and I went 'off roading' on the way home from practice yesterday. Sally doesn't like having dirt caked into her undercarriage." He strokes the ute like it's a horse.

"Like father, like son." I cock my head at the Porsche, locked in its glass cage.

"Funny," Jake says, unamused.

"Taylor wants to finalize our prom plans," he says and his face twists.

The Friday before spring break, Jake had hijacked the media center at school, allowing him to ask Taylor to Prom via a live feed from the roof of the science building. Every television in the entire school tuned in during 4th period. Poor Jake, with that type of pre-prom hype, Taylor's expectations of the actual night had to be sky high.

"I'm so tired of all the prom talk. I know it's exciting for you girls, but really there is more to life."

"Don't lump me into that group. I have never been to a prom or a dance or whatever you call it."

"You've never been to a school dance?"

"I was the girl who was supposed to go to the dance but ditched it to go night surfing." I spray down Sally's backend.

"Why can't all girls be like you?" He lifts his hand in the air and a soap bubble lands in his hair. "You say what you mean and you don't care what people think."

I laugh to myself. His approval wasn't something I needed or wanted but I found myself very keen to have it. How had things changed so quickly?

"So, if Grady asked you to prom what would you say?" he asks, changing the subject.

"For somebody who hates talking about prom, you sure do like talking about the prom."

"So?" I can tell Jake knows something I don't.

"I'm not heartless. Of course I'd go with him." I try to sound nonchalant.

He picks up a sponge full of soap and rests it on Sally's hood. "Now we move the sponge in small circles like this," he demonstrates.

"You try," he says and chucks the sponge at me, landing suds all over my face.

"Thanks." I use the back of my arms to wipe the bubbles from my forehead.

"Can I ask you a question?" My voice is more serious than I had intended.

"Sure. What's up?"

"Don't you think it is strange that Jane came here looking for your mum, you know, since your mum was supposed to be with her all day?"

"I guess."

"At Greystone, you mentioned your parents had been acting different since returning from their trip to Costa Rica."

Jake nods.

"It didn't mean much at the time, but I started thinking back to some things I saw in San Diego and over spring break."

"What kind of things?"

"I'm sure there are explanations." I swirl the sponge in the bucket of bubbles.

"Shay, what kind of things?" Jake says my given name and it throws me off. "What happened in San Diego?" His eyes anchor to mine.

"The first night at the beach house, your mum and Cassie were on the patio. They were whispering and showing each other their scars." My sponge moves in small circles next to his. "Your mum showed off one on her knee and a new one on her forearm. She told Cassie she was annoyed she had to hide them."

"I've never seen any scars but they've been playing tennis a lot lately; maybe they had a couple really intense matches?"

I can tell he knows his explanation is weak.

"Maybe, but they kind of looked puffy and pink, like burns. And then I found this small black device when we were in San Diego. I thought it was my phone at first but when I showed it to your mum and she said it was a camera Rick gave to Cassie. But later that night, we saw Cassie and I heard your mum tell her that she had to make up something to explain away the device. Then Cassie said she followed you and Taylor to Coronado. I think they might've been tracking you with it."

"Where is it now?" Jake asks, still processing. "The device?"

"I reckon Cassie has it."

"And what about the Grand Canyon? You said something happened during spring break?"

"The morning of the helicopter tour, I saw a handwritten note in the kitchen with the word ECO-Star G888 written on it."

"The tail number of a chopper," Jake says, nodding his head. "So?"

"It was the number of the helicopter that crashed that day."

"Are you sure?" His brows furrow.

"Positive." I stop scrubbing and link my gaze to his again.

"I'm sorry, I shouldn't have told you all this. I have this strange feeling, like your parents are psychic or something." I wince, knowing how crazy I sound.

"I'm glad you told me." He puts his sponge over mine. His eyes are reassuring as he hoses down one of the wheels, rinsing all the muddy bubbles to the ground.

"One last thing? Why are most of the doors in the house closed?"

Jake stops and looks up.

"I've never really thought about it." He cocks his head in thought, then without warning, he turns the hose on me.

"Really?" Dripping with water, I grab a sponge in each hand and throw them at his chest. Covered in soapsuds, he reaches for the nearest towel and wipes away mounds of bubbles.

"Too bad for you, this the only towel," he says and sprays me again.

I grab the handle of the soapy bucket of water but stop as a cold breeze moves over my shoulders. I look down and notice my drenched white t-shirt and try to cover my chest in a mad panic until a towel wraps around my shoulders.

"I'm only doing this so you don't die of hypothermia." Jake holds me tight and my entire body shivers. I rest my head on his chest and he rubs my arms and back, warming me.

"Let me worry about Mary and Sam." He pulls back and the clouds reflect in his blue eyes. "I'll talk to them and make sense of it all. They haven't been your parents as long as they've been mine." He squeezes me tighter. "I know how much they care about you. They wouldn't want you to worry."

I turn my head, knowing if I stare long enough at him something might change; something that shouldn't change.

"So, don't worry. Okay?" he lets go, leaving the towel draped around me and I release the breath that I didn't realize I was holding.

"Oh and we're leaving for Jaden's party in an hour."

I feign excitement, "Brilliant." I had almost forgotten about the party. Since becoming sober, parties no longer held the same appeal.

"Come on, Syd. It will be fun. But before we go, I want to show you something. Get changed and I'll meet you upstairs in five."

CHAPTER TWENTY-FIVE

THEN

I OPEN MY DOOR AND LOOK FOR JAKE, CURIOUS AS TO what he wants to show me. Since we returned from the Grand Canyon, I've seen all his sports memorabilia, including three binders full of mint-condition baseball cards. I faked enthusiasm because I couldn't understand what is so great about baseball when cricket exists. I also marveled at the four shelves in his wardrobe dedicated to his hat collection. He even pointed out his favorite, a crimson one with a black bill, placed strategically in the middle. More recently, he showed me what he called, "the sacred art of constructing the perfect fish taco." I was skeptical at first, having eaten my fair share of street tacos in Sydney, but after devouring four in one sitting, I had to admit he was onto something.

Jake saunters down the hall in a pair of jeans and a fitted gray t-shirt. "Ready?" he asks?

"I guess. Where are we going?"

"Follow me," he says and leads us over the second story landing before stopping at one of the mysterious closed doors.

"My parents started out with nothing. I think sometimes when the doors are open it makes them feel like they are flaunting their success." Jake turns the knob then lets it open slowly.

"This is my dad's study." The room is paneled in mahogany and has four towering bookshelves. A navy velvet sofa is centered between two gold wall sconces. It is luxurious, but not in the least mysterious.

The next door opens and the smell of stale smoke spills into the hallway. "Dad's cigar room." Similar to the study, the room is paneled in dark wood. Six chairs covered in faux zebra hide are tucked into a large green felt poker table. Behind the table, navy velvet curtains frame a large picture window. In the corner, a glass humidor displays a vast collection of cigars.

Door after door, there are no real surprises. Two opulent guest rooms, decorated in ivory and gold, are sandwiched between a small library, complete with a fur rug and fireplace. A grand piano sits proudly in a sunroom behind a pair of french doors and a magnificent ballroom with crystal chandeliers and a dance floor is behind a door off of the huge great room downstairs. Apparently it's where Mary learned to salsa dance a couple years back.

"Do you want to see the bowling alley?" My eyes light up and I nod. Jake shakes his head and grins. "There's no bowling alley." I peg his arm with my fist.

"There is one more room I want to show you. It's one of my favorites." Doubting his sincerity, I don't budge. He takes my hand and pulls me down the hall past the kitchen, then opens the door to the backyard and motions me to follow.

"If you're taking me to see the game room in the pool house, I've seen it," I frown. "I saw it the night I arrived."

"That's not the room I wanted to show you." Intrigued, I move next to him and enter through the pool house door. He stops near the air hockey table and I look around.

"Ha ha, very funny. There aren't any doors in here."

He steps closer, and the scent of coconut hits me as he reaches around my shoulder. "You're right," he says and pulls open a pair of massive armoire doors, "look." He nods and I turn and peer into the armoire. Through the wooden doors is a hidden room.

"What's in there?"

"My childhood. My mom went through a Chronicles of Narnia phase when she was decorating this space."

I follow Jake as he crawls through the armoire then through a large hole in the wall to a smaller room filled with shelves of toys. I step over a model plane, and a siren sounds as my foot inadvertently kicks a small fire engine in my path.

"Little Red, I almost forgot about Little Red." The joy of old memories glimmers in his eyes.

"Did you forget about this one too?" I cradle a baby doll, dressed in pink.

"Pinky," Jake says with mild disdain. "Erin cried for days when she lost that thing. Who would have thought it was hiding in here the whole time?"

Jake names his favorites as we look through the stacks of toys. He tells story after story of afternoons spent playing army commander and monster truck driver. I listen quietly from the other side of the room, thinking about my childhood cut short.

"Are you thinking about Alex?" He asks and I wonder if he's psychic like his parents.

"How did you know?" I wipe a welling tear.

"You make the same face when you talk about her. Your mouth smiles but your eyes water."

"She would have loved this place. When we were little, she would set up her room like an amusement park. All of her stuffed things would take turns riding rollercoasters or spinning on a carousel." I use my sleeve and wipe the other eye. Jake moves next to me and I lean my head on his shoulder. We sit quietly for a long time.

"I have a question and I need you to answer truthfully." I say.

"Okay," he says and his fingers fidget with the arms of an action figure.

"Did you really put something in my food in San Diego?" I turn my head and survey his eyes. His mischievous grin gives him away.

"What did you do?" My eyes widen.

"I spit in your bowl."

"Gross! I'm glad I didn't eat it."

"I did it again the next morning at breakfast." He laughs and I pretend to gag.

"Wait, do you hear something?" Jake lowers his voice and puts his hand on my shoulder. I stop, mid-gag and we hold silent. A scratching noise rustles near the door on the opposite side of the room.

"That's a storage closet." Jake jumps to his feet. "There must be a bird or something trapped inside." He turns the knob and tries to nudge it open.

"Something's blocking the door. It looks like a bed." He pushes harder and opens it wide enough to stick his head through.

I crawl up underneath him, poking my head in below his. Two hospital beds, fitted with white sheets, fill the small space. The mysterious scratching sound originates from a small generator powering a humidifier and lamp between the two beds.

———

Music pulses from the open windows of Jaden's house, greeting us at the driveway. I dread parties like this, but I'm glad to get Jake out of the house. Since finding the beds in the closet, he'd been beating his brain, trying to come up with some explanation.

"Do you think Jaden will mind that I'm blowing in? I've never met him."

"You'll be right," Jake replies, like a true Aussie. I laugh and follow him through the front door.

"Jake, what's up?" Jaden yells over throngs of people from across the room.

Jake shouts back and a brunette in Daisy Dukes, runs up to him and jumps in his arms.

He whispers something into her ear, then carefully stands her back onto her feet just to watch her topple over again. On the floor laughing, she grabs one of the red cups littering the coffee table next to her and licks out the last drop.

"You okay with this?" Jake says and glances back; his voice is strangely empathic.

My eyes say no but my head nods yes. It isn't the temptation to drink that makes me want to leave but the memories of my own stupidity. Not long ago, I was the girl, pissed as parrot, drinking the last sip of backwash out of the glass.

Jake casts a reassuring smile and an empty plastic cup slams into my face. I search the room and make eye contact with the sloshed girl on the floor. She mouths the word, "Sorry," then falls over in a fit of laughter.

My eyes narrow then turn to Jake, who is trying hard not to lose it.

"When are we leaving?" I say and he breaks. His laughter makes the humiliation worth it and I can't help but smile.

"Come on Syd," he regains his composure, "everyone knows a party isn't a party until you get pegged in the face with a solo cup."

I sneer and follow him through a dimly lit sea of people to the kitchen. "It's chockers in here," I shout and grab the back of his shirt and he slows his pace then moves to my side. "Let's go outside," he yells back.

We pass a game of beer pong and what I assume is a game of strip poker, before finding the door leading outside. Beyond the flagstone patio, we sit in two empty chairs on a patch of grass near a fire pit.

Jake stares into the fire, lost in thought. He rests his arms on his knees, his eyes intense.

"This is killing me. I can't stop thinking about those stupid beds. Did they look slept in to you?"

"I don't know, maybe? We should talk with your parents when we get home tonight." The anxiety fades from his eyes and they spark with mischief.

"What?" My hand sits on my hip. "What do you know?"

"I know nothing."

"Well, I won't argue with you there."

"So what's up with the tattoo?" he changes the subject and my fingertips freeze in place over the green ink. "Grady is convinced it's some special number only surfers know the meaning of."

"That's because I told him that." I chuckle.

"What does it really mean?"

"Have you ever wondered how many random photos you might be in?" My fingers loop over the numbers again. "Like, if you were sitting behind a couple at a cricket match or near a family at a restaurant and someone took their picture?"

"So you have been in," he turns my wrist, "you've been in 4421 pictures?" His dark eyebrows knit together and his determination to understand makes me grin.

"My mother was the photographer of our family and she insisted we keep old-fashioned photo albums. We had books upon books filled with pictures of every milestone. It was like she wanted proof of every moment, even the insignificant ones." I close my eyes and see the pages unfold behind my lids.

"I had 4421 days with my family; 4421 days of feeling safe and unconditionally loved, 4421 days of knowing where I belonged. I didn't know how important those days were until day 4422. On that day, picnics in the park, beachside holidays, surprise parties, they all died. Photos taken of me after day 4421 reside in random albums, in the strange homes I was forced to live in. There are pictures of me with families who pretended to love and include me, but tolerated me at best; people who have photos of me out of pity, not fondness and who honestly might not even remember my name."

"You belong here, with us. You know that, right?"

His words wrap around me like the warm breeze and I know he's right. I knew it when Mary and Sam asked me to be in the family picture at the Grand Canyon. I want to respond but I don't know how. Admitting he's right makes me feel weak.

"Is Taylor here?" I glance around the yard, trying to change the subject.

"Taylor? She was playing strip poker back in the kitchen. Didn't you see her? She was the one without a shirt."

"She was?" I ask and my eyes and nose scrunch together.

"No, she wasn't." A smile takes over his entire face.

"Why do you do that?"

"Because you are so gullible!"

"Who's gullible?" Grady strolls up behind us and Jake looks over his shoulder.

"Hey dude, glad you could make it." Jake stands and bumps Grady's chest with his elbow. "You didn't see Taylor on the way in, did you?"

"I think I saw her with her shirt off at the poker table." Grady doesn't crack a smile until he looks at me.

"Great, now you too?" My lips pinch together.

"Ready?" Grady takes my hand.

"I didn't expect to see you so soon," I say, lacing my fingers between his.

"See you at home." Jake raises his eyebrows then walks toward the house.

"Let's take a ride." Grady says, pulling me close.

"I'll drive," I say and move for his keys; instead he hands me a blindfold.

"Not tonight."

CHAPTER TWENTY-SIX

NOW

ACROSS THE ART FILLED ROOM, I SEE IT. POWDER-BLUE and black paint are smeared with red, and I know what it represents. I pull it down and stare closely at the wall until I find a slight variation in paint color. I trace the seam with my middle finger. I grab a painter's knife sitting on the drawing table and cut a square into the drywall, I pull it loose. Between two studs, a shoebox hides. I blow the drywall dust off of the box then open the lid. A purple folder rests on top of a manilla file folder inside the box. I recognize the purple folder; I had one like it from when I applied to the foreign exchange program. I move it to the side and open the manila folder. On top is a copy of Jake's birth certificate. Attached with a paper clip, dated two days from today, is Jake's death certificate. I read a copy of his obituary and tears overwhelm my eyes. I pull my phone from my pocket and scroll through five new text messages.

Jake is beyond worried, but I can't respond. I close the manila folder and open the purple folder on the table. My fingers skim down each page until I reach the last few pages of letters written by Mary.

Dear Sir or Madam,

I recently had the privilege of meeting Ingrid Mans, a nurse who currently runs a home for girls in Sydney, Australia. I was thoroughly impressed by the dedication Ms. Mans exudes for those in her care, and I want to assist her in making a difference. I would like to offer a full scholarship to Shay Conrad, one of the current residents in her home. Ms. Mans shared with me Shay's journey of hardships and how she's risen above them. Along with the scholarship, I would like to open my own home to Ms. Conrad. Attached is her full application for the program as well as Ms. Mans' consent. Being a licensed therapist, I have the training and expertise to care for Ms. Conrad and will work closely with Ms. Mans to make sure the transition is seamless.

Sincerely,

Mary Forester, Ph.D.

I don't understand. Ingrid told me someone had offered to pledge money so one of the girl's in the home could participate in the foreign exchange program but I never imagined it was Mary Forester. Ingrid never mentioned any interactions with Mary. I flip to the next letter.

Dear Ms. Mans,

I enjoyed meeting you at the recent grief seminar in Sydney. You spoke so highly of Shay Conrad that I would like to extend an offer to her. I was recently asked by a foreign exchange program to sponsor a student. I mentioned you and the girls in your home, and received approval from the program to award Shay a full scholarship and placement in a home in the United States. Please consider this amazing opportunity for Shay and her future endeavors. Attached is a copy of the application.

Sincerely,

Mary Forester

I take out my phone and begin a text to Ingrid then stop. Ingrid had met Mary but there was no way she knew the Foresters' true agenda. Hell, I don't even think I do. If I text Ingrid, it would only lead her to worry. All of this has been Mary and Sam's doing. Ingrid was only a pawn.

I go to put both folders back in the shoebox and find a loose piece of paper at the bottom of the box; the title to the Spyder. I can't help myself and crumple it into a ball in my hand, wishing the act of destroying the paper would solve everything. I cram the papers back inside the box, then cram the box back into the wall. I shimmy the piece of drywall into place then attempt to rehang the painting. I stop as I notice a wardrobe door hidden behind three hanging paintings. A scratching noise sounds from the other side of the door as I get closer. Painting in hand, I lift it high the air like a weapon then slowly turn the knob. The door eases open and I step into a large closet then stop; the hairs on the back of my neck take on a life of their own. A set of matching hospital beds with crisp untouched white linens are centered under a painting of Jake on the tiny paneled wall. In between them, a small generator hums, powering a humidifier that's run dry. A small green lamp is the only source of light in the tiny room and it casts long shadows. I shudder and shut the door, then walk back down the hall.

I sit back down on the long teal sofa and place the glasses over my eyes. My eyes blink open. Mary is walled in by two rows of mangled cars stacked four high. Rainbows of chipped paint are the only way to tell where one vehicle ends and another begins. I see a gap in the rusted metal and try to step forward, but Mary's feet are glued in place. Her body is heavy and light at the same time, like when I would tread water next to my board waiting for a wave. The wind kicks up and wraps Mary in a thick cloud of dirt. Smells of burned rubber and gasoline whip past, forcing her to move.

Overhead, a ray of sunlight pierces through the haze, casting a wreath of light over the pristine, powder-blue Porsche a few meters away. Mary doesn't turn away. Her heart pounds in her chest like a ticking bomb about to detonate.

The moment passes and Mary sucks in dusty air. Near the sports car, Sam talks to an older bloke wearing coveralls stained with oil and dirt. Mary's shoulders release the tension pinched between the blades in her back and I relax. She walks past a blue van with no doors and a pancaked limo. Sam's mumbled voice rises with irritation and he points to the powder-blue Porsche.

The old man's fingers fumble with his scraggly beard and his head shakes. Mary steps closer to hear and stands a meter or so from the car. A pain pricks in her chest then radiates to her stomach, and her arms instinctively wrap around her waist.

"Get rid of it," she directs, though the comment leaves a sour taste in her mouth.

"With all due respect Ma'am, this car is a collectible and is in perfect condition. Why the hell would you want to crush it?"

"Money? That's what this is about?" Sam's eyes narrow, "I'll give you what I bought it for at auction- $200,000; but you have to obliterate it into nothing, no spare parts, no remnant steel, erase it from the Earth."

The man lowers his head then whistles to the crane operator.

"Make the check out to Don & Sons," he says then clicks his radio to life, "lift and crush the baby-blue classic. Over."

"Sorry boss, I didn't copy. Did you say lift and crush the baby-blue classic? Over."

"Copy that Dan."

"Damn shame. Over. Lift and crush the classic. Over."

The crane moves into position and a giant magnet sways over the shiny blue shell. The operator lowers the magnet at a snail's pace and barely grazes the Porsche as if apologizing for its awaited slaughter. A dull hum moves through the magnet and the car trembles and shakes. It levitates on its own for a moment then connects with the magnet, sealing itself and its fate to the crane.

Sam's phone rings. "Cassie, what do you mean, Bradley knows?" Sam moves his phone back into his pocket then reaches for Mary's hand. His palm is sweaty.

"We have to go." He pulls her arm. She pulls back.

"No, I won't leave until I see it destroyed."

"I promise it will be." Sam looks over at the man in the overalls who winces as the Porsche moves closer to the crusher.

"We can count on you, right?"

"Of course, sir." The old bloke says, holding the check in one hand and shaking Sam's hand with his other. Mary's eyes close and when they reopen she is standing over Jake's lifeless body twisted between two pieces of a mangled orange Porsche.

"I know all of these things will happen." Hot tears sting Mary's eyes. She reaches down and moves her thumb across a piece of scratched orange metal revealing powder-blue flakes underneath.

"I know it will happen and I can't do anything to stop it." I blink three times. When my eyes open, they are filled with tears. I'd lost everything long ago and wouldn't wish that grief on anyone.

CHAPTER TWENTY-SEVEN

THEN

I TOUCH THE BLINDFOLD COVERING MY EYES. "ARE YOU taking me home?" Everything is dark and it feels like the car is moving up the mountain. Grady responds by kissing my hand. The car stops and he opens my door. He helps me to my feet, then turns my shoulders and removes the handkerchief from my eyes.

Small candles flicker inside huge conch shells, lining the Foresters' driveway.

"What's going on?" I ask, chewing my lip.

"Take this," he places a sand dollar in the palm of my hand, "now go find the rest."

I raise a quizzical brow then bound down the drive. Around the side of the house, I follow the candlelit path, ending at the patio in the backyard. A canopy of shells and white lights hang overhead. Dozens of glass urns overflowing with pink coral, purple oyster shells, and pieces of sea glass line the patio. Hundreds of sand dollars and small candles surround the pool.

"Grady?" I search for him behind me in the moonlight.

"Over here." Across the yard, Grady stands in the shadows waving, with a guitar strapped to his shoulder.

"Can you see me?"

"Barely."

A light appears. It shines on Grady, making him squint his eyes. He clears his throat and his fingers pluck the strings as he begins to sing the same song from our first date.

"I know a girl from a far away place,
She has the most beautiful face."

My hands cover my mouth. As I listen to his serenade, the pool begins to glow neon pink and a giant, floating letter P lights up in the center of the pool, followed by an R, O, and M.

I think he is done but realize he's added a verse.

"Girl, you are truly the bomb,
Please, pretty baby, let me take you to Prom?"

He strums a final chord then sets his guitar down.

"Shay, will you go to prom with me?"

I run to him and throw my arms around his neck. "Yes!"

Mary opens the patio door. "So?" she asks.

"I'm going to prom with Grady."

She claps her hands together and looks around.

"I'm going to hire you for my next party," she turns around, viewing the entire display, "this is amazing."

"Mary's right, this is amazing. Did you do all of this yourself?"

"I was planning on flowers but Jake suggested sea shells."

"He did?" I ask, lost in my own thoughts. "Where is Jake? Is he home?"

"We've been talking since he came home," Mary replies.

"Really? Is everything okay?" I try to hide my concern, wondering if Jake mentioned the storage closet to his mum.

"He went upstairs to his room, he seemed pretty tired. I'm going to head upstairs too. I'm waiting for a call from Sam. He likes to check in on me when he's away on business. You two can stay out here as long as you like." Mary says as she closes the glass door behind her.

Grady pulls me close. "We can stay out here as long as we like." He kisses me softly on the cheek, then on my lips. "You okay?" he asks.

"Yes." I smile then bury my face in his chest, afraid he might see the concern in my eyes.

———

The front door closes behind Grady and I turn around. A blanket of darkness hangs over the trees in the atrium and drapes down onto the floor. My foot touches the first marble step and a shadow near the second staircase startles me. A tall slender figure leans, unmoving, against the banister. I step closer and realize it's Jake's lacrosse stick. I chuckle to myself and creep up the stairs. I pass my room and continue down the long hall, hoping to see light streaming from under Jake's door, but the hallway is black. It wasn't like him to go to bed without saying goodnight. Disappointed, I walk slowly back down the hall, wishing I could talk to him. I open my door and almost trip over an urn of coral on the floor. I crawl into bed and pull out my phone. In the midst of all the excitement I missed a text message from Ingrid.

Ingrid:I miss you Shay-Shay. The new girl ran away again.
Shay: Bummer. The Climber asked me to a dance. Gotta get a dress :(

I turn out the light and close my eyes. The night was perfect. It was unforgettable, so why was I worrying about Jake? After an hour of listlessness, I abandon the idea of sleep and decide to get a snack from the kitchen downstairs.

All is quiet except the sound of my own feet padding down the marble staircase. Thankfully, Baby is asleep in her cage at the bottom of the other staircase. I smile when I see Jake's lacrosse stick leaning against the banister, remembering how silly I'd been. I watch my feet closely, afraid I might trip over something and wake the family. I make it to the kitchen without incident. I look up just before bumping into the island. In the dining room, a gray shadow sits, hunched over, at the table. Wondering if my imagination is playing tricks on me again, I blink then step forward. A man, half naked, snores softly; his head rests on the table. The hair on my arms stands on end. Sam is away on a business trip and Jake is in his

192

room. Panic grips my chest. I turn ever so slowly, my only goal is to get to Jake's room. I take five steps into the hallway and the kitchen light flips on behind me. I stop and spin around. Instinct takes over and I grab a glass on the counter. My arms raise in front of my chest, ready to strike.

"Oh blimey. Bloody hell, Sam, you scared the rat piss out of me." My heart feels like it might beat its way out of my chest. "When did you get home?" Using the kitchen counter as a crutch, I slump over with relief. I notice that Sam is slumping too. "Sam, are you okay?" His eyes are sunken deep into the hollows of his face and gray stubble covers his chin. He looks like death.

"Who are you?" his words slur together.

"Sam, it's me, Shay. I was getting a snack. I couldn't sleep."

"Mary!" Sam suddenly wails, "Mary!" his hands fumble over objects on the kitchen counter. "Mary! Call the police! There's someone in the house!"

I put the glass down and step back, not knowing what to do. "Sam, it's me, Shay." He seems completely tossed but I don't smell alcohol.

He yells for Mary again.

"Sam? Is that you?" Mary runs into the kitchen and Jake follows, a step behind.

"Mary, what's going on? Who is this girl?"

"Sam, that's Shay, she lives here."

"Mom, what's wrong with Dad?"

"He came back from his trip early, complaining he didn't feel well." Mary coaxes Sam into one of the dining room chairs. She looks into his eyes then puts her hand on his forehead. He touches Mary's face, confused.

"He's burning up. Come, let's make a bed for you on the couch for the night. I'll take care of him until we can get a doctor to come by and visit."

"Mom, I think he needs to go to the hospital."

"Oh honey, he's fine. Just some mild delusions because of the fever," she says with confidence.

"I'll give him something to bring his fever down and he'll fell much better."

"I'll stay up with you," Jake offers.

"You have a game tomorrow. You need rest. If I need anything I'll come get you. Shay, are you okay? He must have given you quite a scare."

"I'm fine, just worried about Sam. I've never seen anyone so sick. He's as crook as Rookwood."

"He'll be fine. I promise. I'm sure he just caught something on the plane ride home. Go back to bed."

Reluctantly, I follow Jake up the spiral stairs.

"You sure you're okay?" he asks then stops at my door.

"Yeah, a little freaked out. It was dark and I couldn't see. I didn't know it was your dad at first."

"Do you want me to sleep in here tonight?" Jake asks and I put my hand on my hip then smirk.

"On the floor." He rolls his eyes.

"I don't think there's room for you." Swinging the door open, it bumps into a pile of seashells.

"So, prom with Grady?" he asks and I nod.

194

"Thanks for the shells by the way. Grady told me they were your idea."

"Did he?" Jake looks down; his cheeks redden.

"I hope your dad is okay." I change the subject.

"I feel bad, I thought he was drunk." Jake shrugs.

"Me too! But he didn't smell tanked. I know what tanked smells like."

Jake grins."When you talk like that, it makes me curious about all the stuff you haven't told me."

"I don't remember a lot. I'm not sure if I blocked it out or if I was off my face. You'd better get to bed. It's late."

"You sure you don't want me to stay?"

"I'm sure."

"We have a game after school tomorrow. You should come… watch Grady play?"

"Maybe. I'm afraid I might make him nervous. Night."

I shut the door and get into bed. I close my eyes, but I can still see Sam, slumped over. My body shudders under the blanket. Something didn't add up. Sam was sick, but that didn't explain why he looked thinner and had a partially grown beard. I shake the thoughts away and force my brain to rest. I only allow myself to think of Grady and my fairytale night. Soon I pass into a fitful sleep, dreaming of a man with hollow eyes, bending over me in bed. I wake up an hour before my alarm, drenched in sweat, and decide to go for a run to clear my head.

———

"Nice guns, Rambo. You should've put my dad in a headlock last night." Jake stands in the doorway, shirtless. He points to my arms as I curl a kettlebell. Distracted by his chiseled chest, I nod and try to shake loose some words from my mouth.

"I, I couldn't sleep." I finally blurt out.

"Me either."

"How's your dad?"

"Not sure. I went downstairs and he wasn't there. Mom probably had him go upstairs to their room. But who knows, he could be sleeping in the storage room in the pool house, for all I know."

"Did you say anything to your mum last night?"

"Not without my dad there."

"I was worried."

"About what?"

"About you." I feel silly when I say it aloud.

"You were, why?"

"You went to bed without saying goodnight." I frown. "I walked down the hall to see if your light was on after Grady left, but you had already gone to bed."

"I wasn't asleep. I turned out my light because I was afraid my mom would try to talk to me again. She knew something was wrong. You should have knocked."

I place the weights back on the rack. "It's all yours. I'm done."

"You can stay, I didn't mean to kick you out."

"No worries. I need a shower." I wipe the sweat from my brow with a towel.

"I wasn't going to say anything but yes, Rambo, you do." I step forward to punch his shoulder but his hand catches mine before I can make contact.

"You might be strong but I have better reflexes." He drops my hand from his grip, though his eyes hold onto me a little longer.

CHAPTER TWENTY-EIGHT

THEN

I LOCK THE FRONT DOOR AND WALK OVER THE ROCKY drive, scattered with bits of seashells. The pieces of coral remind me of my dreaded task. Three dresses hang in my wardrobe back in Sydney, their sole function to cover my togs at the beach. Finding a formal dress to compliment my mop of orange hair and pale skin might very well prove to be impossible.

A small lizard darts in front of my feet toward a small circular bouquet of yellow wildflowers, just as I walk through the open wrought iron gate. I close my eyes and let the warm sun bake my skin. The breeze shuffles through my hair and I extend my arms, pretending I'm riding a wave.

"Hi there."

My eyes pop open when I hear Jake rev his engine. I didn't even hear the silver ute pull up next me.

"Where're you going?"

"The bus stop. Your parents are playing tennis, I didn't want to bug them." I'd decided the best time to shop for a dress would be when Mary and Sam were out of the house. If Mary knew I'd planned a shopping trip, she would have insisted on tagging along. The Foresters' generosity was more than I could take at times, especially since I knew there was no way for me to repay them.

"Wait, why aren't you at practice?"

"Half the team is sick, so Coach cancelled."

"That's a bummer. Well, I'll see you later." I wave and continue to walk.

"I'll drive if you buy dinner."

"Really? If I buy you dinner you will save me from the perils of public transportation? What a mate."

"Get in," he motions to the passenger side door, "where to?"

I push the button, simultaneously locking all the doors at once and look at him while biting my lower lip. "The shopping center. I still don't have a dress for the prom." I scrunch my nose.

"You mean the mall? That's where you were going? Great, I need some new sunglasses. I thought you needed to go someplace awful, like the library," Jake says, unapologetically.

Most of the blokes I know back home would rather be surfing or climbing, definitely not shopping.

We pull up to one of the larger shops and Jake parks near an entrance.

"I'll text you when I'm done," I say, before walking in the opposite direction.

"I'll come with you," he says, catching up to me.

"Oh, you don't have to." I try to sound casual, though I hate the idea.

"I don't mind, as long as you help me pick out a pair of sunglasses afterward." I nod nervously in agreement.

The tinkling sounds of a baby grand piano follow us through the store and up the escalator.

"Where are your formals?" I ask an older woman with an orange silk scarf tied around her neck.

"Evening gowns are to your right." She points to a barrage of dresses on display and my stomach turns. I approach a circular rack and delicately move the hanging works of art. I have no idea where to begin, or what I'm looking for. Jake finds an oversized chair near a wall of mirrors and pulls his phone from his pocket. Once again, I'm grateful for his apathy.

A sales clerk, with short gray hair and glasses, must see the hopeless look in my eyes and offers to help. I follow her around, weaving through racks of gowns, like an orphaned seal pup. She chooses a dozen dresses in my size, most of which I would never have chosen myself, then leads me past Jake to the fitting room.

"Wish me luck!" I flash a half-hearted smile.

He replies with a quick glance and a sarcastic thumbs up before returning to his phone.

I follow the clerk to a tan stall and patiently wait as she hangs the gowns on two long pegs.

"Let me know if you need a different size, okay love?"

She closes the door behind her and I begin to undress. A single light shines from above, casting unpleasant shadows across my half-naked body. The mirror, made for someone much shorter, only reflects the middle of my body, shoulders to shins. I thumb through the dimly lit dresses and frown as I realize not one catches my eye. Unwilling to accept defeat, I pull the first off the hanger and shimmy into multiple layers of yellow crepe fabric. With my arms finally through, two bright, feathery straps drape loosely over my shoulders. I smooth out the flowing material and rest it over my toes.

"How's it going in there?" the clerk's voice beckons.

"Right as rain," I say cringing at my reflection. "Are there any other rooms?" I crack the door open so only my head peaks out. "Maybe one with a larger mirror?"

"The mirrors are the same in all the rooms but there are full-length mirrors on the storeroom floor. Here, I'll show you."

"No worries." I wave my hand. "I'll be right."

"You look so pretty. Don't you want your boyfriend to see how pretty you look?"

I chuckle. "He's not my…"

"Come on Sydney, your boyfriend wants to see how pretty you look." Jake's voice booms through the hallway. So much for apathy.

I blow a stray hair from my face then walk to the sitting area and find myself surrounded by mirrors. My back to him, I stand in silence and wait for the onslaught to begin. Finally, I give in and turn around.

"Hello, Baby. Polly hates crackers." A devilish grin sits on Jake's lips, reminding me how handsome he is. With one hand on my hip, I scowl in his direction.

"Sorry Sydney, I didn't mean to ruffle your feathers." I ignore him and walk back toward the dressing rooms. His laughter follows me all the way into my stall.

I maneuver out of the bird monstrosity then grab the next gown on the peg. It is a short plum dress with capped sleeves and metallic flecks woven into the fabric. I turn in front of the mirror. The dress shimmers blue and green, reminding me of the shifting colors of a mood ring.

"What's next, Syd?" Jake's musing voice echoes back through the corridor.

"I'll only come out if you promise not to laugh."

"I promise not to laugh, just don't come out looking like another zoo animal."

Behind a strapless black dress, I see a leopard print gown and quickly place it on the same peg as the bird dress. I will not make that mistake. I take another look in the mirror then walk down the short hallway, this time boasting more confidence.

"Not bad," Jake says, nodding his head. "I like the way it changes color but the sleeves," he frowns, "they're no good."

"What's wrong with the sleeves? They're cute." I say and hug my shoulders.

"Let's try something." He motions me over. "Reach up and see if you can put your arms around me." I follow his instructions while he tries to stand as tall as he can. I'm barely able to lift my arms to his shoulders.

"See, it won't work."

I pout. "But it shimmers!" I twirl around him.

He stops me mid-twirl and pulls me to him. "Grady is going to want to hold you close." He holds me tight. "As close as he possibly can and those sleeves are in the way."

I blush. "You reckon?"

"Yes."

The next dress, a short, black number makes my milky white skin look translucent, and the champagne-colored cocktail dress behind it washes me out completely. Only four dresses remain; each one more hideous than the next. I'm ready to concede but a turquoise gown, sandwiched between the last two dresses catches my eye. Hopeful, I know the muted blue-green shade will pair well with my hair. I remove the dress from the hanger and slide into it. The soft satin hugs my body then flares out over my feet as it touches the floor. The gown is simple, the only details are matching diamond straps that loop over my shoulders, leaving my back completely naked. I know the moment the fabric spills onto the floor, that I have found my dress.

I float down the hallway and face Jake. I tap my foot waiting for him to look up from his phone. When he finally does, he's silent.

"So, what do you think?" I turn toward the huge wall of mirrors and pull my wild hair over one shoulder. I can't stop smiling.

"Wow, Shay, you look amazing." Each word comes slowly, as if confined to its own sentence.

I study the diamond detailing on one of the straps and I catch his water-blue eyes, staring.

"Is it too much, the open back and everything?" I turn my head and rest my chin on my shoulder.

"No, it's perfect." He sounds out of breath. "Grady will love you in that dress." He goes quiet; no sarcastic comments or snickering.

"You okay?"

"It's been a long day, I'm tired," he stretches his arms over his head, "and hungry."

"I'm starving too. I'll get changed then do you want to get tea before or after we find you a pair of sunnies?"

"Get what before what?"

"Tea before or after sunnies?" I say slower, then I realize my word choice is the problem.

"Would you like to get dinner before or after we find you a pair of sunglasses?" I recite in my best American accent.

"Sunnies first, mate," he replies in an equally awful Aussie accent then shoos me away to get changed.

———

We have tea at a trendy cafe in the shopping center, since Jake insisted on being properly reimbursed.

"What does Taylor's dress look like?" I ask as Jake fiddles with his new sunnies.

"She won't tell me; wants it to be a surprise." Jake waves his hands in the air. "All I know is I was instructed to buy a hot pink corsage. My guess, her dress is the same color."

"Can I try them?" I point to the sunnies.

"Sure but don't smudge the lenses." I obey and take them gingerly in my hands.

"Am I supposed to tell Grady what color my dress is?" I ask, my eyes hidden behind the dark shades.

"I don't know. Taylor tells me a lot of things. She actually told me that she asked my dad if he would make an exception and let me drive the Porsche to the prom."

"Are you kidding? That girl has got balls." I laugh then take a bite of my sandwich. "What did Sam say?" I ask, still chewing.

"No, of course. But he did offer to pay for our limo."

"That's generous. There are these white stretch Hummer limos all over Sydney. They look pretty sweet. What kind are you going to get? Or does Taylor get to pick that too?" I wrinkle my nose.

"I don't think she cares as long as she doesn't have to pay for it. She told me she wants pumpkin risotto for dinner at the Phoenician, then lemon curd truffles for dessert at the Ritz Carlton."

"Impressive."

"At least she knows what she wants," he shrugs.

"What do you want? I mean, it's your night too."

"I'm more of a steak and seafood kind of guy."

"You must really like her." I dip the glasses down to the tip of my nose and raise my eyebrows up and down.

"Give me those," he says, snatching them from my hand.

"Easy, mate, you don't want to smudge them."

"Do you at least get to choose the after prom activities?" I ask then shake my head, "never mind that, I don't want to know."

"We're heading back to her house with some other couples to hang out in her jacuzzi."

"Sounds like a fun night. I wish I knew what Grady was planning."

"Just look at everything he did to ask you to the stupid thing. It will be the best night of your life, I'm sure."

"I hope so."

"Can I ask you something?" There's a slight hesitation in his voice.

"Sure." I answer, intrigued.

"Why haven't you told Grady about what happened to your family?"

Caught off guard, guilt rises in my gut.

"Forget it. It's none of my business." Jake says then sips his coke.

"Why do you care?" I don't try to conceal the edge of frustration in my voice.

"Shay, he's my best friend and he keeps asking about you. I have answers…"

"So you told him?" I rise to my feet.

"I wouldn't do that," he takes hold of my hand and gently pulls me back down, "but don't you think he should know?"

I hang my head; I know he's right. "It's not easy for me." I say, the edge in my voice dulled.

"I understand, I do," he says and his thumb smooths over my hand.

"No, no you don't." I blink away a threatening tear.

"You're the only person I've ever told." I cringe at my own admission.

"What about Ingrid?" he asks, confused.

"She read my case file. She knew everything before I even moved in."

"So, why did you tell me?"

"Believe me, I've asked myself the same question." I smile and he just stares with the same look of admiration in his eyes as when I told him

206

about my worst day. We sit in silence, not an awkward silence, but a contemplative lull.

"I guess, I decided to take a chance on you," I say.

"I'm glad you did," he says then squints his eyes and looks over my shoulder.

"Taylor?" he moves his hand from mine and I turn my head. The beautiful blonde appears behind us, unamused.

"Well, look who it is, my boyfriend and his new ginger BFF. I saw you as I walked in but didn't want to interrupt; you looked like you were having an intense conversation."

"What's going on?" Jake says, ignoring her irritation.

She points a finger into Jake's chest. "I could ask you the same thing."

"Jake drove me to the mall so I could pick out a prom dress, and I offered to buy him dinner."

"How nice of you both. It's funny that Jake had time to drive you to the mall, since he told me he couldn't hang out today because he had practice." Jake's eyes close and a crease forms across his forehead.

"Practice was cancelled and Shay needed a ride."

"I'm sure she did need a ride. Did Jake give you a good, hard ride, Shay?" Taylor's voice rises with accusation.

"That's enough," Jake says and takes Taylor by the hand and leads her to the front of the restaurant. A few minutes pass and he returns alone.

"What was that all about? Is your girlfriend jealous of me?" I chuckle but Jake is silent.

"The most beautiful girl in school, jealous of me." I use both thumbs and point to myself proudly.

"She's not my girlfriend, and she isn't the most beautiful girl at our school."

CHAPTER TWENTY-NINE

THEN

AS MY NAILS AIR DRY, A HAIR STYLIST AND MAKEUP artist arrive and Mary shuffles them upstairs to her room to set up shop. I have no prior knowledge of prom beauty rituals but this seems excessive. A French man, named Pierre, straightens my wavy red locks with a flat iron then painstakingly re-curls everything he successfully straightened. It makes no sense to me, but his serious demeanor makes me think twice about questioning his technique. He gathers all my hair into a side ponytail and pins it in place at the nape of my neck. Loose curls fall and he masterfully weaves them together to create a beautiful mess of hair. He pins a white dahlia behind my left ear then says, "Viola!"

Nina, the makeup artist whose neon pink lips match her hair, takes over. She rubs moisturizer all over my face and neck then powders and blushes my face, blending the freckles under my green eyes. She uses tweezers to apply fake eyelashes, then lines my upper lids in black and adds gray-blue eyeshadow and jet-black mascara. I bat my eyes in the mirror; I feel more beautiful than I have in all my life and I wonder if it's because I look nothing like the real me. I look like a different version of myself; someone who was unscathed from pain and sadness. No one would suspect that the girl in the mirror had been homeless for months, eating apple cores straight out of the rubbish bin. I smile and snap a picture on my phone to send to Ingrid. After all the years of hell I endured, I fought my way out of the deep canyon and look at me now, standing at the top. Little pools of water well up, threatening to spill over onto my lashes and down my cheeks.

"No, no, no," Nina scolds, shaking her finger at me.

"Take this and lightly dab." Nina hands me a tissue. "No tears!"

I smile and dab. Mary comes up from behind, holding a slender black box.

"I asked Sam if it was okay if I lent these to you for the night. He gave them to me a few years ago for our twentieth wedding anniversary. He thought it was a good idea."

Mary opens the box and places a strand of diamonds around my neck.

"What do you think?" she smiles at my reflection in the mirror.

"It's lovely. Are you sure it's okay?"

"Yes! It completes your look, well almost." She hands me a pair of earrings.

The dangling diamonds look like waterfalls cascading from my lobes.

"Perfect!" Mary steps back. "You are so beautiful Shay; inside and out."

210

"Okay, seriously, no more talk like that," Nina scowls. "If you make her cry, I make you cry."

With a phone in his hand, Sam enters the room and looks around until he finds me.

"Shay, you look gorgeous; which makes what I have to tell you even harder," he says with a grimace.

"Sam, what's wrong?" Mary asks.

"That was Grady's mom on the phone. Apparently he's come down with the stomach bug all the LaCrosse guys have been passing around. He is really sick and won't be able to take you to the prom tonight."

"Oh, Shay," Mary says then bows her head and puts her hand on my shoulder.

I try to process what Sam's said. Around the room, pitiful looks pour from everyone's eyes.

"Oh screw it," Nina says as she hands me another tissue then dabs her own eyes.

"I am so sorry. I'm sure there's someone who doesn't have a date. Sam, go ask Jake, I'm sure he knows someone."

"No, its okay. I've never been to a prom. I don't even know what I'm missing."

"Let me take you then," Sam says and offers his arm.

"That is a very generous offer, but I am afraid Jake would never forgive me if I took his dad as my date to his senior prom."

"You could go by yourself. I did when I was your age and I had a lot of fun." Mary insists.

"No worries. Today has already been more than I could've hoped for."

Everyone is quiet. Unsure of what to say, Mary puts her arm around my waist.

"Well, at the very least we need to get some pictures of you and Jake." Sam says and I nod my head.

"We'll be downstairs when you're ready."

Everyone in the room leaves and I am left alone for the first time since the day began. I look at myself once more and practice hiding my disappointment with a smile. It's the least I can do for all the effort Mary and Sam had thrown into the day for me.

When I'm sure I can convince them, I put on my heels and make my way to the staircase. Uneasy in the stilettos, I hold the banister, slowly taking one step at a time down the marble stairs. Then I look up and a genuine smile finds my lips. Alone in the atrium, Jake fumbles with the bowtie around his neck. Each failed attempt leaves him more aggravated until he finally rips it off. He crams it into his pocket then pulls the black tuxedo jacket up over his shoulders. The clinking of my heels causes him to turn and he stops as if frozen in place. I grab the bowtie dangling from his pocket and face him.

"May I?" I ask then place it around his neck. Tiny sparks warm his deep blue eyes, leaving behind a gentle look I'd never seen before.

"After Alex was born my dad gave up any hope of having a son and taught me all the boy stuff." I tie his bowtie then straighten it as Mary enters from the kitchen.

"Okay you two." She motions us toward the fountain, holding her camera. Jake moves in close and I realize I have never been so aware of his proximity to my body. His left hand holds the small of my bare back while his leg brushes up against my hip. He leans in, swirling coconut and honey in the air around me.

"You don't even know how beautiful you look right now, do you?" I feel like my entire body blushes.

"You don't look too bad yourself." I reply, forcing my voice to sound casual.

He takes my hand and the blue in his eyes intensifies. "I hate leaving you here. Jaden doesn't have a date; I can still call him."

"No, go, have fun. Don't worry about me," I say, brave face intact.

We pose for a few more pictures, then the limo arrives and it's time for Jake to leave.

"Grady is going to hate himself tomorrow," Jake says and leans in and kisses my forehead then walks out the door.

I stand on the front step. I want to turn and walk back inside but I can't leave until the limo is completely out of sight.

"Okay kiddo, we're taking you out for a nice dinner. What sounds good?" Mary tugs my shoulder.

"You both have done so much, really I couldn't ask for more. Can we just hang out and watch a movie? Maybe order in?"

"Great idea. I'll order some Chinese." Sam chimes in.

"Are you sure you don't want to go out, all dressed up?" Mary asks.

"I'm sure."

"Do you mind if I go upstairs and change?" I don't want to ruin my dress with noodles and rice.

"Sure. We'll get everything ready down here," Mary says. "There are a couple chick flicks I've been dying to see. We can make a night of it."

Sam lets out a deep sigh then winks at me.

Heels in hand, I walk up the staircase to my room. I slip out of my dress and rehang it in the same place it had been only an hour or so earlier. I put on my comfy blue t-shirt and a pair of yoga pants, then walk down the hallway and halfway down the stairs.

"Mary, where should I put the jewelry you lent me?" I shout.

"The boxes are on the vanity in my room," she yells back.

I skip up the stairs and open their bedroom door. I look around for the skinny black box on the vanity adjacent to the bed. When I open the box, a piece of jewelry falls to the floor. I lean to pick it up and notice a paper poking out from under the base of the vanity. Curiosity gets the better of me, and I slowly tug the paper out from under the piece of furniture. Printed on the other side is a travel itinerary for a trip Mary took to Australia about five months ago. I remember Mary saying she'd never been to Australia. Why would she lie? I look over the paper again, trying to understand; hoping I misread the information. Reminding myself of the Foresters' kindness and generosity, I put the paper back exactly how I found it and go back to my room.

I decide to leave my hair and make up as is. It seems such a pity to undo everything. The clock hadn't struck midnight yet. I could still feel like royalty for a couple more hours, even in pajamas.

Downstairs, I gorge myself on low mein and egg rolls while watching The Notebook with Mary and Sam. A very apologetic Grady calls halfway through the movie, and I assure him I am fine and having fun with the Foresters. He insists on calling me later but I tell him not to worry and to get some rest.

After the movie, I hug Mary and Sam goodnight and thank them for their kindness.

"Mary, you've never been to Australia right?" The words come out of my mouth before I can silence them. Mary looks perplexed.

"Nope. Never. Why do you ask?" she says coolly.

"I wanted to make you both some Lammingtons, to say thank you for all you've done for me. It is one of my favorite Australian desserts." I say the first thing that pops in my mind.

"That would be great. We love dessert," Mary replies unflinchingly.

With an awkward smile, I head upstairs. Why would she lie about something so trivial? I reach the door and realize I forgot my physics book on the kitchen counter. I turn around and head back down the stairs. At the bottom, I hear Sam's voice.

"There's no way she knows about your trip to Australia; you're being paranoid. And honestly, I don't understand why you had to make such a big deal about prom. You've known all along Grady was going to be sick. We should be keeping our eyes on Jake, not indulging Shay."

"Shhh! She might hear you."

"She can't hear us from all the way up in her room."

"Sam, I told you, Cassie is watching Jake and Taylor tonight and as far as Shay is concerned..."

Mary's voice softens and I lean in to hear. "You know why I made such a big deal out of prom. I wanted her to feel special, even if I knew she wouldn't end up going. We both know she deserves that! Besides, she might have taken you up on your offer to take her."

My mind races as I try to understand their words. It's almost like deciphering a foreign language. I get the gist of the conversation but don't understand the context. How did Mary know Grady was going to be sick and cancel? Did she talk to Grady's mum? Did she know his doctor?

"And Sam," Mary says a little louder, "be more careful what you say around Baby, she's starting to repeat you."

CHAPTER THIRTY

THEN

I WASH THE MAKE UP FROM MY FACE AND REMOVE hundreds of pins burrowed in my hair, but I can't stop thinking about the conversation I overheard between Mary and Sam. There were no explanations for so many things Mary and Sam did, only more questions. Last week, when Jake confronted them about the beds in the storage closet, they explained his grandparents were coming to visit and needed special hospital grade beds because of their ailing health. Before that time, it had never been mentioned that they were sick. When he brought up the notepad with the number of the missing helicopter written on it, Mary said she didn't know what he was talking about and asked to see the piece of paper.

My phone buzzes, alerting me of an incoming text message and I'm thankful for the distraction.

Ingrid: You are beautiful! I hope you have an amazing night.

Shay: Thanks, but I'm not going after all. Grady is sick :(

Ingrid: I told you not to fall for the climber. So sorry love!

Loose curls and false eyelashes are all that remain of my extreme makeover. Deciding to forego Physics, I escape into the novel bookmarked on my night table. A couple pages into the chapter, I stop to answer the phone, hoping Grady is feeling better. He'd sounded so pathetic earlier.

"How you going?" I ask.

"Good, how about you?" The deep voice is not Grady's.

"Jake?"

"Look out your window."

I open the shutters and Jake is leaning against a white, stretch, hummer limo, looking up at me.

"What are you doing here? Where's Taylor?"

"Come down and I'll tell you."

"I have to change first." I tug at the drawstring on my yoga pants.

"Don't change. Just come down."

"Okay." I slip on a pair of shoes and quietly tiptoe down the stairs, trying not to wake Mary and Sam, who'd already gone to bed. I open the front door then gingerly close it behind me.

"Hi?" I say looking around. "Where's your date? It's 11:30, prom isn't even over."

"We made an appearance, long enough to get our pictures taken and for Taylor to get completely trashed off her face. She demanded we take the limo to her friend's party in Fountain Hills. I told her if she wanted to go to the party she would have to find another ride."

"Yikes. How did that go?"

"She slapped me across the face and got a ride with her ex-boyfriend."

"I'm sorry, mate."

"I'm not. It was the best thing that could've happened."

"It was?" I scrunch my nose.

"Yes. Now I get to do what I really wanted to do tonight." His eyes smile then his lips follow.

"What did you want to do tonight?" I ask, still confused.

"Hang out with you," he says and opens the door to the limo and my heart beats fast.

"We have this beast until dawn."

I crawl over the long, black leather seat in the back of the limo, completely gobsmacked.

"This is bonkers." My star-struck eyes double in size. Jake moves next to me and the chauffeur shuts the door behind us.

"It has a hot tub."

"Are you serious?"

Jake shakes his head no. "Never gets old." He laughs and I punch his leg.

"Where are we going?"

He sends a text message and seconds later the driver rolls down the tinted window partition.

"Sure thing, boss."

A couple minutes later we pull into a vacant playground.

Jake hops out of the hummer and holds my hand, helping me to the ground.

"Ready?"

Before I can answer, he drops my hand and sprints toward the empty play yard.

"Come on," he shouts back.

Not to be outdone, I catch up to him near the swings. He's already claimed his swing and motions me to the one next to him. I sit then lean back, holding the chains tight in my hands. I pump my legs and within seconds we're soaring through the air, side by side.

"I bet you I can jump farther," he says, pointing in the distance.

"As I recall, you aren't very good at winning bets." I beam, then, without hesitation, I jump. Flying through the air, I land steps from the merry-go-round.

"That's the best you got, Sydney?" He shakes his head. "I expected better." Gaining momentum, Jake leans forward then back. His feet reach high into the night sky and for a moment I think he might loop around the top. He smiles and his hands drop the chains. With all his might he thrusts his upper body forward but his lower half stays glued to the small seat. It happens as if it were in slow motion; the seat finally releases its hold and he belly flops a short distance into the sand. I run over and hold out my hand, unable to contain my laughter.

"You okay, mate?"

"I think I won." he says and spits sand then wipes his mouth. He takes my hand and pulls me down into the sand, then jumps up and runs over to the slide. Still laughing, I hop up and race after him. Jake barrels down the slide headfirst and I follow, sliding backwards. At the bottom, he waits for me.

"I don't understand you, Jake Forester." I say, looking up at him.

"What don't you understand, Australia?"

"You'd rather hang out at the park with me, in my pajamas, than with your girlfriend on prom night?"

"I told you, she's not my girlfriend. And yes, I would much rather be here with you than with her." He takes one of my hands and sits me up on the edge of the slide.

"I know this might come as a shock to you, since I am an arrogant jackass, barely capable of enjoying the company of anyone other than myself, but I like spending time with you." His eyes are mischievous. "Come on, we have another place to get to before it closes."

I follow him back to the hummer. We drive for about 15 minutes and park in an empty lot.

"What are we doing at a water park? I don't have my bathers."

"We won't need them."

"What?"

He laughs. "That's not what I meant. Come on, over here." He motions to a ticket booth where an older bloke sits on a stool.

"Hey, Jake. How're your folks?"

"Good, thank you."

The man exits the booth and leads us through two gates. Everything is dark except the path lit by the man's flashlight. Down a grassy hill, we reach a sandy beach leading to a giant pool. The glassy water appears black except for a gentle moonlit ripple in the far left corner. The gentleman hands Jake a towel and he spreads it out over the sand before sitting down. He pats the space next to him and I sit. All is quiet except for a churning sound coming from the dark water.

"You have about forty minutes," the man says, looking at his watch.

"Perfect, thank you."

"He was nice," I say, watching him walk away.

"He owns the place."

"Really?"

"This is the best I could do on short notice." Jake shrugs.

Four sets of floodlights spark to life, each tower illuminating a corner of the massive pool. The water swells at the far end and within seconds waves crash onto the sandy shore a meter or so from where we sit.

"Your ocean in the desert." Delight covers his face.

I close my eyes and listen to the water. I fabricate a salty smell in my mind and breathe in. "Thank you," I say and my voice rolls over the sound of the waves.

The sound of footsteps brings me back. An older boy, in red shorts with a whistle around his neck, arrives with a wetsuit in one hand and a surfboard in the other.

"No way!" I jump up and reach for the board then look at Jake to make sure it's okay.

"Have at it. I think there's a place to change over there; just don't come out looking like a bird or something." My head pokes out from behind the board long enough to stick my tongue out at him.

I paddle out to the far right side of the pool in time to catch my first wave. The swells are decent and increase in intensity with each break.

On shore, Jake rolls his pant legs to the knee and rests his feet in the water. I drop in on the first wave then bottom turn before backflipping over the water. He whistles then chants my name as I carve into the next one. I switch my stance, then snap in the opposite direction and finish with a roundhouse. After a dozen more runs, Jake motions me in. I get up one last time and cut back and forth until the wave brings me to shore.

With a grin permanently plastered on my face, I toss my frizzy, red locks into a messy, wet bun. "What a difference a couple hours make." I say and gently pull a dangling set of fake lashes from my right eyelid.

"All that jewelry and makeup; that's not you. This is you," he touches a strand of my hair, "wet from surfing, not a care in the world, and beautiful as hell."

I turn toward him and grin slyly. In my hand, I spin my wet towel. Snapping it hard, I nearly whip his leg.

"Nice try." He grabs the towel near his feet. Staring me down, he spins it fast then moves to strike. I bolt in the opposite direction, my laughter the only thing slowing me down. As I run toward the water he tackles me onto the sand. I squirm, trying to escape the weight of his body. He pins me, arms above my head and I reluctantly surrender.

"What's next?" I ask breathless.

"Hungry?" he says hovering over me; the same gentle look in his eyes.

"Starving."

Jake moves to the sand next to me and pulls his cell phone from his pocket and dials.

"I'd like a large pizza, half ham and pineapple and half..." he pauses to look at me, "half pepperoni and mushroom." I nod in agreement. He pulls a bag of jelly beans from his coat pocket.

"Someone once told me jelly beans are better than chocolate," he says and places the bag in my hand. I try to make sense of it all. How did we get here? When had things changed?

"I'd like it delivered to 6522 East Ocotillo Road."

He turns on his side after ending the call. "Can I have a jellybean?"

"Only if you guess the flavor before you eat it. When we were little, Alex and I would play this game all the time."

Jake grabs a bean from the bag and studies it carefully.

"Hmm, I think this one is cotton candy." He moves the jellybean to his lips and stops short. "To Alex," he raises the bean ceremoniously into the air.

"To Alex." I repeat, and my fingers trace the numbers on my wrist.

Jake puts the bean in his mouth and winces "Crap, that's not cotton candy. It tastes like throw up."

"Grapefruit." I nod, "Gets you every time."

CHAPTER THIRTY-ONE

THEN

"WHOSE HOUSE IS THIS?" THE LIMO PULLS UP TO 6522 EAST Ocotillo and I point to the large white stucco house with an orange, Mexican-tile roof.

"I don't know."

"You don't know?"

"I don't know who lives there now; this was my house when I was little. My bedroom window was the one on the far left."

As he points, a beat up car with a pizza logo on the roof pulls into the driveway. Jake jumps out of the limo and pays the driver then presents me with an oversized pizza box.

"I used to pretend I was superman and climb that tree. One time my cape got stuck and my mom couldn't get me down. She had to call the fire department." He takes a bite of pizza. "Of course, I thought it was the

225

coolest thing ever, but mom never let me climb the tree again. We moved to the house on the mountain a year later."

We continue eating and drive on as I listen to him share his childhood. We stop at a ballpark down the street.

"This is where my dad taught me how to play baseball. In third grade, I hit my first home run on that field. I played baseball every year up until last year. My dad was so angry that I quit. It was his dream to see me play baseball in college, like he did. I like baseball, I do, but LaCrosse is my sport. It was a big deal that he was so supportive when we visited San Diego State." Jake takes another bite then points. "Behind the dugout is where I got into my first fight." Jake closes his eyes. "I was in second grade and it wasn't a fair fight. I still can't believe she won." He opens his eyes and his face is completely serious. I almost spit out my pizza.

The next stop is a school a couple blocks away.

"Behind those dumpsters is where I smoked my first and only cigarette." I crane my head to see.

"It's also where I had my first kiss. Thankfully, not at the same time."

"Shut up. You pashed behind a dumpster? Romantic!"

"We were in the fifth grade, her name was Jenna Silverman and I was a little overly ambitious. I tried to French kiss her but she shut her mouth halfway through the kiss and bit my tongue so hard, I had to go to the nurse."

I gasp and my hand covers my mouth. "You are making this up. There is no way that happened."

"Sadly, it did. There's nothing like listening to the nurse explain to your mom over the phone that you have a partially severed tongue, due to an overly zealous French kiss. Pretty humiliating."

Tears run down my face; I can't remember the last time I laughed so hard. He grins and I wipe my eyes.

"There is one last place I want to take you, unless you're too tired?" I shake my head no.

"Thank you for showing me all of this." I move over and sit next to him.

"I know so much about your past, I figured you should know about mine."

———

The Limo drives up the mountain toward the Foresters' house but doesn't stop at the iron gate. A few streets from the top of the mountain, we pull into the driveway of a partially constructed house overlooking the city. The lights below remind me of my first night in the desert. Jake cranks up the radio and opens the doors, releasing the sounds of an electric guitar into the darkness around us.

"Follow me," he says and takes my hand and leads me to the front door. Using the light from his phone, he steps over the threshold onto a concrete floor. The smell of sawdust sifts through the air and I stumble over a couple empty soda bottles in my path.

"Watch your step. They stopped construction on this place last year when it went into foreclosure. From the second floor, you can see the entire city."

"Is it safe?" I say as a piece of drywall crumbles under my foot.

"Grady and I used to come up here all the time to smoke my dad's cigars." A strange sense of guilt clings to me as Jake says Grady's name. I shake it off and follow him up the wooden stairs to a large room, which opens to an unfinished balcony.

The city lights cluster together, dancing like tiny champagne bubbles rising to the top of a glass.

"If you squint your eyes, it looks like a harbour filled with boats." I step forward.

"Careful, some of those boards are loose." I look over my shoulder at Jake. His blue eyes reflect the moon when he smiles.

I turn back and I hear a board creak beneath me. My foot slips and I fall forward into the darkness until his arms pull me back.

"Easy, Australia. Who's saving who now?" He moves me away from the uneven ledge. "Didn't I tell you, I have great reflexes?" He holds me steady as a shiver courses through my body. His suit jacket finds my shoulders and the scent of coconut hangs around the collar, erasing the smell of plaster and dust.

My eyes lock with his. Everything is still except the breeze carrying the music up from below.

"Dance with me?"

His request throws me.

"Dance with you? Are you serious?"

"Very." He takes my hands and loops them around the back of his neck, then winds his arms tight around my waist. We slowly sway to the music bouncing off the empty walls. As the song ends, our swaying slows but neither of us lets go. Jake finally pulls back.

"I need to ask you something." He winces, like he's readying to take a punch. "Are you sad you are here with me and not Grady?" The vulnerability in his voice tears through me like a rogue wave and I finally understand the gentle look in his eyes.

"When we first met you were a total tosser."

His eyes close, feeling the blow.

"But now you're a tosser, who's somehow become my best mate."

He looks up.

Normally I would have left it at that, not wanting to give away too much too soon, but the way he looked at me, with nothing to hide, sparked a desire in me to tell him everything.

"When you walked out the door tonight, to take Taylor to prom, I was so mad at myself." He stares intently, and I bow my head into his chest to escape.

"I was mad that I felt so much more disappointment, watching you leave, than I did when your dad told me Grady wasn't coming."

Another ballad wafts up the stairs and his hand lifts my chin, aligning my eyes with his. His fingers play with a loose strand of hair touching my cheek.

"You have to know, I hated leaving you." He tucks the strand behind my ear and he leans in. His lips sweep over mine slowly, sending a tsunami of warmth through my chest. It overflows to my arms and down my legs. I pull him tight against me, thinking I might drown. His lips press mine again, this time with hunger and I melt into his arms, safe and exposed all in the same breath.

CHAPTER THIRTY-TWO

NOW

MUSIC MOVES OVER THE GRASS. IT HOPS AND SLIDES WITH each movement of his legs, serenading me until I feel like I am moving next to him on the field. He passes the ball; determination sits on his lips then leads into a full grin as Grady completes the pass. The two mates run at each other. Their chests bump in mid air, knocking Jake hard to the ground. Laughing, Grady extends his hand and pulls Jake to his feet.

"Good game, dude. You want to split a pizza?"

"I would, but I have plans," Jake says and nods in my direction. I blush, embarrassed he would be so bold in front of Grady. A moment of panic hits and I look down. A smile forms on my lips at the sight of my own body. I close my eyes and feel for the glasses for reassurance. I nearly rub the flesh off my nose before I'm convinced. I walk toward Jake. My heart flutters, just as it did when he asked me to dance at the abandoned house. I move a tangled strand of hair from my face and step toward him.

"Hey tosser." I reach for his hand.

A crease forms across his forehead and he pulls away.

"What the hell is a tosser?" His tone is defensive.

"Sorry, mate."

"Whatever, mate." His hostility is wrapped in sarcasm. He pushes past me and walks off the field.

My eyes follow. Taylor jumps into his arms on the sidelines. Pain wells up inside my chest, and my heart feels as if it might collapse in on itself. Jake leans in and tenderly kisses Taylor's neck. Angry tears fill my eyes. I want to turn away but I can't. They walk hand in hand toward Mary and Sam. Sam laughs and tosses Jake the Porsche keys. Something is wrong. They don't know.

Run. Go. Move. My legs kick at the ground and cannot propel me any faster. I hear the rev of an engine and see the powder-blue beast racing toward me.

"Do you have a death wish? Get out of the way," Jake yells.

He swerves and I jog alongside them.

"Stop the car!" I shout. "Jake, stop the car." The car stops abruptly and Jake gets out.

"What are you doing?"

"Please don't get back in the car. I love you." I plead.

"You love me?" Jake mocks.

"Jake, don't be mean, the little ginger girl has a crush on you." Taylor snickers.

"How can you love me? You don't even know me."

"I do know you. I know your first kiss was with a girl named Jenna, in the fifth grade. She bit your tongue."

"Is that true?" Taylor scoffs.

"Shut up, Taylor," he shouts over his shoulder, "Grady put you up to this, didn't he?"

"No. Jake, it's me, Shay." I wipe the tears from my cheeks.

"Jake, don't make the little girl cry." Taylor pouts her lips.

"Jake, if you get back in that car, you are going to die."

"I'm going to die?" He smiles and points to himself then walks back toward the idling Porsche. "And this beautiful machine is going to kill me?" he caresses the Spyder's body with his hand.

"Tell Grady he is going to have to try harder next time." Jake winks and jumps back into the driver's seat.

"No! Wait!" I scream. The wheels of the Porsche spin in the gravel and he peels away. I sprint through the dust left behind in his wake, barely able to breathe. I refuse to stop.

Ahead, sounds of metal twisting and glass shattering jolt my feet into a sprint.

I find Taylor first. Her blonde hair is caked red from a gash over her forehead. One of her ribs has pierced through her skin leaving her pale and barely breathing. I scan the wreckage for Jake. Three meters to the left, he is face down in a pile of glass.

"Jake!" I shout his name but he doesn't respond.

Sirens sound and a helicopter slices through the air. They seem sluggish, like they're taking their time. Mary appears next to me. White-faced, she eyes the chopper with horror. I take her hand in mine.

"I tried to tell him but he wouldn't listen." My words are muffled like I'm speaking underwater. She takes me by the shoulders and squeezes them tight then looks me square in the eyes.

"Only you can save him."

I jolt awake, panting. I sit up. My hands immediately touch my face. The glasses are lifeless on the top of my bag. Even my dreams are corrupted.

"Only you can save him," I repeat Mary's declaration. It pummels me over and over like a wave crashing onto the shore. Each word pushes me away then pulls me back again.

"It's true. Only you can save him," Mary says, staring at me from across the room.

CHAPTER THIRTY-THREE

THEN

JAKE: BEST DAY EVER! WHEN CAN I KISS YOU AGAIN?

I read the text again, then hear a knock on my door and spring to my feet.

"I hope I didn't wake you," Mary says.

"No. I'm up. Is everything okay?"

"Oh yes, sweetheart, I didn't mean to worry you. Sam and I are going to run some errands. We'll be back around dinner. Jake is still sleeping. Will you let him know we went out?"

"Sure."

"How's Grady feeling? Any better?" A pang of guilt rushes through me.

"I haven't heard from him yet today, but last night he seemed to have turned a corner."

"That's good to hear. There are some sandwiches in the fridge, if you're hungry."

I shut the door and reread the text from Jake until another knock on my door brings me back.

I smooth my hair and open the door, anxious to see Jake's face.

"Do you know where Jake put his truck keys?" Sam asks.

I shake my head, "I'm sorry, I don't."

"I can't find them. I was going to ask Jake but I didn't want to wake him. He came in pretty late last night."

"I hope he had fun," I say, hoping Sam doesn't notice the blush on my cheeks.

Sam leaves and I wash my face and brush my teeth then grab my slippers from the wardrobe.

"Morning." Jake leans on my doorframe grinning. A white t-shirt hugs his chest and is left untucked from a pair of gray shorts.

"I thought you were your dad," I whisper then look the length of the hallway and pull him into my room.

"Nope, just the younger, more handsome version." He takes my hand and I close the door.

"Your dad is a pretty good looking bloke for his age." I shrug my shoulders.

"I guess you'll just have to settle for the newer model," he says and laces his arms around my waist.

"I'll suffer through it." I reach up and put my arms around his neck.

"Before I forget, your dad was asking for your ute keys, I mean truck keys, because he and your mum are running errands; they won't be home until dinner."

He pulls me close and kisses me softly. "All I heard is that they won't be home until dinner." His fingers move through my hair and there's another knock.

I shove him behind the door then crack it open with a smile.

"I forgot to ask you if you needed me to pick up anything for you while we're out." Mary has pen and paper ready.

"No thank you, I have everything I need," I say as Jake silently kisses the length of my arm, behind the door.

"Okay. I'm going to see if Jake is awake and needs anything."

"No," I blurt a little too loud. "Sam just checked. Jake is still asleep. I can have him text you when he wakes up?"

"Thanks, sweetie, that would be great."

I shut the door and let out a big sigh. "I just lied straight to your mom's face."

"Come here," he gently commands and pulls me to sit on the bed next to him. My phone buzzes to life on my night table. I read the text message aloud.

Grady: Hey Beautiful! I'm so sorry! I have plans for our very own Prom, next weekend!

"I hate this." I bury my head into Jake's chest. "We have to tell them," I say, defeated. "I never wanted to hurt anyone." I blink away a tear.

"Hey," Jake takes my face in his hands, "I don't want to hurt anyone either." He lifts my chin, "We didn't plan for this to happen."

"We could pretend it never did." I don't look at him when I say it.

"Is that what you want?" he asks and wipes my cheek.

I shake my head, no.

"What do you want?" I ask.

He kisses my cheek. "You," his lips hover over mine, "I only want you." I feel an overwhelming magnetic pull toward his mouth as if our lips are meant to be connected. I kiss him with urgency, then stop abruptly and lean back.

"We need to tell them soon then; before they find out on their own."

"I agree," he tugs at my shirt, pulling me back to him, "but not today; today belongs to us."

I grin. "Our very own day? That sounds brilliant. Can we go for a hike then soak in the hot tub?"

"Yes, especially the part about the hot tub. I have this great speedo; maybe I'll wear it." Jake grins.

———

"I need a little inspiration on what to cook for dinner tonight. What was your favorite dish that your mom used to make when you were little?" Jake takes off his hat and molds the bill in his hands.

"My dad actually did most of the cooking," I say then snatch the hat from him and place it backwards on my head.

"Damn, you look good." I turn the hat around and pull the brim low "Keep it. It looks better on you anyway," he says and taps the bill with his fingers.

"So what did your dad make that was your favorite?"

"Bangors and Mash," I spout.

"What and what?"

"Sausage and mashed potatoes."

He reaches for a pot and begins to fill it with water, "Bangors and Mash it is."

"I heard your mum tell your dad she knew Grady wasn't going to be able to take me to prom. After you left, I overhead them talking downstairs and somehow she knew he was going to be sick."

Jake looks at me intently, "What is going on?" He shakes his head. "Why can't I just have normal parents?"

"You don't think they're really psychic do you?"

"If they can see the future, they're pretty bad at it, because they haven't figured out what's going on between us." He lifts me onto the counter and pulls me close to him.

"And what about the flight itinerary to Australia? Your mom said she's never been."

"I don't think she has been to Australia, but I'll look into it. My parents look through my stuff all the time, I have no problem going through theirs. Tomorrow they're going to brunch with Rick and Cassie. We can try to find some answers then."

———

Out on the patio, Jake soaks in the hot tub. I pull my hair back into a messy bun then step into the bubbling water.

"Do you remember the last time we were in a hot tub together?" He asks, grinning.

"Wait, we've done this before?" I half-smile. "San Diego, Grady's beach house. You dunked Erin," I say.

"And Grady dunked you. He wanted a reason to get close to you, which made no sense to me but now it does." Jake wraps his body around me but I pull away suddenly.

"I heard something coming from the pool house."

Jake looks at the darkened windows of the pool house then sees the lights flicker on in the dining room. "Not the pool house."

"Hey, you two," Mary says and I slowly slide away from Jake to the other side of the spa.

"How was your day? Have you heard from Grady?"

"You just missed him," Jake answers.

"He stopped by? I'm glad he's feeling better."

"Yes, I was telling him about prom and how he missed the best night of my life." Jake's hand finds my leg under the bubbly water and I try to hide the heat rising onto my cheeks.

———

Mary and Sam's Mercedes passes through the iron gate and we rush to their room.

"Where did you see the Travel Itinerary?" Jakes asks.

I catch a glimpse of my reflection in a large mirror over the chest of drawers. Dark circles sit under my eyes. I'd barely slept the night before, tossing and turning, wondering if Mary had seen us pashing in the hot tub. Hiding our true feelings had proven more difficult than I anticipated.

"The itinerary was wedged under the leg of the vanity."

"So you were snooping?" Jake smirks.

"An earring dropped on the floor and I pulled the paper loose when I picked it up." I reply.

On his knees, Jake searches near the vanity and under the bureau.

"They must have moved it. They store most of their documents in a fire safe box in the closet." Jake walks toward the closet door.

"But don't you think that's a little too obvious? If they kept the paper, wouldn't they put it someplace no one would look for it, especially you."

"And where might that be, Sydney?" he asks, unconvinced.

"Does your mum wear lingerie? If so, do you know where she keeps it?" Jake's eyes close and his lips curl in disgust.

"Nope." He shakes his head slowly back and forth.

"Nope, she doesn't wear it, or nope, you don't know where she keeps it?"

"Just, nope." He shrugs and his head continues to shake and I open a couple drawers.

"If I were your mum's knickers, where would I be?"

"Can we please talk about something else?"

"Found it."

"That was quick," he says, eyes opening slightly.

241

"I just thought about my room, and where I keep all my…" I stop mid-sentence.

"Please continue; all your what exactly?" He grins.

I ignore him and search through the undies and negligees. "You were right, there's nothing in here except bras and panties." I shuffle a lacy bra to the one side. "Wait, there's another bottom."

"Shay, I'd appreciate if you would keep all commentary about my mother's underthings to yourself. I don't want to hear about her tops or bottoms."

"No, not panties, a bottom." I clarify and tap the wooden bottom of the drawer.

"Underneath all of this," I lift fistfuls of lingerie out of the drawer, "there's a false bottom." I pull back a thin slat of wood, revealing a locked metal box.

"It's locked," he says, placing it on the bed. I lean over and examine the key lock.

"Get one of your mum's hair pins from the bathroom, will you?"

He follows my instructions and hands me a pin. I wiggle it and the lock pops open in a matter of seconds. Jake stares in awe.

"I was at a home for six months where an older girl made it her mission to abuse some of the younger ones. She kept her toothbrush locked in a silver tin, and each night before I snuck out, I picked the lock and took it with me. Most of the time, I ended up at a party and offered it to the hammered girl who had just chundered. A couple times I let the homeless guy down the street use it. Don't worry I always put it back as I found it though."

"Where have you been all my life, Shay Conrad?"

It was the first time I heard him use my full name. I loved how it rolled off his tongue, so proud. His fingers tug the belt loops of my pants, moving me closer to him.

"Start looking, you don't know when your parents will be home." I point at the contents in the box and he obeys.

"Bills, bills, receipt, bills." Jake names each paper.

"Wait." He stops suddenly.

"Did you find the itinerary?"

"Not exactly." He hands me a boarding pass.

"She has been to Sydney. I don't understand why would she lie?" The look of betrayal on his face makes me second guess our mission, and it hits me that uncovering the answers to all the questions might be worse than the questions themselves.

"I'm sure she had a good reason, Jake."

He's quiet, looking at another page in the folder.

"Did you find something else?"

"It's the piece of paper with the tail number written on it, in my mom's handwriting." He pulls out his phone and searches for the tail number on the internet.

"ECO-Star G888, crashed while flying west toward Las Vegas, Wednesday afternoon. Investigators name an engine malfunction as the cause of the crash. Five tourists visiting the Grand Canyon are presumed dead."

"This is crazy, we need to talk to your parents."

"We will after I figure out what else they're hiding. Will you write out a list of every strange thing you've seen since you've been here?"

"Sure, but it'll be a long list."

"The longer, the better."

CHAPTER THIRTY-FOUR

THEN

THE DAY FEELS LIKE AN UNPREDICTABLE WAVE. IN THE morning, on our way to school, everything seems solid. We agree to confess our relationship to Grady, together, after the Lacrosse game. But I can't shake the feeling that something is brewing underneath the surface like there is a shift in the tide, and if we aren't careful, we'll lose our balance and everything will collapse in on us.

I avoid Grady through the morning, ignoring most of his text messages and taking different routes to all my classes. I hate dodging him, but I know I won't be able to lie to his face when he asks if something is wrong. During lunch I meet Jake in the library.

"I didn't even know this part of the library existed." He looks around in amusement.

"I tried to hide out here during lunch on my first day, but Erin found me and forced me to eat in the cafeteria. Now here I am, hiding again." I hang my head at the irony.

"We're in this together," he takes my hand and taps it against his chest, "you *and* me. Soon it will be over. Grady will be angry for a while but he'll get over it." He pauses then looks into my eyes. "He likes you a lot, but he doesn't love you, you know." I am quiet as I mull over his words.

"Do you want him to love you?" Jake asks. Apparently I was too quiet.

"No, of course not. But how can you be so sure?"

"Seashells and jellybeans," he says, like those two words will solve the world's worst problems.

"What?"

"He doesn't love you, because he doesn't know you; like when you get nervous, you trace your tattoo or play with the sobriety chip in your pocket. You don't have many friends but once you trust someone, you go all in. You love the ocean as if it were an extension of yourself. You are strong and courageous, yet you blame yourself for the accident that killed your family." My eyes well with tears. He touches my cheek then smiles. "You prefer seashells to flowers and jellybeans to chocolates."

"Seashells and jellybeans," he repeats and I nod.

"Have you seen Grady yet today?" Jake changes the subject and I shake my head no.

"You?"

"He found me after Physics and asked if I'd seen you."

"What did you say?" I ask.

"I said, 'Why yes Grady, I saw Shay this morning. Actually I tongue kissed her in the car on the way to school. She was fantastic!'"

I can't help but laugh and Jake pulls me close behind a stack of books and kisses my smiling lips.

———

I sit anxiously in the stands and review the plan over and over in my mind. It's hard to cheer for Grady and not focus all my attention on Jake. I did like Grady very much. He'd been a great mate but Jake was right, he didn't know me. He only knew the version I allowed him to see. He didn't know the girl who got plastered instead of taking her final exams and who slept in a mate's car for an entire week because there was no where else to go. With Jake there were no pretenses, just truth. Any question he asked, I answered. He knew about my worst and still wanted more. I saw him at his worst and uncovered his best. If someone had told me this was the way it would all go, I would have laughed. Jake was never an option, until he was the only option.

The whistle blows and I've never been so thankful for a win in my entire life. I approach Grady.

"Where've you been? I feel like I haven't seen you all day. Are you okay?" I can't answer. The explanation is too long. Instead I bow my head, trying to hide the anguish in my eyes. I know what my words will do to him. Jake walks up from behind. He puts his arm around my shoulder. Grady doesn't flinch.

"Hey dude, good game." Grady punches Jake's arm.

I look up into Grady's face. "Shay, what's wrong?"

"We need to talk to you," I say.

"Okay, what's up?"

"First, I need you to know that we didn't plan for this to happen." Jake says and hangs his head. I can hear the pain in his voice, which hurts worse than the look in Grady's eyes.

"What are you talking about? What happened?"

"I have feelings for Shay, actually we have feelings for each other."

Grady laughs and waits for me to crack a smile, but I look away.

When I look back, his eyes seethe with anger and his lips twist into a scowl. He shoves Jake hard. "Dude, what the hell? You were the one that said she was worthless. You told me I was wasting my time, remember?"

Jake closes his eyes. "I was wrong.," he says it to me then to Grady. "I was so wrong and that was before…" Jake doesn't finish but I know the rest of the sentence. That was before we let each other in and trusted each other, before the Grand Canyon and the skywalk, before the night of prom and the kiss at the abandoned house where I no longer felt abandoned. It was before.

Grady steps back. "And you?" His wrath turns to me. "I waited so patiently, because I wanted to prove to you that I wasn't like all the other assholes in your life. So I waited and you chose the biggest one of them all. Well done, Shay, well done."

Grady raises a fist and Jake doesn't flinch. His knuckles meets Jake's cheek, leaving a purple smudge under his eye.

"You two deserve each other," Grady says and shoves Jake to the ground, then walks over to Erin near the bleachers.

I lean down and help Jake. "Are you okay?"

"You should've picked him." Jake won't look at me.

"He doesn't know me. He only liked the idea of me. Seashells and jellybeans, remember." I bring his hands to my lips.

"Coach says we have to go back to school to review the tape of the game." Jake says and I help him to his feet.

"Grady will be okay." I promise.

"Will we?" he says, barely a whisper.

"Yes, yes we will." I pull him close and kiss him, then watch him jog in the opposite direction.

I pick up my backpack and Erin approaches me, frowning.

"Shay, that was a real dick move." I don't respond.

"How could you lead Grady on like that? He deserves better." She doesn't let me answer. "I'm late for my nail appointment, I can't give you a ride home. Ask Jake, I'm sure he won't mind."

She turns her back to me and walks toward the parking lot.

I don't text Jake, he already felt bad enough. It's only a couple kilometers, so I walk.

When I finally make it home, streaks of sweat stream down my face since I'd decided to run the last kilometer from the Lacrosse field. Up the marble staircase, I close my door and my phone buzzes with a new text message from Jake.

Jake: Grady told my parents about us. Don't worry. We'll talk to them together after practice.

My mouth goes dry and the knock at my door makes my stomach feel like an aquarium sloshing about with schools of fish. I run to the bathroom and turn on the shower, trying to buy some time. Heart racing, I walk to the door and open it.

"Can you come downstairs for a minute? Mary and I would like to talk with you." Sam is in the hallway tapping the doorframe with his knuckles. He doesn't seem angry.

"I'm about to jump in the shower."

"Great, come downstairs when you're finished."

I create a plan while lathering up and rinsing off. I hope Jake will be home by the time I go downstairs, but if not, I will hear them out then speak my piece. Mary and Sam were the closest thing I had to parents. I wanted them to know I could disagree with their objections but still be respectful.

I get dressed, my heart fluttering nervously, then walk downstairs to the great room. I try to calm myself and remember it's only Mary and Sam. They might be frustrated with what transpired, but certainly they wouldn't take it out on me. They had to know we hadn't planned this.

Mary pats one of the stools at the island in the kitchen and I sit. Sam speaks first and the conversation starts as I expect.

"We know what's going on between you and Jake." Sam says, consternation rests on his brow.

"We love you like our own daughter and feel like you should be treated as a member of this family."

The words make me grin. Unlike the other families who had taken me in, I didn't question Mary and Sam's affection. My heart had softened to them the day we played together in the snow.

"There are things you don't know or understand about Jake." Sam's smile wanes.

"We debated whether or not to tell you all this. Jake doesn't know any of it," Mary says.

"Jake is going to die." Sam says, staring out the kitchen window at the 1955, powder-blue, Porsche Spyder showcased in the garage made of glass, "I know because I've seen it happen three times."

CHAPTER THIRTY-FIVE

NOW

"IT'S TRUE. ONLY YOU CAN SAVE HIM." MARY SITS ACROSS the room from me, in her art studio.

I take in Mary's serious tone, hoping that I am still dreaming, but knowing I am not.

"I have one question. You've kept Jake in the dark this whole time. Why did you tell me?" I ask.

"We weren't going to tell you. But you began snooping; making that stupid list. Because we've attempted, and failed, to save Jake three times, the group allowing us to travel in time is watching us closely now. The Echo Initiative knows we are trying to save Jake but has no proof and therefore can't stop us. They're waiting for us to mess up and we didn't want your questions to draw more attention. You never know who is watching."

"But I don't get it. If you're trying to save Jake, why invite me into your home to uncover these secrets? It seems to me, you brought this upon yourselves." Mary is quiet and bows her head.

"So there's more? I don't know what could be worse than this but go ahead, I'm listening." I use my anger as a front and begin mapping my best escape route.

"Dreams are an integral part of connections between past and future events."

"So I've heard, and...?" I say rudely.

"If you study your dreams long enough you can actually learn things about your past or future; things you never knew or things that are to be," Mary explains.

"While trying to save Jake for the third time there was an opportunity for me to attend a grief conference in Sydney. Unsure, I took the advice of a friend and booked a ticket."

"So you have been to Australia. Is there anything you haven't lied about?" I say, rising to my feet.

Mary ignores my outburst and continues, "At the conference I met a woman named Ingrid, who ran a group home. We talked for a long time and she told me about the girls living with her at the time. She explained how each had monumental struggles and hardships and were making impressive strides. She spoke of one girl whose entire family was killed in a car accident."

My brain plays tricks on me, and I feel like I am transported into one of Mary's visions. The art studio fades and I am standing next to Ingrid listening as Mary did.

"This girl overcame addiction and homelessness, all before the age of eighteen and was doing so well. Ingrid wished all the girls such success in life 'just like Shay.'"

I don't know how to feel. Ingrid's proud words make me feel warm all over, but I hate the control Mary has over my emotions and worse, how she invaded my life and lied about it.

"Inspired by how this girl overcame her grief, I left the conference for my hotel and that night had a dream," Mary says and it feels as if I'm lying in a bed.

"My dream began with Jake in the Spyder." I see it as she says it. Jake looks careless and happy, but my attention turns to the death machine he's driving and uneasiness settles in my chest.

"Jake was leaving the Lacrosse game with Taylor. He always dies when he is with Taylor," Mary continues and I see Taylor get into the car. She leans over and kisses him then buckles her seat belt.

"Across the parking he saw someone he knew," Mary says and I watch as Jake beeps the horn, then drives a short distance across the parking lot. Taylor is upset but Jake ignores her so she flips him off, and exits the Porsche. Unaffected, Jake revs the engine and speeds down the road. I feel sick to my stomach. The car loses control and Jake turns to the passenger seat. I expect it to be empty but it isn't. There's someone wearing a hat but I can't make out a face. Everything blurs as the car flips over. Two bodies fly through the air like ragdolls, then lie facedown on the asphalt. One of the bodies begins to twitch awake and I see Jake sit up slowly. I share Mary's relief. He looks around and when he sees the other body, he crawls over to it through the glass and shards of metal. He hovers over the body and cries as he begins CPR.

"Shay, Shay, Shay!" I hear him yell.

I jolt back to reality, still sitting on the teal sofa in the Art studio with Mary and gasp for air. She stares at the floor and refuses to look at me.

"So you orchestrated all of this?" I say panting, "You brought me here to fall in love with your son, then die in his place?" I try to stand but I feel dizzy.

"We didn't mean for you to fall in love with Jake. We never imagined that would happen," Mary says and I laugh bitterly.

"Of course you didn't. But you did bring me here to die?" I choke on my own words. "And all of it, all of this-" my hands wave frantically in the air, "it was all a lie?" My eyes burn with unwanted tears. "I opened my heart, you were my family… and for you it was all a game."

"The day you arrived at the airport, Sam stood outside the baggage claim watching you. He walked away. He couldn't do it. This wasn't a decision we took lightly. Sam told me that the reason he turned around and returned to the baggage claim the day you arrived, wasn't because we needed you to save Jake, but because we wanted to give you the life you never had."

"Bullshit," I shout.

"We knew it wouldn't make things right, but it could make things better, for you." Mary moves next to me and my skin crawls. "We wanted to give you everything that had been stripped away from you as a young girl. During the first couple months we thought we'd failed, we saw how miserable you were and almost sent you back to Sydney. But then you saved Jake at the Grand Canyon and..." Mary wipes the tears streaming down her cheeks. "We couldn't let you go," she sobs and I cringe.

"You have to know that we love you! You are our daughter; that's why the choice is yours now." I stand and clutch my bag. I refuse to look at her as I walk toward the front door.

"He's our only son, Shay." I pause, then walk out.

CHAPTER THIRTY-SIX

NOW

MARY FORESTER'S PARTING WORDS, "THE CHOICE IS yours" plays like a soundtrack in my mind.

My choice? My lips curl and a laugh breaks free. I'd witnessed the choices they'd made; I experienced the way they manipulated everyone and everything so they would appear generous instead of ruthless. I look over my shoulder. The choice was never mine. A shiver of panic bleeds down my back as I loosen the knife of their betrayal.

I sit behind the driver on the bus. Out the window, groups of palm trees and cactus flicker between cream colored stucco houses, but I can't see beyond my own warped reflection. In the darkened, dingy glass, my freckled skin looks gray and the puffiness around my eyes, hot from angry tears, appears black as if I'd lost a fight. In a way I had. Untamed orange and red locks cling to my face like jagged scars, reminding me of the man dressed in black with the puffy, pink scar raised high across his temple. The thought of him causes my whole body to shudder. I shake my head and try to regain control.

The bus stops and I worry if I'm making a mistake. I run up the switchbacks without stopping until I reach the Forester's driveway. The gate is closed and all seems quiet. I dart past and hide behind a giant palm. It feels incredibly stupid to be in such a close proximity to the Foresters, but my best place of refuge is nearby.

My pace slows as I see the partially constructed home. It seems fitting for me to end up here. Alone, in an abandoned house, dilapidated and falling to pieces; much like my own life. I enter through the open front door, and the smell of plaster and sawdust reminds me of the last time I was here with Jake. My heart aches. Why does everything I love have to leave? Why is happiness so hard to keep?

I sit in the open room on the second story overlooking the city. I roll an empty bottle back and forth between my feet and a vision overtakes me.

Mary unrolls a long piece of paper and reads the words next to a dash marked with a date. I follow along and read the rest of the timeline that lists each travel departure and arrival date, or dig as they're called. Beneath each dig, there is a short description of the happenings of each trip:

-Trip to San Diego 2/24-28, Moses stays at the condo to watch the coma patients.

-Grand Canyon Trip 3/25-4/8 Cassie and Moses stay at the house and keep watch over the coma patients.

-Sam travels with Cassie to help save Stone 4/15

I notice the last entry. The date is the same as when Sam was supposedly out of town and I found him sick in the kitchen. A shiver crawls up my spine as I realize the Sam I saw was not the Sam I knew.

The vision ends and all I want is to be in Jake's arms. I hate myself as I reach for the glasses, but I'm a glutton for instant gratification. I know there's no guarantee I will see his face or smell his coconut aftershave but I can't help myself. I feel so alone and so lost. I place the glasses over my eyes and I pray to see his blue eyes on the other side.

"Last time we were here, I was so nervous. I realize now, this is the easy part." Mary's shoulders hunch over and I can feel the loose skin under her eyes stretch and wrinkle as she rubs her temples.

"Deja vu?" Moses winks, then pulls a white sheet over one of the identical hospital beds. His shoulder rubs against the wall, flaking paint chips onto the brown carpet.

"Are you going to try to destroy the car again?" he asks.

"We were so close last time. The Porsche was about to be crushed but Coma Sam escaped and Bradley almost caught him." Sam says.

"I hate it when you call him Coma Sam." Mary frowns.

It's probably for the best. Cassie doesn't like the idea of destroying the car. With the eyes of The Echo Initiative watching, she is afraid we will be showing all our cards at once, risking expulsion. She thinks destroying the car should be our last resort, but watching him die again in that damned car..." Sam's jaw clenches tight.

"The first time he died in the Spyder, it was because we let him drive it; we handed him the keys to his own death. The second time he died, it was because we didn't actually see it get destroyed. We left the junkyard and the old man kept the car for himself but repainted it orange. The next week Jake was driving Taylor home after practice, and the orange Spyder hit Jake head on killing him and the old man instantly. The last dig, we watched it happen right in front of our eyes." Mary's body shudders, "we can't make the same mistake this time. I won't watch him die again." Mary tucks a piece of the white sheet under the mattress.

"Listen to Cassie. Focus on keeping the Porsche locked up. Don't let Jake drive it and keep him away from Taylor. Who knows, if you're lucky that could make all the difference." Moses shrugs then powers up the generator on the floor.

"Did Cassie give you the glasses?" he asks, searching through his black leather bag.

"Yes, last night. Most of my memories have already been downloaded."

"You will need to continue to update new memories daily so your past self will understand everything she missed."

"If we are successful."

"No ifs...when," Moses says and I blink three times. Blackness swallows everything around me and my fingers touch the frames resting on my face. The sun begins to set in the distance. Long rays of orange light shine over the city below. I put the glasses in my backpack and the sound of footsteps turns my head. Jake stops when he sees me and I lose sight of him through my tears.

CHAPTER THIRTY-SEVEN

NOW

JAKE'S EYES SPILL RELIEF AND ALL THE FEELINGS OF LOSS and abandonment leave. I forget all the fear and hopelessness and find myself in his gaze. For the very first time in my life, I know without a doubt that I love this boy. Butterflies flutter in my stomach, then twist painfully in my chest as the reality of our love finds me.

I stand and walk into his open arms and he takes hold of me. He grips my shoulders and searches my eyes.

"You can't just leave and not let me know what has happened to you." His voice is trumped with sadness. He takes my hands in his. "When you left yesterday, I realized something," he says then clears his throat.

"I love you," he shakes his head, "no, its more than that." His eyes close and he brings my hand to his lips. "I'm in love with you."

His words have a divine effect. The heaviness in my chest lightens, and for the first time since using the glasses I can see clearly. My entire body tingles with warmth and I feel safe and complete. His declaration changes everything and nothing, and I realize I have nothing in common with the old abandoned house. My epiphany deafens, for a moment, the knowledge of our fate.

"Come watch the sunset with me?" he says and I follow him to the edge and the air feels cooler with the smell of rain approaching. Clouds unfurl different hues of orange, pink, and purple as the sun descends below the horizon. I lean into his arms.

"I love you too," I whisper the words, afraid of what they might mean.

He turns me toward himself so I'm looking into his eyes. "I didn't hear you." The smirk on his lips tells me he heard every word. "Can you repeat that?"

"I love you. I love you more than I have ever loved anyone, and I'm terrified I'm going to lose you." I begin to cry and his arms hold me tight. He kisses me tenderly at first, then harder. It's as if his lips have been charged with pulling years of pain from me. The wind picks up, rushing around us and I archive the taste of his mouth and the smell of the coming rain as it blends with the scent of coconut around his neck.

He pulls back and takes my left wrist in his hand. With my palm facing up, he gently raises my sleeve, exposing the ink. His fingers methodically trace the numbers over and over.

"Today is a new day," he says and brings my wrist to his lips. "Day one."

I remember the conversation we had at Jaden's party, and my mind is flooded with all the homes I've lived in but had never been a part of. Insincere faces pass before my eyes and then there is his face, close enough that I can feel his breath on my cheek.

"This is only the beginning, I promise." The clouds open and rain pours through an open skylight above us. I bury my head in his chest and pray his words are true.

———

We approach the garage made of glass and an invisible cord tugs at my legs, veering me off course toward the Porsche. Haloed in white light, atop a circular platform, the caged machine mocks me. It knows its place and purpose in the world more than I know my own.

The trance is broken when Jake opens the front door to his house. A flicker of the image of two bound bodies, fighting to free themselves, makes me pause. I linger outside a moment, knowing a step inside equals a decision. Running would only lead to self-preservation and losing love. I'd been down that road. When I chose myself over those I loved, I'd lost everything. Pride wasn't worth the cost.

"It'll be okay," Jake says, seeing my struggle. "My parents aren't mad, just worried."

As I step into the atrium, I feel like a timid animal being led to slaughter, ensnared in a trap set for me months ago.

I lift my head high and try to hide my surrender. Footsteps from the other room make me cling tight to Jake's arm. Over my shoulder, Sam stands in the entryway. The urge to run at him and shove him to the ground is so strong but Jake steps in my line of sight and I remember why I came back in the first place.

"We need to talk to you both in the other room," Sam says and my body stiffens at the sound of his voice. Unable to trust myself, I take Jake's hand, and sit next to him on the sofa. I refuse eye contact and stare only at Jake or the floor near my feet.

"Shay, we feel it's in your best interest that you go back home to Sydney as soon as possible." I look up. I'm sure I didn't hear him correctly.

"In light of the present circumstances, we know it's the right thing to do." Mary's back is to us as she stares through the window at the city lights and all the breath is pulled from my lungs, like a long line of scarves tied together in a magician's trick.

Jake stands to his feet in defiance. "This isn't fair," he says, and Mary turns around. For the first time, I connect with her blue eyes and watch her tears fall without shame, pooling puddles of salty apologies.

I had written them off. I was convinced they had never loved me, that they were only looking out for their son. But why then, would they choose to send me home? It didn't make sense. I look away.

Jake folds his arms tight in front of his chest. "Shay's done nothing wrong. We still have three weeks."

"We've made our decision," Sam says, face blank.

"Your decision is a bunch of bull."

I look at Jake, in all his rage, and my lips form the words.

"Let me stay, please... let me stay!" The plea escapes before I can stop myself. I don't look at Mary or Sam. My words take courage; bravery that can only be found when I look at Jake's face.

"Please!" I implore. Mary's hands cover her mouth to choke back a sob, and she turns back toward the window.

"We love you, Shay, and this is what's best for you. Your flight leaves tomorrow at 10 am," Sam says, unyielding.

"I will never forgive you for this." Jake storms out of the room and his parents follow. I walk upstairs, my body and mind numb as I crawl into bed, not knowing how to process what just happened. I was right; the choice was never mine, the decision has already been made. I will be on a plane back to Sydney tomorrow at ten. A sigh of relief escapes and I hate myself. I weep until I fall asleep.

Jake is next to me when I wake up. "I hate this," he says as his forehead grazes mine. "I don't understand. They love you. They've never even liked any of the girls I've dated."

"Maybe they have reasons?"

His eyes narrow. "You're defending them? Do you want to go home tomorrow?" His words pour salt into an already open wound and my entire body grimaces.

"I don't know why my life turned out the way it has. I've often thought it was my fault; I must have done something wrong. When I came here, I had no intention of becoming a part of your family and falling in love with all of you. I never wanted anything like that again. But here I am, in the same place I was all those years ago, on the losing end."

"You can't lose me." He takes my hand and kisses my fingers. "You won't lose me, I promised, remember?" His fingers touch the numbers on my wrist.

"I want to believe you." I stop myself, afraid I might tell him everything and I can't break. If I were to step off that ledge and spill my guts, it wouldn't change our fate. It would only make facing the inevitable that much harder.

I lean in and kiss him. "I believe you." I can't let him suspect anything. "Come help me pack."

Jake follows me into the wardrobe and lies on the velvet sofa while I load all my new clothes into an extra-large suitcase that appeared in my wardrobe with my surfboard luggage tag attached.

"So, where are you going to take me to, when I come to visit you in Australia?" Jake asks, unaware of the torture he's inflicting.

"First, I'll take you to the beach by my house." I force myself to play along.

"Will you teach me to surf?"

"Of course," I fold a pair of trousers, "but I don't think you'll be very good at it." I shake my head and smile.

"I will most definitely prove you wrong," he says, tickling my side.

"Then, I'll take you to the skywalk at Sydney Tower."

"Wait, there's a skywalk in Sydney?" he stops me from folding another jumper.

"Yes, but I've never been."

"A skywalk in Sydney, what else aren't you telling me?" My body tenses and I avoid his question as I nervously pick through my pile of clothes.

"Next, I'll take you on a tour around the city." I steer the conversation back to sightseeing. "We can visit the Chinese gardens then have tea at Cafe Sydney overlooking Harbour Bridge." I turn my back to him so he can't see the grief falling off my face.

The later it gets, the longer the lulls in conversation. He stretches out over the velvet sofa and I snuggle in next to him. "I love you, Jake," I say and kiss his lips.

"I love you more," he says in a tired slur, before falling asleep.

I close my eyes and find myself in the Porsche. The wind throws Jake's hair in all directions, and I pull the brim of his favorite baseball cap down over my forehead. He looks over at me. "I love you, Shay Conrad." One hand is on the wheel, the other on my leg. "I love you more than anything." I put my hand over his. "How much do you love me?" He revs the engine and the car rages over the road. He turns my hand over and traces the numbers on my wrist. "You won't lose me, I promise," he says and a loud thump sounds from under the front tire. He grips the steering wheel but loses control, and we cut hard to the right. Jake overcompensates and turns hard to the left. The back end of the Spyder fishtails then flips up in the air, first to its side then upside-down so that when I look up I see the ground charging toward my face. I quick-glance to my left and Jake's seat is empty. I don't even have time to scream before the crushing pain of impact. My head is forced to my feet and everything goes black. I feel nothing but the cold darkness.

CHAPTER THIRTY-EIGHT

NOW-MARY

I NUDGE SAM, WHO IS STILL HALF ASLEEP.

"Come, it's time to get up. We can't hide in here all morning."

Sam groans and moves over to my side of the bed.

"Today will not be as bad as you think, I promise," he says, looking up at me with tired eyes.

Sending Shay back to Sydney was the right decision. A few months ago, I wouldn't have been so sure. It would have felt more like defeat, but that was back when I'd convinced myself that I was doing the right thing. Sam and I would rescue this young orphaned girl while saving Jake in the process. Desperation had a way of making very wrong things seem right. But something happened that even I couldn't have foreseen. Love had taken root, and my heart opened to the redheaded girl from my dreams. Now those dreams didn't seem as foolproof as they once had. There were no guarantees Jake would be saved or that Shay would actually die in his place. We had mistaken a chance for a guarantee; a chance we manipulated in saving the life of our son. However daunting, losing Jake always seemed inevitable, but now the thought of losing Shay, the girl who had become like my own flesh and blood, made me ache.

After a quick shower, I begin preparing breakfast in the kitchen. Eggs and bacon sizzle on the stove while I ready the coffee maker. The brewing urn sends me into a trance. I look out the kitchen window, dreading the drive to the airport. Sam was insistent that Jake stay home, not wanting to tempt fate one last time.

"Did you get the newspaper?" Sam asks as he sits at the kitchen table. My eyes scan the side yard.

"No, I thought you got it." The coffee gives its grand finale of spits and sputters and I reach for a mug in the cabinet. My hand finds the one with Jake's initials carved into the handle. I smile and shut the door then look out the window. I gasp and the mug drops from my hand.

"Mary, what's wrong?" Sam looks at the shards of clay on the floor.

I point out the window, afraid the words won't form, "The Spyder," I shout, "it's gone!"

"Where's Jake?" Sam is already sprinting to the next room shouting Jake's name.

My body quakes, rattling all common sense from me so that I can't decide what to do next.

"Jake!" Sam calls and runs up one set of stairs while I look up from the bottom of the other. The urgency in his voice terrifies me.

"He's not in his room," Sam yells from the landing. My body crumples onto the first step.

"His bed hasn't been slept in."

I stand slowly, knowing I can't abandon Sam. I pull myself up the stairs and I brace myself on the banister with each step.

"I found him. Mary, he's in here." My legs almost give as I run to the sound of Sam's voice. I cross through Shay's room where I find them in her closet.

"I'm here." Jake sits upright on the couch, still groggy from sleep.

"Why are you shouting?" I sit next to him and take his hand.

"Where's Shay?" he asks and an uneasy glance passes between Sam and I.

"What's going on?"

Sam ignores Jake and calls out for Shay. I chime in and we search again, this time for Shay.

"Where is Shay?" Jake asks, following behind me.

"Would someone tell me what is going on?" Jake puts his hands on my shoulders and spins me around. He gets in my face, but I refuse to answer and yell out her name again. Sam comes up from behind and loosens Jake's grip on me.

"Son, Shay took the Spyder. She's gone." My head drops and I can't breathe. This was what we wanted for so long. It's what we planned, to save our son. I realize in that moment that I'm not the savior; I'm the villain. I'm the murderer.

"No way." Jake shoves Sam's hands away. "She barely knows how to drive. She hates cars." He shakes his head. "Her entire family died in a car wreck. There is no way she took the Porsche."

"Jake, the car is gone and so is Shay."

"Last night, she was defending you guys." A pang of guilt hits my chest, knowing Shay's defense was rooted in love for Jake, not for us. She begged to stay and save him last night—how could we have been so stupid not to assume she would try to save him by stealing the car this morning?

"There is no way she would do something like this." Jake is confident.

"I know it doesn't make sense, but I need you to listen carefully because I'm not sure how much time we have," Sam speaks slowly.

"What are you talking about?" Jake asks.

"Shay is in extreme danger. I can't explain it to you right now, but you need to trust me. We need to find her as quickly as possible. Do you have any idea where she would have gone?"

Confusion sets in on every wrinkle of Jake's forehead.

"Where would she go, sweetheart?" I put my hand on Jake's shoulder.

"Is there a friend she would visit or a place she loved? What did she talk about most?"

Without an answer, Jake puts on his shoes and sprints out the door.

"Where are you going?" I shout.

"I know where she is," his voice trails back.

"Jake you need to stay here!" Sam yells, "in case she comes back." We chase him down the stairs to the door.

"Jake, wait!" But my pleas are in vain. By the time we reach the Mercedes, Jake's truck has already peeled out of the driveway. I call his cell phone as we speed out behind him.

"Where are you going?" I put him on speaker.

"The ocean. She went to San Diego."

"Are you sure?"

"I'm trusting you! Now trust me."

We follow Jake closely to the freeway going west toward Los Angeles. Jake speeds ahead and weaves in and out of traffic until he is completely out of sight.

"Damn it Jake, you are not invincible." Sam hits the steering wheel hard with his fist then slams on the brakes to avoid a stopped car. I call Jake again. No answer.

"No. Sam, look." I put my hand over my mouth as a police car races past us on the shoulder with its lights flashing. An ambulance follows. Sam steps out of the car.

"Is it Jake?" I ask frantically.

"I can't see." Sam steps onto the car doorframe while I open the moon roof and stand on the console.

"Can you see his truck?" Sam shouts.

"It's not him!" I say and shimmy back down. Peace sets in for a moment and I sit back into my seat.

I call him again. There is no response. I send a text message.

Mom: Jake if you see her, call us right away.
Jake: K

Mom: And don't text while you are driving!

No response.

"Good boy!" I say aloud. But he isn't a boy. Not anymore. He's a man and he's in love with a woman, and one of them will die today and it will be my fault. I let go of the thought and scan the road for Jake's truck.

"Mary, send Cassie a text message. Tell her Shay is missing and that she needs to enact the kill switch on the glasses. We can't chance them getting into the Echo Initiative's hands."

I follow Sam's instructions and send the text. A moment passes and I receive confirmation from Cassie.

Cassie: The glasses are inoperable. Where's Shay?

I ignore her message, knowing she is of no help to us now.

"Now all we need to do is find the car and save our kids." Sam says. I know how much I love Shay, but it is in that moment that I understand Sam's connection to her. I feel like my heart might break and burst at the same time.

"We'll find her. No one dies today." I squeeze his hand.

we keep in close contact with Jake and a couple hours later we near La Jolla.

Jake calls me on my cellphone, "Mom, did you find her?"

"Not yet. Where are you?"

"Getting gas near Mission Beach." The thought of Jake parked at a gas station puts a smile on my face. The moment passes as I think of Shay, scared and completely alone. What if Jake is wrong? What if she went in the opposite direction? She could be anywhere.

"Jake, do you have any idea where she could be?" Sam asks.

"Somewhere on the beach." I can hear the frustration in his voice.

"Great, that narrows things down. Don't go anywhere. We will come to you."

We head toward Mission Beach to find Jake. Sam drives past Crystal Pier and I spot a powder-blue sports car driving in the opposite direction.

"Mary, was that her?" Sam asks.

My heads follows the car until it turns out of sight.

"I'm not sure, it could be. The car turned down a side street; one that leads to the beach," I say and Sam makes a u-turn.

I send a text message to Jake.

Mom: We think we saw her. Meet us at Crystal Pier.

We pull into a spot close to the pier, and Jake pulls in across the street. He jogs past us and shouts, "I'll check the beach, you guys check the pier."

CHAPTER THIRTY-NINE

NOW-SHAY

SHAKY FROM MY DEATH GRIP ON THE STEERING WHEEL, my hands tremble as they dip into the water. The salty air fills my lungs and rustles my hair, calming my frayed nerves. Driving the Porsche to San Diego felt much like being held prisoner in Mary's body while wearing the glasses. Early in the morning, the roads were empty but I kept seeing things. Mary's memories had overtaken my subconscious, making it close to impossible to judge what was real. At times, it felt like the car had a mind of its own which only fed my fears.

I almost lose my balance as the waves crash into my shins. I laugh at myself and for a moment, my fear is washed away. I find a vacant spot near the pier and sit. I lay back and dig my toes into the warm sand. My mind wanders to Jake, probably still sleeping on the sofa in my wardrobe.

Stealing the car had been easy compared to leaving Jake. Cocooned in his arms, I was safe. But the death-dream I had helped me decide. If Mary's dream theory was right, it was the confirmation that I needed to take matters into my own hands. As I watched his chest rise and fall, sleeping soundly, I found the courage to leave. I knew if I stayed, he would not see his eighteenth birthday or graduate from high school. He would never marry or have a family; his chest would never rise or fall again. It was torture to unwrap myself from his arms. I whispered goodbye, and wiped the stray tear that fell on his cheek as I leaned over and kissed him one last time.

I made it through the house undetected, hoping Mary and Sam's clones were being properly drugged at a different location. I approached the garage made of glass and found the hidden keypad Jake had told me about. He tried entering codes one night with Grady but they were unsuccessful. I assumed the code had something to do with Jake or me, but it wouldn't be something obvious—Jake would've tried that. I tried my birthday, nothing, then the day I arrived in the US; the glass panel didn't budge. I looked down at the number 4422 inked in my skin, then entered it into the keypad. The panels unlocked and the spike of their betrayal dug deeper into my already wounded heart. I had seen the visible remorse in Mary's eyes. It curbed my anger. And the fact they couldn't finish what they started satiated my desire for vengeance. But here in San Diego, hundreds of miles away, they aren't in control anymore. The choice really is mine.

I allow the warm sand to run between my fingers. I scoop the grains and watch them shift and move. They remind me of an hourglass; my hourglass. After my family died, there were times that I would have easily let it all go, wishing for my own death, but things are different now. I am different. The remaining grains of sand sift to their final resting place on the shore and my heart fills with sorrow. I know, in my heart, I will never see Jake again; the only stitch of light is the thought of reuniting with my sister and parents on the other side. I pull my phone from my pocket and send a text message to Ingrid.

Shay: Ingrid, I miss you and love you always.

I say goodbye as I press send.

I type and retype message after message to Jake but can't find the right words to say. Goodbye is inevitable but goodbye isn't enough. Soon, he will wake up and I will be gone, no longer a part of his life or this world. He will be wounded but he'll move on and, more importantly, he will live. After typing and deleting, I send my final message.

Shay: Jake, I know you don't understand now, but I hope in time you will see that everything I did was because you are my greatest love.

I allow myself one last deep breath, one last touch of salty water, one last feel of the sand. I know I must go back to the car. I've tempted fate by staying away this long. Meandering through the sand, I take in every second, clutching each moment to me as protection from what lies ahead. Proudly parked on the street, the Spyder taunts me, tempting me to run away. But I move toward the powder-blue beast; each step a declaration of love, until I start running to the car as if it were Jake himself.

I open the driver's side door, sit down, and lock myself in. I hope death will be quick. I dread the coming pain and try to keep my imagination from terrorizing me with the different ways I might die. Mary's memories of Jake's death pop to the surface, and I shake my head to ward them off, but it's no use. I place the key in the ignition and start the car. Out of the corner of my eye, I see someone running in the distance. I put the car in gear and that's when I realize—Jake is sprinting straight towards me. I can hear him yelling my name and all I can think to do is scream.

CHAPTER FOURTY

NOW-MARY

FROM WHERE I STAND, I WATCH AS JAKE SEARCHES THE beach. He begins on one side of the pier then runs to the other.

Jake: She's not on the beach.

Sam runs back to me, shaking his head and I send a message to Jake.

Mary: Dad says she's not on the pier either.
Jake: I see her one street north.

I look north to the street that dead-ends at the beach. No words are exchanged; Sam and I just run. One block away, Jake is sprinting toward the Porsche, parked in a spot near the beach. We get closer and I see Shay in the front seat. She waves her hands wildly and screams the words I so desperately want to yell, "Stop! No! Don't!"

I want to scream; to warn him, but I don't, I can't.

We stop running and I can't decide whether to close my eyes or take it in. Our feet freeze in place and Sam takes my hand as Jake opens the passenger side door. His eyes focus on Shay's face. I know what will happen; like a reoccurring nightmare, it is a different version of the same tragedy. Sam squeezes my hand. The helpless feeling that has become a part of who we are, binds us together again. We should be horrified. We should be running toward the car. Instead, we stand still and surrender to fate.

Beyond the intersection, a MAC truck barrels down the narrow street with brute force. The driver sounds the horn; it is obvious he's lost control. Increasing in speed, the truck is headed straight for the Spyder.

Seconds pass but it feels like the length of a motion picture. I see my son's life painted out onto a canvas, starting with him in my arms as a baby; it's how I cope. Paint still wet, the image changes to a boy in a superhero cape. He grows and the brush stokes became blunt like his chiseled jaw and body, tall and muscular. The final strokes of his life are beautiful; emphasizing the dimple I love, in the corner of his smile.

The driver's horn continues to blare, bringing me back. It sounds, right up to the point of impact. The collision unfolds like a paper map, spreading out in different directions. The Porsche flips two times, propelling Jake through the air. He lands in a pile of glass and is nearly run over by the runaway truck. Screeching sounds of steel on steel combine with the popping sounds of glass on asphalt. The car flips again and Shay is ejected. Her limp body lands face down a couple of feet from where the car comes to rest on its side.

For a second, there is peace and a quiet stillness. I take a breath, then run into the chaos. Weighed down with shame, I force myself to find Shay first. Kneeling in a pile of glass, I hold her hand, still warm to the touch. I inspect her mangled and twisted body. Her blood smears on my legs and arms like I am the canvas. I can't bring myself to check for a pulse.

"Mary." Sam's voice doesn't startle me.

I know what he will say. It is always the same two words; "He's gone". I lower my head and close my eyes and brace for the blow. I turn slowly, still holding Shay in my arms.

Eyes open, I can barely see through the blur of tears. In front of me, Jake stands, blood-soaked. An audible gasp comes out of my mouth and my entire body trembles. He looks at me, but it's as if he doesn't see me. I fall back, in shock as Jake pushes past. I feel like I'm in a dream. My eyes follow Jake, who removes Shay's body from my arms and pounds steadily on her chest.

"Do something!" he shouts as blood drips from his nose.

"Someone help her!" Jake pumps his hands into her chest and Sam moves in to help with CPR.

Sirens sound from all directions and paramedics rush in beside me; two of them pull Jake from Shay.

"No, I won't leave. Don't touch me." He struggles to break free of their grip but he too weak.

An EMT holds Shay's limp wrist searching for signs of life. I know the outcome, even before his head shakes. He turns his eyes to his watch.

"Time of death 3:13 pm." Jake's body falls into a heap on the pavement beside her. He moans then hits the ground with his fist.

I move to his side and put my hand on his shoulder. Sam mirrors me on the other side. It's the first time I've touched him since the accident. Relief courses through me and I hate myself even more. Murderer!

Respectfully, the paramedics step back. Jake takes Shay's lifeless hand in his and finds the tattoo hidden on the inside of her wrist. With his finger, he traces the numbers then kisses them softly. "I'm so sorry I didn't keep my promise. I will love you forever."

"Son, it's time to go." Sam's words choke in his throat. "The paramedics need to get you to the hospital." He loosens Jake's grip and gently places Shay's hand next to her broken body. I hold Jake as his entire body tremors; each touch of his warm flesh reminds me of the role I've played in his suffering. They load him onto a stretcher and into the back of an ambulance. I climb in behind him and, out of the back of the rig, I see Mr. Bradley standing on the beach. Transparent ripples shift over his chest and arms as the direction of the wind changes. I shudder and look at Sam. "What have we done?"

EPILOGUE

NOW

IT'S THE FIRST DAY OF CLASSES AT SAN DIEGO STATE, AND I am up before sunrise, driving to the beach. Not the damned beach where she took her last breath, but a Southern stretch of sand she would have loved. I'd been putting off the inevitable for as long as I could. Her gray backpack needed to be opened, but it felt like reading the last page of a book. Going through all her belongings is the final acknowledgment; she's gone.

Bag in hand, I shuffle my feet through the sand for about a mile, before sinking into a dune close to the water. A bitter smile forms on my lips as a surfer rides an orange and yellow wave to shore. The ocean makes me feel closer to her. I pull the backpack between my legs and unzip the top. Inside, my favorite crimson hat sits next to her green purse. She looked so good in that hat; brim pulled low, with a sly grin on her lips. An ache spreads over my chest and I stop and breathe in the salty air. I open her wallet and a picture slips into my hand. The small black and white image takes me back to the day at Mission Beach. I cringe, remembering what an ass I was. If I could go back, I would've loved her from the beginning. I wouldn't have waited until she saved me. I would've saved her first.

I tuck the picture into the billfold and find another photo hidden between two bills. Gently, I pull it loose and a knot forms in the back of my throat. Shay is wearing the turquoise prom dress and I have my arms wrapped around her. I knew I loved her then, and it took everything in me not to kiss her. I wish I had. I bring the photograph to my lips and gently kiss her face. My fingers move over what feels like writing on the opposite side. Handwritten is a note from my mom: We love you, Shay! You will forever be a Forester.

The accident had wrecked them too but they refused to talk about it. I had plenty of questions, but they remained silent and asked me to trust them. I kept my mouth shut but, one thing was certain—I no longer trusted them. They both knew Shay was in some sort of danger. They knew and they kept it from me. From my back pocket, I pull out my wallet and slip the prom photo in next to the list Shay made. My head shakes with frustration as I add another piece to a puzzle that doesn't fit together.

I reach down and bring her plum sweatshirt to my face. Like a drug, I breathe in deeply, holding her scent in my lungs for as long as I can. When I exhale I feel a steady vibration coming from somewhere inside the sweater. I turn it over and dig through the pockets. A pair of glasses fall into my lap. As I inspect the thick frames, black ripples move outward from the middle of each lens, keeping in time with the water crashing near my feet. I don't ever remember Shay wearing glasses. I lean back in the soft sand and rest the frames on the bridge of my nose; the vibrations cease. A voice in the distance catches my attention; it cuts through the roar of the breaking waves. I turn my head in both directions. No one is on the beach. I blink my eyes and everything goes black.

A moment passes and I jolt upright. Out of breath, I tear the glasses from my face and grab the cell phone from my front pocket. Fingers shaking, I type a text message to Erin's stepmom.

Jake: Cassie, I need your help.

She responds within seconds.

Cassie: I've been waiting.

ACKNOWLEDGMENTS

Writing can be a lonely journey but I am so thankful for those who have trekked alongside me and encouraged me over the last decade.

Mike, I am so grateful for your unconditional love and unwavering support. Without you none of this would be possible.

E and B, thank you for believing in me and cheering me on every step of the way. You are my favorite boy and girl forever!

Jim and Kathy, it is one of my biggest honors to be your daughter. Your prayers and constant encouragement are life-giving.

To the rest of my amazing family, thank you for your kind words, prayers, and well wishes. I am more grateful than you know.

To my biggest fans and beta readers, Lenka, Angela, Patti, Ashley, Doni, Jon, Hannah, my friends from Mountain Valley & AZ Happy Hour, my amazing teacher friends, my WEC family, and Yorktown Write Night, I am indebted to you for your prayers, constructive criticism, and enthusiasm for this project.

A special thank you to Scott Whiteman for sharing your rock-climbing expertise and to Hannah, Isaiah, and Shay for being the "face" of Broken Echo's cover.

Brooke, thank you for your faithful friendship and for believing in me.

Ashley, your countless texts of encouragement and words of wisdom are a true blessing.

Shana, it has been such a blessings to ignore you while we write together. You inspire me.

A huge thank you, to my editor and friend, Taylor Allen. Thank you for making sense of my words and helping me to sound more intelligent than I really am.

Erin, Broken Echo belongs to you as much as it does to me. Thank you for loving my characters and my story as much as I do. The cover you created is more than I could have ever hoped for. Thank you for being my makeup artist, photographer, and biggest cheerleader. Your friendship is one of my greatest joys. #kerin4ever

Jesus, thank you for your presence and your perfect love that casts out fear and makes all things new.

ABOUT THE AUTHOR

K R Hancock lives in Virginia with her husband, two children, and sweet dog, Sydney. She loves science fiction, photography, and slow-burn romances. She believes that hiking is better than chocolate but not gummy worms and that book characters often make better friends than real people. It is her dream to one day visit Sydney, Australia.

Look for Saving Stone, the sequel to Broken Echo, available in 2020.

Learn more about K R Hancock at thekrhancock.com
Instagram: krhancock
Facebook:@thekrhancock

Made in the USA
Middletown, DE
15 July 2019